Darrel Nelson's *The R*  compact, quickly paced tucked into a revealing of mental and physica builds page by page as a ⟶⟶⟶ ⟶⟶⟶ ⟶⟶⟶ ⟶⟶⟶ ⟶⟶⟶ upon the wits and courage of the ultimate underdog to escape the wrath of a man consumed by hate born of ego and desperation. This is a book that is impossible to put down and a story that lingers long after the final page has been read.

—ACE COLLINS
AUTHOR OF *REICH OF PASSAGE*

I said I'd read this manuscript for endorsement if I had time, though I seriously doubted I would. Then came a flight to Michigan—the perfect opportunity. I became riveted by the story line, the characters' dilemmas, and the real-life dialogue. I hardly remembered to change planes during the layover. I read every free minute I had, often so fast I could hardly keep up with myself because of the heart-stopping action and emotion. In other words: I loved it! I'm a forever-fan.

—EVA MARIE EVERSON
AUTHOR OF THE CEDAR KEY SERIES

I loved Darrel Nelson's debut novel. *The Return of Cassandra Todd* is even better. The multilayered characters, the complex relationships, and the strong suspense thread all kept my attention until the very last page. This one is a keeper.

—LENA NELSON DOOLEY
AWARD–WINNING AUTHOR OF *CATHERINE'S PURSUIT*,
MARY'S BLESSING, *MAGGIE'S JOURNEY*, AND *LOVE
FINDS YOU IN GOLDEN, NEW MEXICO*

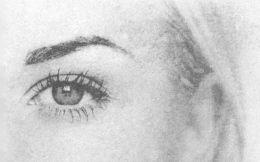

DARREL NELSON

AUTHOR OF *THE ANNIVERSARY WALTZ*

THE RETURN OF
Cassandra Todd

A novel

REALMS

Most CHARISMA HOUSE BOOK GROUP products are available at special quantity discounts for bulk purchase for sales promotions, premiums, fund-raising, and educational needs. For details, write Charisma House Book Group, 600 Rinehart Road, Lake Mary, Florida 32746, or telephone (407) 333-0600.

THE RETURN OF CASSANDRA TODD by Darrel Nelson
Published by Realms
Charisma Media/Charisma House Book Group
600 Rinehart Road
Lake Mary, Florida 32746
www.charismahouse.com

Unless otherwise noted, all Scripture quotations are from the King James Version of the Bible.

Visit the author's website at www.darrelnelson.com.

Cover design by Nancy Panaccione
Design Director: Bill Johnson

Library of Congress Cataloging-in-Publication Data:
An application to register this book for cataloging has been submitted to the Library of Congress.

International Standard Book Number: 978-1-62136-021-6
E-book ISBN: 978-1-62136-022-3

The characters portrayed in this book are fictitious unless they are historical figures explicitly named. Otherwise, any resemblance to actual people, whether living or dead, is coincidental.

13 14 15 16 17 — 9 8 7 6 5 4 3 2
Printed in the United States of America

acknowledgments

*W*HEN IT COMES to thanking those who have helped me with this novel, knowing where to start is the easy part. The hard part is knowing where to stop. I am reluctant to name names for fear of missing someone truly deserving. But name a few I must. And I apologize in advance for missing anyone I should have mentioned.

First of all, thanks to my wife, Marsha. It's been forty wonderful years. You have been, and remain, my biggest supporter and toughest critic. You are my official sounding board, and nothing is committed to final manuscript form until I have discussed it with you and received your take on it. You pick me up when I get discouraged, and you keep me grounded when I get carried away. As with all my writing, this book is dedicated to you. Thanks for always being there, love. Let's make it forty + forever years more.

Next, a huge thanks to my children—Tami, Chad, Kim, and Shawn—and to their spouses—Jeramy, Lisa (my website manager), Peter, and Christy. I appreciate your love and support. Also, love and appreciation go to my grandchildren: Hunter, Emerson, Cassidy, Ella, Avery, Weston, Finn, Cambree, Chase, and Brooklyn. Ten future writers! Grandpa is so proud of you.

Thanks to Liana, Cari, and Martha for reading the manuscript and offering timely suggestions. Friends who can remain objective are a wonderful asset.

I would also like to thank my agent, Joyce Hart, for signing me to a contract back in May 2009. It has been four eventful years that we have worked to bring *The Anniversary Waltz* and *The Return of Cassandra Todd* to light. Thanks, Joyce, for believing in me from the beginning. I look forward to more eventful years of working together.

The team at Charisma House has my undying gratitude. You are amazing to work with, and you truly exemplify the principles upon which Charisma House is based. This time around I worked most closely with Debbie Marrie, Adrienne Gaines, Leigh DeVore, Althea Thompson, Debbie Moss, and Atalie Anderson. But I know many others were involved in the process, and although unnamed, you are not unrecognized, and you have my sincerest appreciation.

Also, thanks to Rebeca Seitz and LeAnn Hamby of Glass Road Media & Management. I appreciate your work, along with Althea, in helping promote my books. It is humbling to realize how far the ripples spread when a stone is cast into the water.

As always, it has been a pleasure and a learning experience working with Lori Vanden Bosch, my editor. You are top-notch in my books, Lori. No pun intended. When asked recently who gives me the best feedback on my novels, I answered without hesitation: "My wife, Marsha, and my editor, Lori Vanden Bosch. I wouldn't dare submit anything for publication without first obtaining their stamp of approval. And even though their stamp of approval is sometimes hard to come by, I am a better writer because of it. So far I have been unable to slip anything by either one of them—I know because I keep trying—but they hold me accountable to their exacting standards." Lori, I acknowledge my indebtedness and thank you and Marsha for your unwavering expectations.

prologue

S HE LAY BESIDE her husband, listening to his steady breathing. A sliver of moonlight peeked through a gap in the curtain and illuminated his features. He lay on his back with his mouth partway open, his hair disheveled, a two-day growth of stubble on his chin. He snored softly but otherwise remained asleep.

She rolled onto her side and glanced at the clock. 1:27 a.m. After waiting to make certain her movement hadn't disturbed him, she eased back the covers, her bare feet soundlessly touching the floor. She grimaced as the bedsprings protested her departure. Remaining still for a moment, she studied her husband. He continued to snore, and his silhouetted shape did not stir.

After tiptoeing into the bathroom, she quickly changed in the darkness, slipping into the clothes she'd purposefully laid out before going to bed. She rehearsed what she'd say if her husband unexpectedly came in and discovered her...dressed.

Then, with her heart in her throat, she stepped into the hallway as cautiously as though walking through a minefield and went directly to the bedroom next door. Opening the door slowly so the hinges didn't squeak, she listened to see if her husband had noticed her absence.

All remained silent, except for the blood pounding in her ears. Exhaling slowly, she crossed the room and gently touched the little figure huddled beneath the covers. "Sweetie," she whispered. "It's Mommy."

The little boy, only four, rolled over in protest to the interruption.

"Time to wake up."

He opened his eyes and stared questioningly at her.

"Come with Mommy."

"Where?" he asked. This was followed by an extended yawn and catlike stretch.

"We're going on an adventure."

"An adventure!"

"Shhh! We don't want to disturb Daddy. Hurry and get up, but be very quiet."

Another yawn. "Isn't Daddy coming too?"

"No, he has to work. So it's just you and me, sweetie. Now hurry."

After helping her son get dressed, she guided him to the door and peered into the hallway. "Remember," she whispered, "Daddy needs his sleep, so be very quiet."

"Okay."

They went into the kitchen, and she opened the refrigerator door. Grimacing as the refrigerator light blazed on, she grabbed the bag of food she had prepared earlier and closed the door quickly and quietly. Then she went to the home security controls near the interior garage door and entered the code to disarm the system.

"Mommy, I have to go potty."

Sighing, she whispered, "All right, but we won't flush the toilet. We have to be very quiet."

When that chore was finished, she led him into the garage and pressed the remote button on the key fob. The trunk lid opened with a soft *click*, revealing a single suitcase inside. She lifted out the suitcase and then lowered the trunk lid, not daring to latch it shut. In the stillness every sound seemed magnified.

"Aren't we going to drive, Mommy?"

"No, we're going on this adventure by bus."

The little boy's eyes lit up, and he sucked in his breath.

"But we still have to be very quiet, sweetie."

They exited through the side garage door, and she paused to make sure their departure hadn't been detected. The house remained dark and silent.

She pulled her son close and embraced him. "Dear God," she prayed, "please guide us and watch over us. We need Your care and protection. Amen."

"Amen," her son repeated.

She kissed him on the cheek. "Ready for our adventure?"

"Ready."

Avoiding the streetlight, they crossed to the other side of the street and headed down the sidewalk, remaining in the shadows.

Ahead lay the bus depot. Behind only heartache.

chapter 1

*A*S THE DIGITAL clock sounded its invasive alarm, Turner Caldwell hit the snooze button with a well-practiced thrust of his arm. Five more minutes to sink back into his pillow, he decided. There would be time to shower and grab some breakfast before beginning his day. The jobs on his to-do list would still be there. Like they were every morning.

The alarm sounded again five minutes later, and Turner staggered out of bed, running a hand through his short, brown hair. He stretched the kinks out of his six-one frame and then dropped to the floor and did fifty push-ups. He followed this with a hundred sit-ups. He was glistening with perspiration by the time he made his way into the bathroom and turned on the shower.

He adjusted the temperature to as cool as he could stand and let the water soothe his burning muscles. The last few days had been fairly busy, and he needed to get back to the gym.

After drying off on a musty-smelling towel—he made a mental note to do the laundry soon—he put on his work clothes. As he reached for a pair of socks in his dresser drawer, his hand brushed against a book he had stashed there. Gideon's Bible. Picking it up, he looked sullenly at it for a moment and then tossed it back into the drawer.

A photograph fell out of the Bible and fluttered to the floor. As he retrieved the photograph, his scowl deepened. It showed him standing with a group of other guidance counselors in front of a large wooden sign that read *Camp Kopawanee*.

He flipped the photograph over and noted the dates written on the back, denoting the four years he had worked there following graduation from high school. Camp Kopawanee was a Christian youth camp for troubled teens. Canoeing, hiking, and camping activities in the summer had given Turner a chance to develop outdoor skills, while helping the participants straighten out their lives. And in the winter he had done maintenance work, which had given him a chance to develop handyman skills. It was a great situation...until church budget cutbacks occurred and he lost his job.

"Laid off by God!" he muttered, flicking the photograph into the drawer and kneeing it shut.

He went into the kitchen and grabbed a container of blue raspberry protein powder. After putting a scoop in the blender, he added one cup of cold milk and made a protein shake. He studied the protein powder container as he drank the foamy mixture, wondering if he could believe what the label stated. He should have energy to spare and a smile to go with it according to the advertising.

Problem was he didn't feel like smiling. Seeing the Camp Kopawanee photograph was a downer, and he wondered why he'd bothered to keep it. Having it around was like rubbing salt into an open wound. Still, it was all that remained of the best four years of his life.

He finished the protein shake and then gave the blender jar and his glass a token rinse, placing them in the drainer to dry. After wiping his hands on a dishtowel that hung from the handle of the oven, he headed for the door.

As he stepped outside, he paused to survey his surroundings. Morning had brought a fresh wash of color to the Mountain View Motel, a two-story structure located just off Highway 6 in

Lakewood, Colorado, a western suburb of Denver. During the past two years he'd worked as the motel's resident handyman and had begun attending college. The motel was owned and operated by Harvey and Loretta Jones, and showed signs of recent refurbishment. The exterior walls had been freshly painted, and trim had been added around the doors and windows. Sunlight glinted off the new asphalt shingles and backlit the well-maintained lawn and flowerbeds.

Turner headed for the maintenance room.

Harvey was already there, waiting with list in hand. His customary windblown appearance, magnified by his large forehead and a fringe of hair that stuck out at odd angles, made him resemble the stereotypical image of a mad scientist. "There you are," he said, rubbing his shoulder and wincing dramatically. "I thought I was going to have to send out a search party."

"Sorry, sir. But I got in late from last night's mission."

Harvey stopped rubbing his shoulder. "Not that old joke again."

"Yep, protecting the good citizens of Lakewood from crime and danger."

Rolling his eyes, Harvey muttered, "We should be so lucky."

Turner traced an H on his own chest with a finger. "Handyman at your service, sir. Just promise not to reveal my secret identity."

Harvey clicked his teeth and handed Turner a piece of paper. "Here's today's job list. I'd help you out but my shoulder is giving me fits. My arthritis is acting up again."

Studying the list, Turner said, "Not to worry, sir. I'll just grab some duct tape and chewing gum and get right to work."

"Duct tape and chewing gum," Harvey grumbled. "And to think I pay you good money."

"Not to mention the free rent."

Harvey shook his head and walked away, mumbling to himself and rubbing his shoulder.

Turner watched him go and smiled affectionately. He loved the guy. No matter how bad things were for other people, Harvey had it worse. If Turner complained of a headache, Harvey had a migraine. If Loretta had a sore back, Harvey had severe muscle spasms. In the game of one-upmanship, Harvey was a true champion.

Turner grabbed his toolbox and headed for the first job on the list. He knocked on the door and called out, "Maintenance."

A middle-aged woman answered the door, scrutinizing Turner from head to toe.

"I'm here to fix the sink," he said, holding out the toolbox as evidence.

"The faucet is constantly dripping," she said. "It kept me up half the night. I have a good mind to check into a different motel."

"No need to do that, ma'am." He switched on his smile. "I'll have it fixed in a jiffy."

She opened the door hesitantly, and Turner marched into the bathroom. He noticed her husband in bed, still sleeping.

The woman followed and stood in the doorway, watching him work. Turner didn't mind. He was used to motel guests making sure their specific concerns were addressed. Fixing the problem to *their* satisfaction was the key.

As he reached under the sink to shut off the water supply, he said, "The problem is, they don't build things to last anymore, do they?"

"Isn't that the truth," the woman replied, glancing at the sleeping figure of her husband.

"Planned obsolescence is what it's all about. You buy something, and it only lasts for a while before it wears out and you have to replace it. Not like in the good old days. Back then things were built to last."

"I still use the same toaster I did ten years ago."

"Mine didn't last a year." He grabbed a wrench from his toolbox. "But don't worry about the tap. It's an easy fix." He glanced at her from the corner of his eye and saw her expression soften. That was important. Repeat business was good for...business.

By now the woman was standing over him, watching as he removed the tap, replaced the worn rubber washer with a new one, and put the tap back together. Turner reopened the water supply and motioned toward the sink. "Try it now, ma'am."

The woman turned the tap on and off several times and nodded in satisfaction. "It doesn't drip anymore."

"You'll sleep much better tonight."

"Thank goodness."

"Anything else I can do while I'm here?"

"No, that's everything. Thank you, young man. You're very good at what you do."

"Just don't tell my boss. He might insist on giving me a raise."

The woman chuckled. "I'll be sure and mention you when we check out."

Turner picked up his toolbox. "Thank you, ma'am. You have yourself a nice day now." He headed for the door. His job here was done.

As he stepped outside, his smile faded. Doing even simple tasks around the motel required him to be "on" whenever a guest was nearby. And that took a great deal of energy. But that's not why he felt out of sorts this morning. No, it was the photograph. It stood as a painful reminder of where he had been and what he had lost. Now his life consisted of fixing taps, unclogging toilets, and repairing broken air conditioner units. He was cooped up in a small motel suite and attended crowded classrooms at college. But there was a time he had been surrounded by nature's grand architecture, when a simple glance in any direction inspired awe. A time when he lived with purpose. And made a *real* difference. Unlike now.

By two thirty Turner had the chores on Harvey's list completed. This included securing the handrail in the bathroom of Room 23, replacing several tiles on the backsplash in the kitchenette of Room 4, and fixing the coin-operated washing machine that had an appetite for quarters.

When he returned to his room, Turner washed up and changed into a clean pair of blue jeans and a T-shirt. He gulped down a sandwich and guzzled a glass of milk, and then headed for his late afternoon classes.

The September sky was clear and bright as the sun tilted westward. Because Lakewood has an elevation of 5,500 feet, the air was thin and shimmered like wrinkled curtains over the sunbaked pavement. The storefront windows became retina-searing mirrors.

He kept to the shady part of the sidewalk and made his way passed the Wells Fargo Bank while listening to music on his iPod nano, his backpack slung over one arm. A slender band of shade lined the south side of the street, and the foot traffic negotiated the sidewalk as if it was a narrow ledge.

A taxi pulled up in front of the bank, and a woman climbed out, followed by a little boy. The woman wore sunglasses, but Turner recognized her instantly, although seven years had elapsed. It was Cassandra Todd. He had gone through high school with her and always thought she was the cutest cheerleader on the squad.

Turner ducked around the corner of the bank. Like a

detective in a dime novel, he peered around the edge of the building and watched as she waited while the taxi driver retrieved her luggage from the trunk, which turned out to be a single suitcase. In appearance she hadn't changed a great deal and had lost none of her beauty. Straight, blonde hair touched her shoulders, and she still had her petite cheerleader figure.

She paid the fare and fired glances in all directions. Then, taking the boy by the hand, she quickly led him toward the front door of the bank and disappeared inside.

Turner let out his pent-up breath slowly. Memories resurfaced, sharklike, and razor-sharp teeth tore at the old wounds.

He was suddenly back in the high school cafeteria. The student council was sponsoring an early morning pancake breakfast, and Turner had just loaded his plate with a stack of pancakes dripping in syrup. Brad Duncan, All-American and captain of the football team, was sitting at a table as Turner walked by. Brad stuck out his foot, and Turner stumbled forward, doing a face-plant into his food.

As he frantically wiped the pancakes and syrup from his eyes, Turner saw faces contorted in riotous amusement. Brad was laughing his head off, along with the rest of the football team. People like them were on this earth to preserve the natural pecking order of things. They were at the top, Turner at the bottom. If this were a food chain, he was in serious trouble.

"Smooth move, Pancake," Brad said, apparently determined to twist the knife after plunging it into Turner's self-esteem.

"Pancake?" repeated one of the other football players. "As in pancake turner?"

That got another rousing round of laughter. How clever of him to make a play on words with Turner's name.

Pancake Turner was not how he wanted to be known, so Turner quickly shrugged off the incident as if to say, "Clumsy

11

me," and left to clean himself up. However, Brad was not about to let it go, and so the nickname stuck...like syrup.

But worse than the embarrassing face-plant, worse than the nickname, was Cassandra Todd, blonde cheerleader and object of a long-time secret crush, observing the whole thing— her face the picture of pity. And every time he saw her after that, whenever she looked at him, her expression said just one thing: pity for Pancake Turner, loser of Lakewood High.

Turner was angry about the whole thing, but what could he have done? Brad was used to making mincemeat out of others, particularly on the gridiron, and being cheered for doing it. Turner couldn't stand up to him, or he'd just be giving the spectators in the cafeteria more to cheer about at his expense.

As for Cassandra, how could Turner deflect pity? He couldn't simply ask her to stop pitying him. Respect had to be earned. And in high school that was the most difficult achievement of all.

Turner pulled himself back to the present and shifted his backpack, fighting to suppress the onslaught of resurrected memories. He thought he had gotten over that incident, but seeing Cassandra Todd again proved him wrong.

He glanced once more at the bank and then continued on his way to classes, no longer aware of the music on his iPod nano. Time was supposed to heal all wounds. But how could it when memories kept picking the scabs?

chapter 2

CASSANDRA WEARILY LED Justin into Mel's Diner, a small brick-fronted building two blocks from the Wells Fargo Bank. The diner had once been a shoe store but had been renovated to give it a retro look from the fifties. Padded booths lined the windows, and a counter with stools extended in front of the kitchen.

Two men, seniors by their appearance, occupied a booth near the front door. A young couple sat at the counter, sharing a milkshake and a hot dog, oblivious to the world around them. A jukebox in the corner softly played hits of the fifties in the background, adding to the atmosphere.

Cassandra ushered Justin to a booth near the back of the diner. She placed the suitcase on the seat and slumped down beside it in frustration. The business at the bank was going to take longer than she had expected. At least two more business days before everything could be processed. That meant she had to lay over longer than she wanted. She felt vulnerable being back in Lakewood because it was the logical place for her husband to look for her.

"I'm tired," Justin said, his eyes drooping. He stuck his thumb in his mouth and leaned against the back of the booth.

"I know," she replied, picking up a menu. "I'm tired too. But we need to eat first, okay?"

It had been a twelve-hour bus ride from Las Vegas to downtown Denver, and a thirty-minute taxi ride to Lakewood. Then it had taken another forty minutes to start the proceedings at the bank. All she wanted to do now was find a motel room and get settled in. Only she couldn't. Justin needed something more than the snacks she had brought for him to eat on the bus. A full stomach would help him feel more comfortable.

The waitress—an overweight woman in her forties—approached, her order pad poised and ready. "Afternoon," she said cheerfully. "What can I get you?"

Cassandra lowered her voice. "Do you accept credit cards here?"

"Yes, ma'am, we sure do."

Breathing easier, Cassandra referred to the menu. "In that case, I'll have a cheeseburger for my son."

"And fries," Justin added.

"And fries," the waitress said, smiling as she wrote down the order.

"With a cup of coffee and a glass of milk," Cassandra said. "And I'll have a spinach salad, with vinaigrette dressing."

The waitress finished writing and said, "I'll be right back with your coffee and milk."

As she waited, Cassandra let her mind drift to the subject she had managed to avoid during the bus ride. Her husband. She tried to envision his reaction when he woke up and discovered that she and Justin were gone. He would have wandered from room to room, calling to her, growing angrier by the second. Next he would have looked on the whiteboard in the kitchen for a message as to her whereabouts. When he found nothing, he would have become angrier still. But his anger would have reached eruptive proportions when he eventually discovered that the large envelope was missing from the wall safe. He would have flown into a rage, and his fists would have broken things as he shouted threats to the vacant room, promising what he would do to her when she returned home. She would experience his unbridled wrath!

But she wasn't *returning* home. Not tomorrow, not ever.

Seven hundred fifty miles now separated them, and she wanted to increase that distance as soon as possible. Once she completed her business at the bank, she and Justin would use the money to go somewhere her husband would never find them.

Her resolve was accompanied by a gnawing sensation in the pit of her stomach. Despite leaving him, despite the number of miles that currently separated them, she felt a degree of guilt for abandoning him. She had made a wedding vow to love and to cherish him, and that was important. But wasn't it even more important for Justin to have a good father?

Tears welled in her eyes, and she grabbed a napkin from the dispenser, careful not to attract Justin's attention. Her son was amusing himself with a sugar packet, pouring a small amount on the table and licking it up with his wet finger.

When the waitress arrived with the cup of coffee and the glass of milk, she paused and looked at Cassandra. "Is everything all right?" she asked, genuine concern evident in her expression.

Cassandra forced a smile. "Yes, thank you. We've just had a long bus ride and are pretty tired."

"Where did you come in from?"

Cassandra hesitated.

"Never mind," the waitress said before Cassandra could reply. "Mel always says I'm too nosy for my own good." A bell rang, signaling an order up. The waitress said, "I'll be right back."

The waitress's cheerfulness was refreshing, and it reminded Cassandra of better times. She remembered when she and her husband had first married and moved to Las Vegas. Their future was as bright as the lights on The Strip. Already trained in construction by his father, her husband had jumped head-long into the housing boom. Before long he was contracting million-dollar homes. They were able to build a house in a

15

respectable neighborhood, purchase two cars, and acquire all the toys that hard-working Americans were supposed to have.

Cassandra took classes at the local art school in interior design. On the surface at least, life was fulfilling her girlhood fantasies. But that was before things began to change. The crash of 2008. The drying up of credit. And the drought in construction projects. Not to mention her getting pregnant and the terrible morning sickness that followed.

The waitress returned with their order, smiling as she placed the hamburger and fries in front of Justin, who had licked up the pile of sugar. "Here you are," she said. Then she placed the salad in front of Cassandra and turned to leave. Hesitating, she said, "It's none of my business, but are you sure everything's all right?"

A tear trailed down Cassandra's cheek before she could restrain it. "Not really."

"Is there anything I can do?"

"Not unless you know how to speed up bank transactions."

The waitress shook her head. "I'm no good to you there. But I know how to make a mean banana split. On the house."

"We'll take a rain check, if you don't mind. We need to be on our way soon. But thanks for your kindness."

"My pleasure." She patted Cassandra on the shoulder and whispered, "It's tough, isn't it?"

Cassandra looked at her in surprise.

"I've been there," the waitress added. "Leaving him was the best thing I ever did."

Instinctively raising a hand to her cheek, Cassandra wondered if her makeup was beginning to fade, revealing the bruise.

The waitress smiled at Justin, who was smacking his way through the hamburger and fries. "You'll be fine, dear," she said, squeezing Cassandra's shoulder. "Good luck." Then she left to wait on the two men in the booth near the door who were waving to get her attention.

Toying with her salad, Cassandra considered what had just happened. She could still feel the warmth of the waitress's touch on her shoulder and hear the words of encouragement. The gesture had been small, but it meant a great deal. A sense of gratitude tingled through her, and tears threatened to fall once more. The experience in the diner was a witness that people were being positioned along the way, like signposts, to guide and comfort her on her journey. Her prayer *had* been heard.

chapter 3

*T*URNER SAT RESTLESSLY in his Psychology 201 class. The professor was one of his favorites, but Turner found it difficult to concentrate on the lecture. During his walk to class he had been unable to reach the escape velocity necessary to leave his high school memories behind. As a result he hardly heard a word the instructor spoke. Hopefully the contents of this day's lecture would not find their way onto the midterms.

The subject was on dream determinants. The professor projected some notes on the screen, and Turner opened his backpack and removed his laptop. He powered it on and absent-mindedly copied down the notes.

The professor explained that determinants are factors in the environment that play a part in the causation of a dream and lend it a particular flavor. Turner smiled grimly as he considered the dream determinant he'd just experienced on the way to class. Surely Cassandra Todd and the memories of high school she evoked would invade his dreams for weeks to come.

Following class, he went to the library to work on a reading assignment for one of his outdoor education courses. But he had a hard time concentrating and kept rereading the same paragraph about the essentials of running an effective outdoor education camp. Finally he slammed the book in frustration, causing several students to look at him in disapproval. Shrugging apologetically, he grabbed his backpack and headed for home.

A note from Harvey was waiting for him, pinned to the door. Turner sighed and snatched up the note and read:

> Tenant in Room 21 wants safety chain fixed. Do right away. Not tomorrow. Right away!

Turner glanced at his watch, not because he needed to know the time, but to emphasize a point. It was late, and there were the remains of a half-eaten pizza waiting in the refrigerator. But it was a futile gesture. To Harvey everything needed to be done *right away*, as far as motel guests were concerned. Even if it was past nine o'clock and would undoubtedly be disruptive, Harvey probably had an eye pressed against the peephole in his room, checking to make sure the job got done ASAP.

Free rent came with a price.

Turner went to the maintenance room to get his toolbox and headed for Room 21, planning his apology for the late disturbance.

Sorry, sir, but someone must have forgotten to undo the chain before trying to yank the door open. Happens all the time. Don't worry, though, we've got plenty of new parts.

In retail the customer is always right. In the motel business it was the same. Turner would apologize for not having anticipated the damage to the safety chain.

He lugged the toolbox up to the second floor, reminding himself to throw out a few tools sometime. The only problem was, whatever ones he took out to lighten the load were the exact ones he'd need for the next job.

Grunting as the toolbox banged against the back of his leg, he walked down the hallway and paused in front of door

21, waiting for the throbbing to subside. No sense having the occupant open the door to a face twisted in pain. It might send the wrong message.

He knocked on the door and waited. Occupants came in various shapes and sizes, as well as temperaments and demeanor, and he never knew what to expect. Someone could as easily answer the door toting a gun as they could with a drink in one hand and an open invitation in the other.

"Who is it?" came a voice from inside.

"Maintenance," he replied.

There was a brief pause and the doorknob turned. A moment later, the door opened...and so did Turner's mouth. He stood blinking at Cassandra Todd.

He had recognized her when she emerged from the taxi. But now at close range he realized she was even more beautiful than he remembered. Blonde hair framed high cheekbones, and her large, brown eyes were perfect in shape. Her nose was thin and straight, and her lips were full. She had maintained her petite figure, and Turner sensed that she could still do the splits while waving her pompoms vigorously. But in spite of her beauty something lurked beneath the surface—a tension in her countenance that competed for coveted facial space.

Did she recognize him? Was that the reason for her tension? No, he could see by the neutral expression in her eyes that she didn't recognize him. And the reason was obvious. He'd waited until after graduating from high school to grow six inches and put on forty pounds. Ducking around the corner of Sharpe's Pharmacy so she wouldn't see him had been unnecessary.

"I'm...uh, maintenance," he said numbly.

She glanced up and down the hallway. "Come in," she said, opening the door wider. "It's the safety chain. Can you fix it?"

He stepped into the room, stared blankly at the safety chain, and mumbled, "Yeah, sure."

What were the odds of having her turn up here? It was unbelievable. If fate was dealing the hand, he didn't like how it was shaping up. It came with too many painful memory cards.

He thought of telling her who he was but decided against it. That would only make things more awkward than they already were. Too much of the past would be dredged up. *Remember the time when...? And Turner wanted to keep the past where it belonged. In the past.

He fumbled in his toolbox for a screwdriver, anxious to do the job and clear out. With luck she'd leave the next day, and the memories of high school that she evoked would become dormant again.

"Thank you," she said. "I really appreciate it. I hope I'm not being a pain about this."

Nope. Only the memories you've conjured up. "No problem," he replied with practiced politeness.

As he loosened the screws to the door latch, he glanced at her as she crossed to the window and lifted the edge of the curtain, peering down into the street below. Then she dropped the curtain and paced the floor, glancing toward the bedroom door of the suite where, Turner guessed, the little boy was sleeping.

He wondered why Cassandra wasn't staying with her parents. Perhaps they had moved away...like his had. In that case why wasn't she staying with friends? There were probably several still in town. He stole a glance at her ring finger. She was wearing a wedding ring, and he wondered where her husband was.

As he removed the old safety chain and installed the new one, he struggled to keep his mind on his work. It proved difficult, especially when she peered over his shoulder to check on his progress. He caught the scent of her hair, and he could feel her breath on the back of his neck. The screwdriver slipped, and he banged his knuckles on the edge of the door.

"You okay?" she asked.

He nodded stiffly, refusing to show the pain he felt in his throbbing knuckles.

As she turned to leave, her hair brushed against his shoulder. His hand shook as he tried to reposition the screwdriver.

She went back to the window and peered out again.

When the new safety latch was in place, he tested it to make sure it was secure. As he slid the chain into the slot, the bedroom door of the suite suddenly opened, and the little boy emerged. He had curly blond hair and large, blue eyes. A thumb was stuck in his mouth, and he wound and unwound a curl of hair around his finger. When he saw Turner, he stopped twisting his hair and walked directly to his mother, hiding behind her legs.

"What's the matter, sweetie?" Cassandra asked.

He peered from behind his mother and studied Turner cautiously. "I can't sleep," he replied. "I miss teddy."

Cassandra groaned and scooped him up in her arms. She held him tightly and looked at Turner. "I forgot to bring his teddy bear," she explained.

"Can I have drink, Mommy?"

Cassandra carried him into the bathroom but returned in a moment. "There are no cups," she said.

"The cleaning staff must have forgotten them," Turner said. "We're in the middle of training a new crew. I can grab a couple of glasses for you if you like."

"If it's not too much bother."

"No bother."

Turner stepped outside and closed the door, leaning against it momentarily. Drawing in several deep breaths, he shook his head in an effort to dislodge the memories, barbed and sharp, that vied for a place in his consciousness. Dormant images that had lurked behind his mental firewall were now moving along revitalized circuits, invading his brain. For the most part he had managed to repress the memories...until Cassandra reappeared on the scene.

He went to the supply room and grabbed two plastic cups, each wrapped in cellophane. He held them up and studied them, remembering a time in the high school cafeteria when Brad winked at his buddies and offered him a drink of apple juice in a plastic cup. Turner had been suspicious and rightly so. It turned out to be a urine specimen for biology class.

Other memories followed. He remembered being invited to a party for Jen McCaffery, one of the cheerleaders. When he arrived, he saw Cassandra and was just building up the courage to talk to her when Jen intercepted him and told him his job was to walk her dog so it didn't bark when the *fun* started. He also remembered the time in his junior year when he opened his locker door and a dead cat, with bulging eyes and a misshapen body, tumbled out and landed with a splat on his shoes. Brad and the other pranksters laughed for a week over their roadkill joke. The same length of time it took for the scent to disappear from Turner's locker.

Shaking off the memories, Turner looked down at his hand. It had closed into a fist, crushing the cups. He tossed them in the trash and got two more. Then he made his way back to Room 21 and knocked on the door.

It opened until the safety chain pulled tight.

"It's me," he said.

The door closed so Cassandra could undo the chain. Then it reopened, and Turner handed her the plastic cups. She took them gratefully and went to the sink in the bathroom.

As Turner retrieved his toolbox, he saw the little boy peering at him from behind the couch. Turner smiled and wiggled his fingers in greeting. The corners of the little boy's mouth curved into a half smile, and he wiggled a finger in reply.

Cassandra returned with the cup of water and knelt beside her son, offering it to him. He took a long, slow drink, and Turner could hear the little boy's muffled breath coming in short gasps. It took him a full minute to drink the cup of water, and he did a great deal of backwashing in the process. The water kept moving in and out of the cup. Perhaps he was stalling, looking for an excuse to stay up later, curious about who Turner was. Or perhaps he was delaying going to bed without teddy.

Finally Turner heard a slurping noise and the sound of hollow breath into the empty plastic cup.

"Say good night to the nice man, Justin," Cassandra said patiently, kissing her son on the cheek.

"Nighty night," the little boy said, wiggling two fingers at Turner this time.

"Good night, Justin," Turner replied, gathering up his toolbox and opening the door.

"Thanks for everything," Cassandra added.

"You're welcome," Turner said, stepping into the hallway and closing the door. He waited for his heartbeat to decelerate. Talking face-to-face with Cassandra Todd had been surreal...like an episode of *The Twilight Zone*.

He wanted to head to his room and suppress the memories of high school by watching TV, but he knew Harvey would be waiting for him. Whenever Harvey said, "Right away," he expected a report when the job was done. Otherwise he would worry, and that was not good for his blood pressure.

As Turner dropped off his toolbox and headed for Harvey's room, he imagined his boss keeping a giant to-do list taped to the door of his refrigerator. Harvey's mission in life was to continually add items to the list. Turner's was to make sure they were crossed off, one by one.

~~Safety chain on Room 21.~~

Harvey could now get a good night's sleep, his blood pressure percolating on normal.

Turner did have an ulterior motive. He wanted to pump Harvey for information and find out how long Cassandra was staying. Hopefully only overnight.

Harvey answered the door, his hair disheveled and his chin speckled with grey stubble. "Done?" he asked, economizing words.

Turner nodded, economizing even more.

"Good, good. Everything okay?"

"Perfect, sir," Turner replied.

"Then I'll turn in. But for all the good it's going to do me. Know what I'm saying?"

Turner did.

His boss kept a second list, one enumerating his personal aches and pains, which he reviewed and recounted daily. If Turner got an earful, he could only image what Loretta heard. She was a woman of epic proportions, which conveniently provided room for the saint within her to grow.

"This arthritis is killing me," Harvey said. "I go to bed, but all I do is toss and turn, toss and turn."

"And don't I know it," came Loretta's voice behind him. Apparently she still had a ways to go on the path to sainthood.

"I ache in every joint and finally get up and pace around. But it doesn't help. You'd think by now they'd have a cure for arthritis."

"It's a tribulation, sir."

"Tell me about it," Loretta muttered.

Harvey spoke on, describing other tribulations. Turner sometimes wondered if Harvey endured the aches and pains so he'd have something to gripe about. Harvey loved to complain, and he did it in his own unique way...in triplicate.

When he had listed enough complaints for three people, Harvey waved his hand in dismissal and began to close the door.

"Wait," Loretta called, appearing behind him moments later. She wore a housecoat and had her hair done up in curlers. She held a plate of homemade chocolate chip cookies, Turner's favorite. "Have some cookies," she said. "I made them earlier this evening."

"Thanks, Mama Retta. They look heavenly."

This was no overstatement or attempt on his part to be polite. Loretta—he affectionately called her Mama Retta—couldn't spoil a recipe if she was blindfolded, suspended upside down, and required to work with one fleshy arm tied behind her back.

"Better try one first," she said. "I'm not sure I used enough sugar."

Turner ate the cookie slowly to give the impression he was preparing a verdict. A wine taster of cookies. "I'd love another one, ma'am."

Satisfied, she handed him the plate. As Harvey reached for a cookie, she swatted his hand. "These are for Turner. Yours are in the cookie jar." She winked at Turner and stepped back inside.

Turner waited a moment and then discreetly offered Harvey a cookie, priming the pump in order to siphon what information he could from his boss.

"So what's the story with Room Twenty-One, sir?" Turner asked, leaning against the doorjamb and savoring a second cookie.

Harvey chewed quietly. "I don't poke my nose where it don't belong."

Turner maintained a poker face even though a line like that deserved a good laugh. "What brings her here?" he asked, knowing that if he could find the right combination, his boss would open up like a vault door.

Harvey took another bite. "I don't ask those kind of things."

"What about the boy? Hers?"

"I only ask about pets, not kids. She doesn't have a pet, so I didn't ask. But I will tell you one thing, she's nervous about something."

Turner had noticed it too. She had peered out of the curtains several times and paced the floor like a caged animal. "Nervous, sir?" he repeated in encouragement, offering Harvey another cookie.

"She said she was in town on business, and she paid for two nights in advance. Her credit card went through, that's all that matters."

Two nights.

Armed with that information, Turner took the last of the cookies and handed Harvey the empty plate. As he approached his room, he wondered if Cassandra, one floor above and three doors down, was still peeking out of the window and pacing the floor, while her son slept restlessly, missing teddy.

After consuming another cookie, Turner brushed his teeth and climbed in bed. He finally fell into a restless sleep, his dreams centered on the biggest dream determinant he'd experienced since graduating from high school. The return of Cassandra Todd.

chapter 4

*C*ASSANDRA SAT ON the couch in her motel room, gently rocking her son. With his thumb stuck securely in his mouth, Justin made soft sounds as his eyes grew heavier and finally closed. She paused to shift his weight but his eyes opened, so she continued rocking him.

She looked into his face and smiled as he worked on his thumb. Brushing a strand of curly, blond hair from his forehead, she fought to hold back the tears of relief that were welling in the corners of her eyes. This was the first moment she'd been able to relax in what seemed like days, although less than twenty-four hours had elapsed since they left Las Vegas.

Their departure had been planned for months, but she had not actually put her plan into operation until two nights ago. Until after the most recent beating and her husband's ultimate threat to direct his anger at Justin. Later, when her husband went to "cool off" at the bar, she quickly packed a suitcase with everything she could fit inside: two changes of clothes for her and Justin, her wallet—containing what little money she could scrape together, along with a credit card her husband had forgotten about—and her passport and a large envelope she had taken from the wall safe in the den.

She hid the suitcase in the trunk of her car, certain it was safe from detection. She prepared a sack lunch, along with an explanation should her husband make inquiries. She and Justin were going on a picnic with some church friends, she would say. It wasn't true, of course, but her husband wouldn't question it.

After checking the bus schedules—she didn't dare take her car for fear it could be easily traced—she decided to catch the early bus for Denver. But she couldn't leave while her husband was at the bar because she needed a bigger head start. So she waited until he returned home, drunk and incoherent, and fell asleep. That gave time for her to get Justin and slip away unnoticed.

A cold chill crept up her spine. She had crossed a line by leaving her husband and had passed the point of no return. She couldn't simply go back home, apologize for even thinking of leaving, return the envelope, and resume her life as if nothing had happened. The consequences would be too severe, beginning and ending with her husband's fists. No, she had no choice but to forge ahead.

She noticed a copy of Gideon's Bible sitting on the end table beside a brochure advertising the Mountain View Motel and its amenities. She picked up the Bible and thumbed through the pages. Her eyes fell on a passage in the Book of Ruth:

> Intreat me not to leave thee, or to return from following after thee: for whither thou goest, I will go; and where thou lodgest, I will lodge: thy people shall be my people, and thy God my God: where thou diest, will I die, and there will I be buried: the LORD do so to me, and more also, if ought but death part thee and me.

The tears began to fall as Cassandra pondered the words. She knew people who had used this verse during their wedding ceremony. Now a sense of guilt pierced her because she had broken her wedding vow. But her husband had broken his vow too. *To love and to cherish, to love and protect* had become meaningless to him. His fists proved that.

After laying the Bible aside, she carried Justin into the bedroom and put him on the bed. He didn't stir as she slipped him between the covers. She lingered to look at him, worried about what the future held, but certain she was doing the right thing.

She had been willing to stay with her husband for the sake of their marriage and try to work things out. She could have put up with the heartache he put her through while she tried to change him with love. She was willing to do this and more. But when he angrily threatened to turn his fists on their son...

chapter 5

*T*URNER AWOKE THE following morning, blurry-eyed and brain-weary. He grabbed a bite to eat and then got dressed and went downstairs to the maintenance room. There was a list from Harvey, starting with a plugged toilet in Room 15. Unclogging drains and toilets was not at the top of Turner's fun-to-do list, but that's why Harvey paid him the *big bucks*, as his boss called it.

Taking his toolbox and a plunger with him, Turner went to Room 15. "Maintenance," he called, knocking on the door.

A woman appeared in the opening and explained that her daughter had flushed a toy before she could stop her. A yellow rubber duck was "swimming" in the toilet bowl at the time. One hour and some bruised knuckles later, Turner retrieved the duck, which the mother promptly threw in the trash.

The next job sent him to Room 25, four doors down from Cassandra's. He passed her room on the way, praying the door didn't suddenly fly open and she'd emerge. Hopefully she was still in bed, recovering from a sleepless night. Maybe she'd already left with her son to take care of some personal business. Perhaps visit friends. But somehow he *knew* she was still here. Her presence seemed to register in his bones like a psychic vibration.

He knocked on the door to Room 25. When no one answered, he let himself in with his passkey to replace a burned-out light bulb in the bathroom. The job didn't require a master's degree in engineering, but someone had to do it. He put the light bulb in his tool kit to drop off at the maintenance room later so Harvey could see physical evidence of a completed job and happily cross off another item.

He followed this up with a visit to Room 28, where the air conditioner was blowing only warm air. Harvey wouldn't be happy if the unit had to be sent out for repairs or, heaven forbid, a new one had to be installed. Keeping his boss's blood pressure down, which meant being creative and inventive, was a top priority. He was only half kidding when he referred to duct tape and chewing gum as part of his arsenal of tools.

Turner started down the stairs, on the way back to the maintenance room, when he heard voices from the level below. There was no mistaking them. Cassandra and Justin.

He tried to retreat the way he'd come, but it was too late.

"Good morning," Cassandra said, carrying a small grocery bag. Her hair hung loosely at her shoulders and glistened in the morning sun.

"Hi," Turner replied, careful not to stare at her. Attractive packaging notwithstanding, the mere sight of Cassandra was a painful reminder of the past.

She looked at her son. "Justin, you remember the nice man who fixed our safety chain."

"Good morning," Justin said, his face the picture of innocence.

Turner managed a smile.

"The safety chain worked fine, by the way," Cassandra said.

"Any more problems, let the front office know," Turner replied. This was a standard line he frequently used, but this time he hoped the offer would remain unredeemed.

"I'm sure things will be fine. We're leaving tomorrow morning anyway."

"We're on an adventure," Justin said, his bright, blue eyes widening in excitement.

"Sounds fun," Turner said. "Where are you going?"

Cassandra spoke before her son could answer. "We shouldn't keep the nice man from his work, Justin. I'm sure he has lots to do." She took Justin by the hand and hurried to the top of the stairs. With a backward glance at Turner she disappeared down the walkway.

Turner paused, mulling things over. *Adventure!* What sort of adventure? He didn't know. But it had to involve more than coming to stay at the Mountain View Motel, recently renno-vated though it was.

He descended the stairs, still in thought. Despite the uncertainty, there was one thing he *did* know for sure. Cassandra was the hinge upon which the floodgates to his memory swung. And the sooner she left the motel, the sooner he could close them again. Hopefully for good.

As he dropped off the light bulb in the maintenance room, something caught his eye. A stuffed monkey sat in the junk box—a large cardboard box filled with lost and found items left by occupants.

He pulled the monkey free. It wasn't a teddy bear, but perhaps the little boy would regard it as an adequate substitute for the night. Cassandra may have triggered painful memories, but that was no reason to withhold a degree of comfort from the little boy.

Minutes later Turner knocked on the door to Room 21. Muffled sounds came from within, like someone rushing across the floor. Then everything became quiet.

He could feel an eye peering at him from the peephole, scanning him like an electronic device at airport security. Then the safety chain rattled and the door opened a crack.

"Yes?" Cassandra asked with noticeable tension in her voice.

Turner held out the stuffed monkey. "I noticed this in our lost and found. It's not a teddy bear, but I was wondering if it might work."

She opened the door wider and called to Justin. "Sweetie, look what the nice man brought you."

Justin sucked in his breath and rushed forward.

Turner dropped to one knee and handed him the stuffed monkey. The little boy's eyes glowed as he clutched it. "This is for you," Turner said. Then to Cassandra: "It looks brand new, so it should be sanitary."

"Thank you so much," she said. "That's so thoughtful of you. I—we—really appreciate it." She turned to Justin. "What do you say, sweetie?"

"Thank you," Justin replied, cradling the stuffed monkey against his cheek.

"You're welcome, little man." Turner backed into the walkway. With nothing more to offer, he turned to leave.

Cassandra smiled in gratitude again and slowly closed the door. This was followed by the muffled sound of the safety chain being engaged.

He headed for the next job. There were still two items on the list, and he hurried to finish them so he could get to his afternoon classes. Some days were like that. He worked until it was time to go to school. Other days he could actually relax while waiting for a tenant to damage something. So far, this morning had not been an example of the latter.

Mercifully the final jobs were easy, and by one o'clock he had cleaned up, eaten, and was on his way to classes.

In outdoor education the instructor showed a PowerPoint presentation sponsored by the Colorado Wilderness Coalition, supporting a bill to protect Colorado's mountain wildlands and preserve the natural wildlife. It was proposed that some two hundred thousand acres be designated as a sanctuary. A stirring soundtrack accompanied the message, and the presentation was a slick, professional production.

Turner thought of his experiences at Camp Kopawanee,

with its majestic mountain scenery, the crystal-clear lake, and the fresh scent of pine and spruce. He had loved hiking and canoeing and working with troubled youth in order to help them grow in self-confidence and appreciation for nature. The participants were taken far into the mountains, away from the convenience and familiarity of their world, and allowed to experience hunger, fatigue, and deprivation. They were pushed to the breaking point and then were helped to rebuild new attitudes and outlooks. It was rewarding to see phoenixes emerge from the ashes of teenage angst and confusion.

It was a time of personal growth for Turner too. He had received some initial training, but the first trip into the mountains had been more difficult than he had expected. But by the time of the next camp, he had prepared himself better. He read a pile of outdoor education books, watched endless hours of instructional videos, and attended sessions on survival training. For the first time in his life he felt like a person of worth. And it felt good.

Until the church budget cutbacks. Then he returned to feeling like a nobody, and this had jolted his faith severely.

But the fatal blow occurred a short time later when his mother was diagnosed with cancer and died within six months. And to make matters worse, his father remarried soon after to a woman half his age, sold the family house, and used the money to go on a permanent vacation, far from the memories. Turner was not invited along. His father and stepmother occasionally sent him postcards highlighting their travels. But at no time did they write: *Having a wonderful time. Wish you were here.*

Bitter and in need of temporary accommodations Turner checked into the closest motel he could find, the Mountain View.

Harvey Jones was attempting to fix a broken chair when Turner entered the front office that May morning, over two years ago. The seat had become detached, and Harvey wasn't having much luck. With his experience doing maintenance at the youth camp, Turner knew immediately what needed to be done. So while Loretta checked him in, Turner helped Harvey put the seat in place and fasten it with four screws. A simple task but his gesture impressed the Joneses.

Loretta drew her husband to one side and conferred with him. Following the one-sided discussion, she approached Turner and explained that the motel was in need of help because the former handyman had just moved away. A nudge from her left elbow brought a nod from Harvey. Turner was offered a suite on the ground floor, rent free, and a salary commensurate with his experience as a handyman.

The perk was a standing invitation to dinner with the Joneses every Sunday afternoon. Loretta described menus consisting of southern fried chicken, roast beef, lamb chops, mashed potatoes and gravy, vegetables dripping in butter, homemade rolls, and an impressive list of desserts. Turner accepted the Joneses' offer and moved in to Room 13, the former handyman's suite.

The following year, at Loretta's urging, Turner enrolled at Red Rocks Community College. He had only this semester to go before gaining his two-year degree... and figuring out what to do with the rest of his life.

Now as the PowerPoint presentation continued and his thoughts focused on his experiences at Camp Kopawanee, bitterness welled inside him. It was bad enough that Cassandra Todd had returned, reawakening painful memories. But it was even worse to know that God had pulled the rug out from under him and swept the remnants of his self-esteem under a corner of it.

Turner gathered up his books and slipped out of the room in the dimness and was gone.

chapter 6

*L*ATER THAT EVENING, as Turner watched the late news in an effort to distract himself from the memories, a knock, soft and urgent, came on his door. He hit the mute button and crossed the room, grimacing as he thought of Harvey, list in hand, requiring another job to be done. Right away!

When he opened the door, he gawked in surprise. There stood Cassandra, holding her suitcase in one hand and Justin with the other.

"I'm so sorry to disturb you, but can we come in?" she asked breathlessly, glancing back down the walkway. Without waiting for a reply, she stepped into the room, pulling Justin behind. "Quick, close the door," she begged.

She dropped the suitcase and folded her son into her arms. Sitting on the couch, she slowly rocked back and forth.

"What's the matter?" Turner asked.

His first thought was that something was wrong with her room. He had visions of an electrical short shooting sparks in all directions or a backed-up toilet flooding the bathroom. Something told him though that there was no physical problem with the facilities.

"They found me!" she said, her eyes wide in alarm.

"Who?"

"Some men, hired by my husband."

Instinctively Turner glanced toward the door, as though expecting the men to suddenly appear.

"I don't know how they found me, but they did," she said, as her shoulders slumped noticeably.

Turner could guess how. She had paid for her motel room with a credit card. The paper trail was as evident as a path indicated by notched trees, colored flag markers, and rock cairns. "What do they want?" he asked.

"Me." She drew Justin closer. "Us."

"Why?"

She placed a hand to her forehead as though trying to squeeze a migraine into submission. "It's a long story," she said vaguely.

Turner swallowed hard and waited. There was desperation in her eyes and uncertainty in her expression that disarmed him. His gaze wandered to Justin, who sat sucking his thumb and clinging to the stuffed monkey.

We're on an adventure. The words echoed in Turner's head. "Shall I call the police?" he asked, reaching for his cell phone.

"No!" she replied. "I can't go to the police. It'll just be my husband's word against mine."

Turner had checked the motel register and noticed she'd signed in using her maiden name: Cassandra Todd. Whether she was trying to maintain anonymity or had elected to keep her maiden name, he wasn't certain. "What are you going to do?" he asked.

They were interrupted by a loud knock on the door.

The situation was becoming increasingly surreal, and Turner found himself reeling. Events were unfolding faster than a child going through presents on Christmas morning. Only this wasn't morning or Christmas, and there certainly were no presents.

His thinking became cloudy as a desperate thought crossed his mind. He could end his part in the matter by flinging the door open and letting events take their natural course. But explaining the woman and boy's presence would be a problem. If she were in trouble with the law, he might be painted with the same brush that colored her situation, and the colors were growing increasingly murky. He would be guilty of harboring fugitives, although it was hard to think of the little boy as a *fugitive*.

Turner had to make a split-second decision: reveal their presence and claim they had invaded his room unexpectedly, which was true, or hide them until he could get more facts and work things out in his mind.

Cassandra looked at him imploringly as another loud knock sounded on the door. Holding her son protectively, her arms a womb of safety and love, she sat on the couch like a small child herself, desperate and frightened.

This was not the Cassandra Todd he remembered from high school. She had been Miss Popular—cheerleader, homecoming queen, and center of the teenage universe. Laurels and bouquets were hers. The world lay at her feet. Turner could only wonder what life with her husband had done to bring her to this point. But there was no time for contemplation.

Lurching into action, he pointed to his bedroom door. "Quick, in there."

She took Justin by the hand and hurried toward the bedroom.

"The suitcase," Turner whispered urgently. "And close the door."

She grabbed the suitcase and Justin and rushed into the bedroom.

As the knocking grew more urgent, Turner ruffled his hair to make it appear as though he had fallen asleep on the couch, watching the news. "Coming," he called, reaching for the doorknob.

Harvey's windswept countenance appeared in the doorway.

He looked worried. His wrinkled forehead resembled a topographical map. "The woman in Twenty-One," he blurted. "Have you seen her?"

"Yes, when I fixed the safety chain." Turner spoke in a matter-of-fact tone, afraid that a change in pitch or a nervous squeak would be a dead giveaway. He also hoped a calm reply would help calm himself.

"What about today?" came a deep voice from behind Harvey.

A stocky man stepped into the opening. His hair was slicked back and glistened dully in the hall light. He had a permanent scowl, and his eyes bored straight into Turner. There was an air about him that conjured up images of car trunks, docks at midnight, and cement shoes. "Did you see her today?" Slick repeated.

Turner tried not to squirm. A bug sandwiched between glass plates under the glare of a microscope would have felt less conspicuous.

Deciding to be as truthful as he dared, he said, "Yes, I passed her on the stairs when I was heading to the maintenance room."

"Did she say anything about leaving?" came another voice, almost a whine. A second man, taller, with black hair and a scruffy beard, appeared behind Slick. He had a tic and continually twitched his head to the right as though constantly needing to check over his shoulder. Slimmer than the oily-haired man, Twitch was still someone Turner wouldn't want to go nine rounds with, mostly because he suspected the taller man would knife him in the first round to save himself the trouble.

"No, sir," Turner replied.

Slick and Twitch had now muscled Harvey off to the side. All Turner could see of his boss was his anxious face, peeking between the two men when the opportunity presented itself.

"Did she say anything about where she might be going?" Slick asked.

Turner shrugged. "She didn't say. Why?" He hoped the casualness of the question would bolster his pretense of innocence.

"We need to find her, that's all," Twitch replied shifting restlessly.

"Is she in some kind of trouble?" By playing it cool and at least appearing to be willing to help, Turner hoped to tease additional information from them.

Slick was having none of it. His jaw tightened, and his voice fell to a hoarse whisper. "Curiosity killed a rat, my friend."

Turner decided not to remind him that it was *cat*. Slick's version was probably more accurate.

"We just need to talk to her," Twitch said, his head jerking again.

"Sorry, I haven't seen her."

Slick made a face reminiscent of a glowering mask in a Japanese Noh drama. And Twitch looked like he was ready to end the round by drawing his knife.

Harvey peered over Slick's beefy shoulder. "You didn't notice her again after meeting on the stairs?" he asked. Undoubtedly Harvey wanted to make certain the facts were established. Cooperation meant that the men would go away and unnecessary repercussions would be avoided. Bad publicity was bad for business.

"She must have left while I was at class," Turner replied, sidestepping the question.

Slick looked at him narrowly and then let his eyes wander around the room. Turner followed his gaze and noticed the oily-haired man's eyes come to rest on the stuffed monkey lying on the floor. Justin must have dropped it in the mad rush from the room.

"That yours?" Slick asked dryly.

"I found it in one of the rooms this morning," Turner replied, willing himself to remain composed. "It's going in the lost and found."

Slick grunted. "Maybe you'd better pick it up so you don't trip over it in the dark."

"Thanks," Turner said as calmly as possible. There was something intimidating about these two men. He worried that they could see through him well enough to read the inside label of his boxers.

Slick held out a business card. "If you see or hear anything, give me a call. My number is at the bottom."

Turner studied the card like he was preparing for midterms. It was easier to focus on it than maintain eye contact with him or Twitch. There were truths behind his corneas waiting to blaze forth like twin beacons from a lighthouse.

Harvey escorted the men outside and gave Turner a parting glance. He was not happy. Turner knew that it was because he had not been more helpful in getting rid of them. *Remember your blood pressure, sir,* he wanted to call after Harvey, as he closed the door and waited for *his* blood pressure to stabilize.

He entertained visions of Slick and Twitch standing outside, ears pressed against the door, waiting for him to make his first mistake. If he hadn't made it already. He'd once read that someone who commits a crime makes twenty-five mistakes in an effort to cover it up.

Exhaling slowly, he considered the possibility that he had exceeded that number and was approaching triple digits. There had to be more red flags waving than those at the Chinese embassy.

chapter 7

ASSANDRA FLINCHED AS the bedroom door swung open and her host, the handyman, stood silhouetted in the light from the living room. She was sitting in the darkest recesses of the room, cuddling Justin. Looking up at the man anxiously, she whispered, "Are they gone?" She couldn't believe she'd intruded on this stranger, but she'd had no choice.

He nodded and turned on the lights.

"Thank you," she said in relief. "I didn't know where else to go. I had gone downstairs for some ice this afternoon and saw you come out of your room, and I remembered your room number. I hope you don't mind."

The handyman sat on the edge of the bed and looked at her solemnly. "They saw the monkey," he said, holding it toward her. "I told them someone left it behind and it was going to the lost and found."

She caught her breath. "Do you think they know I'm here?"

Justin climbed out of her lap and reached for the monkey, cuddling it against his chest and talking to it.

"I don't know *how* much they know," the handyman replied. "Or how little."

"But you told them you didn't know where I went, right?" She was frustrated at having to entrust her life to a stranger. A kind stranger, true...about her age and handsome enough. But one who certainly didn't owe her anything.

"Yes, I told them...but I don't know if they believed me."

She moaned and slumped back against the wall, wondering

when the merry-go-round would wind down and the room would stop spinning. "I'm sorry for getting you involved in this. I'll leave in the morning."

"That might not be a good idea. They're probably waiting, hoping you'll make a run for it."

She looked up at him in desperation. "Then what am I going to do?"

Her host ran a hand through his short, brown hair. "Stay here in my apartment. Lie low for a couple of days. Let them think you *did* leave."

Shaking her head wearily, she said, "If we stay here, it will only make more trouble for you." She was stating the facts, but she was also gauging the seriousness of his offer. Was he actually willing to shelter them?

"I don't see you have a choice." He glanced at Justin and lowered his voice. "Run now and they'll nab you. Go in the morning, they'll follow you in the light."

"But what about"—she dropped her voice to a whisper—"my son? I can't keep him cooped up for two or three days."

"You're going to have to."

She looked at Justin briefly and then nodded in agreement. But it was an uneasy agreement. She was getting her host seriously involved in this, and the situation was becoming complicated.

"Exactly why are they after you?" the handyman inquired at length. "What's going on, if you don't mind my asking?"

Instinctively her hand went to her tender cheek as she tried to figure out how best to answer the question. She owed him an explanation because of his kindness. But how much did she dare tell him? The more he knew, the more dangerous it could become for him. She needed to protect him as much as she needed protection herself.

She brushed a stand of hair from her forehead and dropped

her gaze. "I'm running from my husband. He's become physically abusive. And just lately he even threatened..." Her voice choked on Justin's name. But the horror and disgust on the handyman's face told her he'd understood.

Tears welled in her eyes and ran down her cheeks.

Justin dropped the monkey and hurried over to her. "What's the matter, Mommy?" he asked, concern etched in his young countenance.

Wiping her eyes with the back of her hand, she said, "Nothing, sweetie. Mommy's okay."

She distracted her son with the monkey and then got to her feet, crossing to the window and standing with her back to her host. "I can't believe I'm involving you in all this," she said, turning to meet his gaze. "I don't even know your name."

"It's Layton," he replied.

"I'm Cassandra," she said, extending her hand.

She felt him tremble when they shook hands. His touch was warm and gentle—everything she wished her husband's could be. "Thanks for what you're doing, Layton," she said. "I can't tell you how much I—we—appreciate it." She released his hand and dropped her gaze. "I dumped a lot of stuff on you tonight," she said apologetically. "You must think I'm crazy or something."

"Of course I don't."

His response seemed genuine, and she felt a wave of relief spread over her. It was difficult to hold back the tears. She sniffed into the back of her hand. "It means so much to hear you say that," she said.

He reached out to wipe her tears. Alarmed, she backed away, and he dropped his hand. An awkward silence followed. Her gaze darted to him, then away. Could she really trust him? She'd been around enough men to recognize the lust that often flashed in their eyes when they looked at her. This guy, however, seemed to be genuine in his offer to help. But there was something else too—something she couldn't quite put her finger on.

"Look," he said at length, "I'm going to go talk with my boss and see if I can get any more information out of him. I need to find out what the men know, if anything. Will you be okay until I get back?"

"Yes," Cassandra said. "Justin and I will be fine. Just make sure to lock the door, okay?"

"Of course." He walked to the door and turned. "You and Justin use my bed, okay? I'll turn out the lights so the apartment looks unoccupied."

"Okay. Thanks again for everything, Layton."

He nodded and closed the door behind him. When they were left alone, Cassandra cradled Justin in her arms and whispered nursery rhymes to comfort him. She felt more secure in the darkness where prying eyes couldn't see them. Daylight was the worrisome time.

She rocked Justin until his steady breathing practically lulled her to sleep. Her head bobbed several times.

After getting to her feet, she carried him to the bed and lay down beside him. As she settled on the mattress, she felt herself beginning to relax. Whoever this Layton was, he appeared to be a good man, one she felt instinctively she could trust. She thought of the prayer she had offered before heading for the bus depot. A warm feeling came over her, as it had in the diner, and she realized that her prayer had been answered again. Another signpost. She had been led to another angel of mercy, someone to help and guide her.

The last thought she had before drifting off to sleep was how she was being guided along, step by step. The going might be slow, precarious, and dangerous. But she had been led to this place. Now she needed to find out where to go next.

chapter 8

*T*URNER ROSE EARLY the next morning following an unsuccessful attempt to get more information from Harvey. He sat on the edge of the couch and massaged his sore muscles and stretched his back. The couch was lumpy, and he'd had to sleep in a curled-up position.

Besides the poor sleeping accommodations, it was unsettling to have Cassandra and Justin in his apartment. The memories continued to disturb him—it was becoming increasingly hard to stuff them into the back recesses of his mind. And to hear her address him as *Layton* made him feel awkward. He had known she would eventually ask his name, and he had already decided how he would handle it. He used his middle name so he didn't have to reveal his high school connection with her. It would keep things simpler. She had been open with him about her relationship with her husband, but he still felt it best not to be open with her.

As he got dressed, he heard two bare feet hit the floor in the bedroom. Moments later the door opened and Justin appeared in the doorway, wearing his pajamas. He wandered into the living room, thumb in his mouth, arm wrapped around the stuffed monkey.

"Hey there, little man," Turner said. "Did you have a good sleep?"

"Uh-huh."

"Would you like some breakfast?"

"Uh-huh."

Turner rummaged through the cupboard and brought

out two boxes of cereal. The packaging held little kid appeal, but he decided he could make the contents more enticing by adding lots of sugar. "Which one would you like?" he asked.

"This one," Justin said, pointing to the box with a picture of a man smiling over a heaping bowlful of the cereal.

"Good choice." Turner poured a small amount into a bowl, added milk, and garnished it with a generous dose of sugar. He smiled at Justin and watched as the little boy stuffed a heaping spoonful into his mouth, milk dribbling down his chin. "How's the cereal, little man?" he asked.

Justin chewed for a minute. "Crunchy."

As Turner looked into his angelic face, he wondered what kind of father would jeopardize his relationship with so innocent a being. Deciding this might be the only chance to get information that was pure and unbiased, Turner asked, "When did you and your mommy leave home?"

"I don't remember."

It was an honest answer. Was Turner expecting the little boy to cite the day, hour, and minute?

"Where are you and your mommy going?"

"On an adventure."

"Are you going back to see your daddy?"

A housefly caught Justin's attention. He watched it zigzag back and forth across the table, amused by its indecisive direction.

Turner shooed it away. "Does your daddy play with you?"

"Sometimes we wrestle."

"Wrestle, huh? You're such a strong boy. Do you beat him up?" Turner kept his tone purposefully light and melodramatic.

Justin took another mouthful and giggled.

"Does your daddy ever beat *you* up?" Turner's throat went dry in anticipation of Justin's response.

"Nope, I'm stronger than Daddy."

Turner watched him eat, smiling at the thought of the little guy grunting and groaning in an effort to pin his father to the floor and make him beg for mercy. "But does your daddy ever *hurt* you?"

Justin took another mouthful and didn't answer.

Hesitating a moment, Turner asked, "Do your daddy and mommy ever wrestle?"

"Uh-huh."

"Does your daddy hurt your mommy?"

"Sometimes Mommy cries. She comes to my bed, and I kiss her better."

Turner was about to probe deeper when the bedroom door opened. Cassandra came into the kitchen, wearing a T-shirt and jogging pants, her hair slightly tangled. She looked at him self-consciously, and then, when she spotted Justin, she looked a little embarrassed.

"I didn't hear him get up," she said, padding over to the table and kissing Justin on the head.

"I hope you don't mind me getting him breakfast," Turner said.

Justin smiled at his mother and loaded his spoon for another mouthful.

"Not at all," she said, smiling gratefully at Turner as she pulled up a chair. "I must have been more tired than I realized. I slept like a log."

"No problem," Turner replied, willing Justin not to say anything more about *wrestling*. The little boy remained busy with his cereal, slurping the milk from his bowl.

"How was the couch?" she asked.

"Great," Turner lied, resisting the urge to massage his stiff shoulders.

She looked at the cereal boxes sitting on the table. "I appreciate everything you're doing for us, Layton. And I want to help pay for the groceries. Soon as I can get things worked out at the bank."

When Turner looked at her questioningly, she explained, "I have a safety deposit box in the bank here. It contains some stocks and bonds my dad left me when he died. I'm just waiting for the bank to process them."

Her dad had died? When had that happened? And where was her mom in all this?

Without warning, she touched his arm lightly. "Thank you so much for everything, Layton. You're a godsend."

Aware of her gaze, Turner stared straight ahead, refusing to meet it. "I'm just trying to help out."

"God directed us to you."

Turner pushed away from the table. "I doubt that."

She looked at him apologetically. "Sorry, I hope I didn't offend you."

He shrugged lightly. "God and I aren't exactly on speaking terms."

"I'm sorry to hear that," she said sincerely.

He rose from the table. "I—I'd better be going. My boss will be waiting for me. And then I have an afternoon class to attend."

"College?" she asked.

"Red Rocks Community College. Outdoor education, with a minor in psychology. I'm in my last year."

"I went to college until little Mister Buster came along. He changed everything, but I don't regret it for a second." She laughed under her breath. "Sorry, I'm rambling and I know you're busy. I'd better let you go."

"Will you be all right? Is there anything you need while I'm gone?"

She shook her head. "I don't think so. We'll just camp out and watch the Cartoon Network."

"Make yourself at home. Help yourself to whatever you can find to eat. There's not much, but I'll bring more tonight."

She nodded. "Thanks, again, for everything."

"You're welcome," Turner said, looking into her eyes momentarily before shifting his gaze to Justin, who was slurping the last of the milk from his bowl. "See you, little man," he said, wiggling his fingers.

"See you," Justin replied as he wiped his mouth with the sleeve of his pajamas and wiggled his fingers in return.

After nodding awkwardly to Cassandra, Turner headed for the maintenance room, struck by the morning routine he had just experienced. It felt so...domestic. But discomforting too. Out there somewhere were an angry husband and two other very threatening men who wanted to find her. But why was she the center of such an intense search? Turner pursed his lips. Cassandra wasn't telling him everything.

chapter 9

*T*URNER SAT IN the library later that afternoon, working on an assignment for his outdoor education class. He had to plan a hypothetical one-week recreation camp for a group of twenty-six people. The plan had to include a diagram of the camp setup, an outline of activities for individuals of all ages, a nutritious but budget-conscious menu, and a list of first aid supplies and emergency contact numbers.

But he was having a hard time concentrating. Two people were hiding in his apartment, and that was *not* conducive to helping him focus on his studies. His life had suddenly become complicated. And he found it more challenging planning for the three of them than for the twenty-six people in his outdoor education assignment.

His cell phone vibrated a short time later, and he flipped the cover open. "Hello?" he whispered.

"It's me," Harvey's voice sounded in the earpiece. "Look, I'm sorry for bothering you at school. Loretta would kill me if she knew. But something's come up."

"Trouble, sir?" Turner asked, retreating to a corner of the library so he could talk.

"You could say that, yeah." Harvey's voice rose in pitch. "You remember the woman and her kid that those two guys were inquiring about?"

Turner felt a chill creep into his bones. "Yeah."

"Well, her husband's here now, and he's looking for her. Said he just flew in from Vegas because of a family emergency. I

55

don't know, maybe there's been a death or something. Anyway I told him I didn't know anything about her or the kid. He asked if anyone had talked to them, and I told him you did. And now he wants to talk to you. Let me put him on. Tell him what you know, and then maybe he'll go away. Maybe they'll *all* go away."

"All, sir?"

"I just saw one of those two guys again who came calling last night."

"The oily-haired guy?"

"The other one, the nervous one. He was going through the trash out back. Can you believe it?"

Turner caught his breath.

"Something's definitely fishy," Harvey said. "Why would those guys show up looking for one woman and her kid?" He sighed. "This business sure is stressful."

If you only knew. "I can talk to the husband and make him go away, sir. But I don't want to do it over the phone. Have him wait. I'll be there in twenty minutes."

"Okay, hurry."

As Turner stuffed his books and laptop into his backpack, he thought of the approach he was going to use. A plan was already formulating in his brain.

When he arrived, he found Harvey in a state of agitation. The older man's hair was even more unkempt than usual, and he was practically wringing his hands in anxiety. He quickly conducted Turner into the back office, where a figure with dark hair and broad shoulders sat in a chair across from the desk, his back to them.

"This is our maintenance man, Turner Caldwell," Harvey said. "Maybe he can answer your questions."

As the man spun around in his chair, a shockwave coursed through Turner. It was Brad Duncan!

A flood of memories struck Turner with the force of a tsunami, and his muscles tensed as he faced his old nemesis. This was the jerk who tripped him in the cafeteria and made him do a face-plant in his food tray, who offered urine in place of apple juice, who put a dead cat in his locker and laughed when it came tumbling out. This was the football jock who took delight in punishing his opponents on and off the gridiron.

"Turner Caldwell?" Brad said, staring hard at Turner. Then his eyes widened in recognition. "Pancake?"

"*Turner.* Hello, Brad."

Brad looked him up and down. "Man, you've changed."

Obviously you haven't, Turner thought bitterly, remembering the details Cassandra had told him.

"You two know each other?" Harvey asked in surprise.

"We went through school together," Brad said, rising from his chair and extending a hand that was just one size smaller than a baseball glove.

Turner reluctantly shook Brad's hand, aware of the raw power in the larger man's grip.

Brad Duncan was Cassandra's husband!

He had thinned a little on top and had thickened in the middle, but he appeared to be in good shape. Well-groomed and smelling of strong aftershave, he flashed the same smile that had appeared in the local sports page over the years. "How you doing, buddy?" he said enthusiastically, applying pressure to Turner's hand. "It looks like you've been working out."

Turner was not swayed by the phony courtesy. Brad wanted something, and they both knew what it was. "A bit, yeah," Turner replied, returning equal pressure to the handshake.

"Turner is our maintenance man, and he goes to college too," Harvey said, like a proud father. "Outdoor education, with a minor in something or other."

"Great," Brad said, feigning interest.

An awkward silence fell on the room. Harvey looked from one to the other and then cleared his throat. "Well, I'm sure you two have a lot of catching up to do. I'll be out at the front desk."

When the two men were alone, Brad flashed another smile. "So you work as the handyman here?"

Turner nodded stiffly. "You can't beat free rent."

"Handyman, student—you've got quite the thing going." Punching him playfully on the arm, he added, "Who would have thought we'd be here right now, catching up on old times."

"Yeah, who would have *thunk* it," Turner replied, barely masking his sarcasm.

"So how are things going?"

"Good. You?"

"Good too. Can't complain."

Yeah, right. Turner stopped himself just short of gloating. This was the man who had tormented him mercilessly. And now here Brad was, down and out, looking for his wife and child. He could tell Brad was dying to fire point-blank questions concerning Cassandra's whereabouts, and he enjoyed watching him struggle, shooting randomly with light artillery. He wondered how much longer until the full metal jackets came out.

He found out the next instant.

"Look, Turner," Brad said, growing serious. "I know Cassandra's in town. Or was. I know she stayed here at the Mountain View Motel, and that you saw her and Justin. Did she say where she was going?"

"She didn't tell you?" Turner queried, unwilling to camouflage the dig.

"Think, Turner," Brad said, his mouth thinning to a lipless slit. He got in Turner's face and then caught himself, backing away.

Turner stroked his chin as though trying to remember, employing as much conviction as he could. Brad wasn't the only one good at playacting.

"She must have said something," Brad persisted.

Turner tightened his thespian belt another notch. "Well, she said something about Kansas City." He drew out the syllables as he spoke the last two words, letting them hang in the air.

"She's heading for Kansas City?"

"That's what she said," Turner replied, noticing Brad's hand curl into a fist.

Brad sat on the edge of the desk and gritted his teeth. "She took something from the safe that belongs to me, and I need to get it back. It's very important."

The family emergency, Turner thought.

"Can you remember anything else she said? When she was leaving or where she was going to be staying?"

Turner shrugged innocently.

Brad studied him menacingly for a moment.

Standing his ground, Turner prepared for an assault but it never came. Instead, Brad's expression suddenly softened. "She's changed since high school, you know." He looked at Turner earnestly. "She's...schizo."

Turner hid his skepticism. "You mean schizophrenic?"

"Yeah, she's just plain nuts. She claims *I* have violent outbursts, but it's the other way around. She's crazy, man. I've got to find her before she hurts our son."

"People with schizophrenia aren't prone to violence," Turner said, remembering his psychology class.

"She's okay as long as she's on her meds," Brad continued, ignoring him. "But when she forgets to take them, she gets crazy. She changes without warning and becomes...dangerous." His countenance darkened like a lunar eclipse. "She attempted suicide while I was at work." He paused for several seconds as if struggling with his emotions. "Justin was in the house. Can you imagine the damage that might have done to our son? Naturally, I confronted her and told her she had to get help. She promised she would. But that night she kidnapped Justin and took off."

Turner studied Brad, who slumped against the edge of the desk, looking nothing like the former high school football hero. His demeanor was reminiscent of the time he'd been carried off the field during a game, a crumpled form writhing on the stretcher. Gone was the arrogance, the swagger, the air of contempt—all by-products of high school godhood. Brad was either one chastened individual or he was giving a performance that was worthy of an Academy Award.

"She's got my son, Turner," Brad said, shaking his head sadly.

"And the thing from your safe. She's got that too, right?"

Brad's jaw muscles bulged as he clenched his teeth. "She stole it from me, and I need it back." He stood up and fumbled in his pocket for a business card. "Take this. Call me if you remember anything else or if she shows back up here. Okay?"

"Sure," said Turner, masking his contempt. The agreement was as empty as the regard he held for Brad.

After studying Turner a moment longer, Brad spun on his heels and exited the room, pounding his fist against the doorjamb on his way out.

chapter 10

WHILE JUSTIN NAPPED in the bedroom, Cassandra swept the floor and then cleaned the kitchen countertop with a damp rag, smiling in bemusement at the lack of organization in this bachelor pad. The place needed the touch of a woman's hand.

A spatula and a plastic ladle sat near the stove, and she opened several drawers in order to find where they belonged. She shook her head at the hodgepodge of utensils, dishtowels, and odds and ends they contained.

In one drawer she found a postcard lying on top of a pile of papers. The picture featured a scene from the Bahamas, and she looked at it longingly, wanting to find just such a place for Justin and her. She could see the two of them settling in to the tropical climate and lifestyle quite nicely

She absentmindedly flipped the postcard over. A short note written in an untidy hand read:

> Weather's great. Went snorkeling yesterday. Going boating tomorrow. Take care, Dad.

The name in the address section caught her attention, and she exhaled in surprise. It was addressed to *Turner Caldwell*. She wrinkled her brow in confusion. What was Layton doing with a postcard addressed to Turner Caldwell? She knew a Turner Caldwell. Had gone to school with him, in fact. He was a short, skinny kid who had been bullied mercilessly. But what were the odds of there being two Turner Caldwells in Lakewood?

Driven by curiosity, fueled by suspicion, she searched through the drawer and found a cell phone bill and a credit card statement, both addressed to Turner Caldwell. She also found a college transcript from Red Rocks Community College belonging to *Turner Layton Caldwell*.

She picked up the transcript and slumped against the counter, stunned by the realization that Layton was... Turner.

Her head reeled. The Turner she had known in high school was nothing like the young man who identified himself as Layton. Turner had been skinny and awkward and, well, a real dweeb. Layton was taller and huskier and more handsome.

She thought for a moment longer, holding them in a split-image comparison. Their height, weight, and physiques were completely different. But their eyes! There was definitely something similar in their blue eyes.

Conflicting emotions tore at her. The gratitude she felt because of Layton's assistance was overshadowed by the anger that rose in her. He had deceived her, and deceit was something she wouldn't tolerate. Not any longer. It had become her husband's trademark. And now this! Her anger increased as she thought about the lies and mind games she'd already endured.

Clenching her teeth, she tossed the transcript back in the drawer and slipped quietly into the bedroom. She emerged moments later with her suitcase just as a key rattled in the outside lock. The door swung open before she could react.

Her host, the handyman, entered and quickly closed the door behind him. He stopped short when he saw her and cocked his head in surprise. "Going somewhere?" he asked.

"Justin and I are leaving," she replied sullenly.

"Leaving? Why?"

"Because we can't stay here any longer, *Layton!*" She wasn't able to keep the bitterness out of her voice. "Or should I say...Turner?"

Swallowing hard, he looked at her guiltily. "How did you find out?"

"That doesn't matter." Her voice rose in pitch. "What does matter is that you lied to me."

"I didn't lie," he replied defensively "Layton is my *middle* name."

Cassandra shook her head emphatically. "When it suited him, my husband could put a spin on things too. Which was always. But I expected better of you."

"And why's that?"

"Because Justin and I were led to you."

Turner's expression tightened. "We've been over this before. I'm not an angel of mercy. I did what any normal, decent human being would do. Besides, it turns out you have a few secrets of your own.'

She traded guilty expressions with Turner and set the suitcase down. "Look, I feel horrible for the way you were treated in high school. I really do. I promised myself if I ever had a chance, I'd apologize...for all of us. And I truly appreciate the help you've given Justin and me. But I trusted you, and you kept the truth from me. Just like my husband always did." She looked at Turner with a determined expression on her face. "I—we—just can't stay. Not when there's deceit."

As she headed for the bedroom to get Justin, Turner took a step toward her. "You can't leave. At least not yet."

Cassandra continued walking. "Why not?"

"Because Brad's here. I just talked to him."

She sucked in her breath and spun around to face him. "He's...here?"

"He was. But I told him you were heading to Kansas City. I

don't know if he bought it, so you're going to have to sit tight until we find out."

Cassandra retreated to the couch, feeling trapped. She was desperate to leave and yet desperate to stay and remain in hiding. But with someone who had deceived her? She turned on him. "Why didn't you tell me who you were?"

She watched his face redden and his eyes turn away in a familiar look of... shame? She'd seen the same expression the day in the cafeteria when he had done the face-plant into his food tray. Of course. He was still ashamed of who he'd been. Of being the bullied one. The victim. And no one knew better than she did what that felt like.

To her surprise he regained his composure and turned the challenge on her. "Brad Duncan! How did you end up with that creep?"

She dropped her gaze. "He made me feel good about myself. You know, the football player and the cheerleader and all that. When my parents divorced during my senior year and my dad moved out and my mom turned to alcohol, Brad and the others were there for me. They accepted me. Hanging out with them was the only way I could handle the divorce."

Turner snorted. "But... Brad! Didn't you realize what a jerk he was?"

In a small voice she said, "He helped me when my world was falling in around me. He was fun. I just thought he liked to play pranks and have a good laugh. He never did anything like that to me."

"At least not until you were married."

"Not until we were married," she echoed dully.

"Look, you have reason to be upset with me," Turner said, softening his tone, "but I did what I thought was for your best good. Can you say the same about him?"

Cassandra stared at the floor and didn't respond.

"Does *he* have your best interests in mind?" Turner asked rhetorically. "He told me you took an envelope from the family safe. And to be honest, he seemed more interested in getting it back than in getting *you* back."

She was surprised at how his words stung. "I took it so I'd have some bargaining power, that's all. He'll get it back when this is all over."

"And he told me you kidnapped Justin."

Springing to her feet, Cassandra stated, "It's not true. I didn't *kidnap* him."

"And he said you have...emotional problems."

Her eyes flashed in anger, but there was sadness in them too. "*He's* the one with emotional problems. My counselor says Brad likely has narcissistic personality disorder. Know what that is?"

"Vaguely."

"It means he thinks he's the center of the universe. He can do no wrong, and I'm always the one to blame. I started to suspect something was wrong after we married, but it really turned ugly after Justin was born. Brad seemed to look on him as...competition." Disbelief and despair laced her voice.

Turner looked at her expectantly, listening. So she continued.

"Brad used whatever means he could to control me. It started small at first. Like the time he got angry because I bought some baby clothes for Justin. I hadn't *consulted* Brad about it first. It was some pants and shirts, purchased at Walmart, no less. They only cost twenty dollars, but Brad went ballistic."

"Did he...hit you?"

"He *shoved* me, but he didn't hit me. Not that time. And he yelled a lot. Talked about money not growing on trees, that sort of thing. He checked our bank statements and charge card statements religiously. If he saw anything that *he* hadn't spent,

I had to answer for it. But he thought nothing of heading to the bar with the boys after work." Her lips twisted in disdain.

"What did you do about it?"

"What could I do? For a long time I just tried to keep the peace, tried to keep the marriage going, for Justin's sake. I started going to church and invited Brad, hoping that would help. He went for a while, but mainly to look good, or get business contacts, I think. We fought a lot, but when I suggested counseling, he absolutely refused. So I went on my own."

"Why did you leave him now?"

She shot Turner a glance. "He started to hit me, that's why. A few months ago. Sometimes it was a week before I could go out in public because of the bruises on my face."

Turner swallowed hard.

"But it got worse. When I wanted to leave, he threatened to have Justin taken away from me if I didn't cooperate. He said he'd tell child welfare services that I was an unfit mother, that I had violent tendencies, that I was a danger to our son." She paused to get control of her emotions, wishing the details of her marriage were not so awful. "Did he say that I tried to commit suicide?"

"Yes," Turner replied, his voice a whisper.

Tears ran down her cheeks freely now. "It was always his word against mine, and he threatened to go to the authorities with his side of the story if I stepped out of line or didn't do exactly what he wanted. He told me he had friends who would testify against me if I ever chose to fight him on it."

Turner placed a hand on her shoulder. "Cassandra, I'm so sorry. For everything."

"Me too, Turner. I'm sorry for unloading on you like that. You didn't deserve it."

Turner removed his hand, and Cassandra shivered at the lingering warmth of his touch.

Just then a knock came on the door. Cassandra stared at Turner, both of them sharing the same thought. Brad!

The knock came again and a woman's voice called out, "Turner, it's me."

Quickly motioning Cassandra into the bedroom, Turner replied, "I'm coming, Mama Retta."

Cassandra grabbed the suitcase and slipped into the bedroom, willing Justin not to moan or cry out in his sleep. She pressed her ear against the panel and listened as the front door opened and Loretta greeted Turner with, "We need to talk, young man."

chapter 11

URNER SAT ON the couch with Loretta, who faced him squarely and asked, "Exactly what do you know about the woman with the little boy?"

Shrugging nonchalantly, he replied, "I fixed her safety chain and talked to her on the stairs. But I—"

Loretta held up a hand. "Don't play innocent with me, young man. Two guys have been snooping around looking for them, and they talked to you in the process. Then the woman's husband came here today and talked to you too. Do you see a pattern here?"

Turner feigned innocence.

"Are you going to sit there and pretend you don't know what I'm talking about?" Loretta said, staring directly into his eyes.

He squirmed beneath Loretta's piercing scrutiny.

"I can read Harvey like a book." Loretta continued, "and I know when he's genuinely worried about something. I learned long ago how to finagle things out of him. But I only know the story from his perspective, which both you and I know can be pretty warped. I want to hear the story from yours. So are going to be a good boy and spell it out for me, or do I have to cancel Sunday dinner privileges?"

"I *want* to be a good boy, Mama Retta."

"Then start spelling."

Turner glanced apprehensively at the bedroom door. For obvious reasons Cassandra had trust issues. How would she feel if he told Loretta about her? How much of her story dared he relate without her permission?

Loretta patted his knee. "She's here, isn't she?"

Looking at her in surprise, Turner said, "How did you know?"

"I didn't until I came in and saw how neat and tidy your apartment is. I knew that wasn't your doing." She motioned toward the bedroom door. "Ask her to come in here so we can talk."

Bowing to Loretta's keen detective skills, Turner went to the bedroom door and knocked softly. "Cassandra, it's me. You can come out now. Mama Retta's a friend. You can trust her."

The door opened slowly and Cassandra emerged, holding Justin protectively. The little boy clutched the monkey in one arm and had the other arm wrapped around his mother's neck.

"Well, hello there," Loretta said, smiling warmly at Justin. "Aren't you a little cutie!"

"Hello," Justin replied shyly, his large, blue eyes the portrait of innocence and trust.

"I don't want you to be upset with Turner for telling me about you," Loretta said. "But I had to find out what's going on." She looked at Cassandra sympathetically. "I know a person who's in trouble when I see one. And you, young lady, are in trouble."

Tears formed in Cassandra's eyes and obeyed the law of universal gravitation. She clung to Justin with the fervor and pathos of a Michelangelo sculpture—mother and child captured in living stone. "It's true," she said, her voice breaking.

Justin craned his neck to peer up into her face. "Why are you crying, Mommy?" He stroked her cheek gently.

As Turner watched the living sculpture, the painful memories of his experiences in high school seemed to pale in comparison. He handed Cassandra a tissue.

"Mommy's fine," Cassandra said, stroking her son's head.

"Let's get him something to eat," Loretta said. "Occupy his attention while we talk."

Turner poured a bowl of the *crunchy* cereal and set Justin up to the table. While Justin focused on his cereal, the three sat on the couch and talked.

"What's your story, dear?" Loretta asked, taking Cassandra's hand.

Cassandra told it, chapter by chapter.

When she finished, Loretta had tears in her eyes too. "Do your parents live in town?" she inquired, her voice filled with emotion.

"No, they divorced several years ago and went their separate ways. Dad ended up in New York and died of a heart attack last year. Mom now lives in LA and is an alcoholic. She had problems before the divorce, and it only got worse afterward." Her expression clouded over. "She's in no position to help me."

"Are there any relatives you could contact?"

Cassandra wiped her eyes, folding and unfolding the tissue. "They all live back east."

"Then we're going to have to proceed without their help," Loretta said. "We've got to get you and your son to a safer place until things can be worked out. If your husband finds you and forces you to return home..." She paused, letting the ominous silence suggest possibilities.

"I know where Cassandra can go," Turner said, anxious to make a contribution. "To a women's shelter."

"Women's shelters can be a haven for abused women, true," Loretta said. "But the local one isn't. My friend Mary Sweet worked there as a volunteer. She quit when a drug-crazed woman threatened her with a knife. The shelter admits addicts, alcoholics, freeloaders, and abusers. It doesn't have proper screening or accountability." She glanced at Justin, who was eating contentedly at the table. "That's not where we want to send that little boy."

Turner nodded in agreement.

71

"However, you may be on to something," Loretta added. "Mary still counsels abused women privately, in her home. She can help you contact a lawyer, fill out the police reports so charges can be filed, and—"

"I can't go to the police," Cassandra said, cutting her off and glancing at Justin, who was wiping a drop of milk from his shirt.

"But you've got to protect yourself and your child," Loretta protested.

Cassandra shook her head determinedly. "Last year a friend of mine went to the police and told them she was being abused by her husband. A restraining order was issued, he was kicked out of the house, and she got sole custody of the children. He was charged with assault. But while waiting for his court appearance, he broke into their home, severely beat her, and took the children and disappeared. She was in the hospital for three weeks. I can't risk losing Justin. Brad would do the same to me. Or worse."

The saturated tissue was back up to her face. Then biting her lip, she slid her shirt partway down over her shoulder. Dark bruises were evident on her back and upper arm.

Loretta sucked in a sharp breath, and Turner scowled grimly.

"Justin was playing with Brad's trophies and didn't put them back in the right order," Cassandra explained. "When Brad got home, he went ballistic. I told him I had been dusting them. He said I had violated him and didn't respect his accomplishments. And if I ever touched his trophies again"—she lowered her voice to a whisper—"he'd make me pay."

"Over something that minor?" Loretta gasped.

Cassandra pulled her shirt back over her shoulder. "It wasn't minor to him. He punched me several times and stormed into the bedroom, waiting for me to come and... *apologize*. If he'd found out it was Justin who had disturbed his trophies, there's no telling what he would have done to him. That's when I knew I had to take Justin and leave. And never go back."

Turner felt himself growing angrier by the minute. He knew Brad and what he was capable of doing. Brad had been a champion on the gridiron. But what kind of champion beat up women and threatened children?

"Mary lives in Colorado Springs," Loretta said. "You need to visit her so she can counsel you and help you decide what to do."

"I don't want to be a bother," Cassandra said. "Your friend doesn't even know me."

"She knows you…because she knows many other women in your position."

Cassandra hesitated. "I don't have any money for bus fare. Not until I can finalize things at the bank."

"Money is no problem," Loretta said.

"You can buy a bus ticket at the depot and—" Turner began.

"The bus depot is probably being watched," Loretta said, interrupting him. "You'll have to drive instead."

Turner didn't own a car, but he knew Harvey and Loretta did. A silver 1992 Buick Century, in mint condition. It had been an inheritance from Loretta's uncle, now deceased. She had never learned how to drive, but she was still the keeper of the keys.

"You're offering the use of your car, Mama Retta?" Turner asked.

"It'll do the old girl good to get out on the road again. Harvey just putters around town in it." At the mention of her husband, she paused a moment. "By the way, I'd just as soon he didn't know about this for now."

"Understood," Turner said.

"You can leave tonight," Loretta said, and Turner noticed she was looking directly at him.

"Ma'am?"

"You need to go with them. See that they arrive safe and sound. I'll call Mary and let her know you're coming. Let me use your cell phone, Turner."

When Turner looked at her questioningly, she added, "In case the motel telephone lines have been tapped."

Turner decided not to mention that although there was a time that it was impossible to monitor cell phone conversations, everything changed with 9/11. Technology now existed to trace and listen in on cell phone conversations with the ease of the proverbial fly on the wall. But there was still a chance their pursuers didn't yet have access to equipment that rivaled Homeland Security's.

He handed her his cell phone and then turned to Cassandra, awaiting her response. She looked at Loretta, who held the cell phone poised for action, and then slipped into the bedroom momentarily. She returned carrying a single white envelope. "I'll do it," she said. "But if anything happens to me, see that the police get this. It's very important."

"What is it?" Loretta asked.

"Justice," Cassandra murmured. "Promise me you'll send it to the police."

Loretta slipped the envelope into her pocket and said, "I promise." Then she motioned toward the bedroom door as she punched in Mary's number. "Get your suitcase, Turner, and your school backpack. And remember to pack clean—"

"I'm on it, Mama Retta," Turner said quickly, sparing himself the indignity of being told to pack clean boxers.

chapter 12

As the sun dipped below the mountains to the west, Cassandra sat with Turner on the couch and waited for the night to deepen. Justin lay on the area rug, his chin resting in his hands, watching the Cartoon Network. The stuffed monkey lay beside him, similarly positioned.

Cassandra couldn't concentrate on the TV, not even as a pleasant distraction. It was as if total darkness would come only if she gave it her full and undivided attention. As a result she continually glanced toward the window, willing clouds to roll in and mask the moon and the stars.

She looked at Turner at one point and their eyes met. She felt an unspoken anxiety and was grateful to have him as an ally. But what was she getting him into? Did she really have the right to impose on him in this way?

Wanting to do something to keep busy, she went into the kitchen and began sweeping an already clean floor.

Turner joined her. "My apartment is going to miss you," he said.

She smiled at the notion, but in a way she was going to miss it too. Though small and unadorned in comparison to her house in Las Vegas, it had a better atmosphere. And despite the danger lurking outside the motel walls, she felt strangely safe and protected in this shoebox. That was something she *was* going to miss.

"I read a survey recently," she said. "It asked whether or not we would want to know our future if we could, including how and when we die. You know the surprising thing?"

Turner shrugged. "A made-for-TV movie is in production, based on the results."

"No, wise guy. Eight out of ten people said they wouldn't."

"I'm with the eight."

"Not me, I'm with the two."

Turner made a face. "I bet when you were a kid you snuck into all your Christmas presents early and then carefully rewrapped them so no one would know."

Cassandra smiled guiltily. "I don't handle suspense well. I just had to know what was inside. Just like if I had a choice, I'd like to know how this day is going to end." She swept a moment longer and then looked pensively at Turner. "I really appreciate your help, Turner. But I'm wondering why you're doing it."

Motioning toward Justin, who was glued to the TV, Turner said, "When I was ten, my parents split up for a while. To this day I don't know all the issues. I was bounced back and forth between home and the apartment my dad rented. I've experienced both sides of the story. I know what it's like to be caught between your parents' differences and to have your heart slowly torn in two."

"What finally happened?"

"They eventually worked things out and got back together."

"That's good."

"Yeah." But his grim face told her that wasn't the end of the story.

"Where are they now?" she prodded.

"A few years ago my mom got cancer."

"Oh, no."

He nodded, his eyes downcast. "I prayed hard for God to heal her. I bargained with Him, went to church, put all the money I had in the collection plate. But she died anyway." He slumped down on a kitchen chair and rested his elbows on the table. "That's when God and I parted company. And when my father remarried and moved away, I had to leave our family home. That's how I ended up here. God took everything away from me."

Cassandra set the broom aside and laid a hand on Turner's arm. "Not everything. Don't you see? He *led* you here. You've got a job, and you have good people in your life. Loretta's amazing. And you're enrolled in college. Look at what you've accomplished with God's help. "

Turner stared at the tabletop bitterly. "Where was He when my mother died?"

"We all lose loved ones, Turner. That's part of life—part of the plan."

Shifting in the chair, Turner said, "Time for a better plan, I'd say."

She sat at the table and pulled her chair close to him. "You're not the only one who's wondered what God is up to, Turner." Tears welled in her eyes. "I prayed that Brad's heart would be softened and he would stop hitting me. I prayed to know how to help him, to know how to save our marriage." She exhaled and looked around the room. "Yet here I am."

Turner looked at her sullenly. "And yet you still think there's a plan?"

"I found the strength to do what I needed to do." She reached over and took his hand. "I don't know what's in store for Justin and me. But I believe we were led to you, just like you were led to Loretta and to your job here. And I believe we'll be led to where we need to go next."

Turner squeezed her hand. "I wish I had your faith, Cassandra." He got up from the table and crossed to the window, where he lifted a blind to look out. "It's just about dark enough. We can leave soon."

She flashed him a look that blended anxiousness, tension,

and hopefulness. They maintained eye contact for a long moment, and then she glanced around the room, wanting to take in everything one last time. Truly it would be harder to leave this tiny apartment than it had been leaving her spacious home.

chapter 13

*U*NDER THE COVER of darkness Turner edged out into the walkway, his backpack slung over one shoulder, the suitcases in hand. He glanced at Cassandra, who held Justin securely in her arms. Before leaving the apartment, they had convinced the little boy that this night's adventure was to see who could be the quietest.

Despite the tense situation Turner couldn't hide a smile when he saw Justin put a finger to his lips as a reminder to be quiet. The little boy's big, blue eyes were filled with anticipation, and Turner could only wonder at the innocence of childhood. But the realities of adulthood were far more pressing, and he, for one, would not draw an easy breath until Lakewood appeared in the rearview mirror.

He stopped breathing altogether when he saw Twitch.

The tall, lean man was silhouetted against a streetlight as he crossed the road. He paused to let a car pass and then proceeded toward the motel.

Turner's mind began to spin. Perhaps Slick or Twitch had planted a listening device when they showed up at his door. Although unlikely, considering the men hadn't raided his apartment, Turner was rattled enough to believe that anything was possible.

Cassandra saw him too, but somehow Turner managed to cover her mouth so she didn't scream. He thought of retreating back into the room and barricading the door, but strategically that was a bad plan. They would be painting themselves into a corner, discovering too late that the paint was a nondrying variety.

The men were not going to go away. They had set up a perimeter around the motel and seemed determined to wait it out.

The moment called for clear thinking and levelheadedness. But reflex action unplugged his brain and muscles engaged automatically. "Run!" he whispered urgently.

Hugging the wall as though attempting to blend in with the stucco, Turner and Cassandra scurried to the garage at the far end of the motel. Loretta was waiting inside to open and close the garage door for them.

Turner glanced in all directions before opening the side door. "One of the men is outside," he whispered to Loretta, ushering Cassandra inside and closing the door quickly behind them.

Loretta exhaled sharply. "Then you'll have to wait. He'll see you driving away."

Turner peered out of the window. "Maybe we won't have to wait, Mama Retta. Not if *you* drive us out of here."

"What?" she gasped.

"We'll hide in the car. Nobody will be suspicious to see you drive away."

"But I don't know how to drive."

"It's just like cooking. Follow the recipe, step by step, and everything will turn out fine."

"Can you stop thinking about food long enough to make some sense."

"It'll work. I'll duck down in the front seat and give you instructions. You know...the recipe."

For the first time since he'd known her, Loretta seemed overwhelmed. "I don't know if I can do this."

"Sure you can," Turner insisted. "I'll call Harvey on my cell and let him know you're going to visit a friend. You have a niece who lives in Castle Rock, right? I'll have her pick you up at Mary's and give you a ride home."

"But driving a car...?" Loretta said, still unconvinced.

"Here are the ingredients, Mama Retta. Insert the key, start the engine, put the car in reverse, press on the gas gently, back out. Simple, like baking a cake."

"It might be our only chance," Cassandra said.

Glancing at Justin, who stared back at her with unblinking eyes, Loretta released her breath slowly and nodded. "Okay, I'll do it." She reached into the pocket of her pants and pulled out a small bundle of money. "Here, take this. You'll need it."

Turner hesitated. "I can't take your money, Mama Retta."

"You can and you will. Now be quick about it. We've got to go."

After pocketing the money, Turner threw his backpack and the luggage into the trunk and helped everyone get seated. Then he quietly opened the garage door and climbed into the passenger side. He had to remind himself that cowering in the front seat with his head ducked as low as anatomically possible was not unmanly. Any dent to his self-esteem could be pounded out once they were clear of Lakewood.

Loretta started the engine and glanced down at Turner.

"Easy on the gas pedal now," he said, "Just back slowly out of here."

Any thoughts Turner entertained of going gently into that good night vanished the moment Loretta put her foot to the pedal. The tires squealed and the car shot backward out of the garage. Loretta spun the steering wheel and did a one-eighty. Then she popped the car in drive and negotiated her way through the parking lot.

In a voice only slightly below that of a scream, Turner offered instructions, all of which Loretta ignored. His crouched position provided a good perspective on her foot action—one foot pressing the brake, the other the gas. Often both at the same time. An upward glance showed that the steering wheel was a windmill of activity. The fleshy part under her arms whipped back and forth as she steered wildly in an effort to dodge obstructions.

Turner braced himself as she cranked the steering wheel to the left, forcing him against the console.

"Wheee!" Justin cried as they descended the driveway leading to the curb and bounced into the street.

Cassandra murmured vigorously under her breath, and Turner wondered if she was praying.

He dared a peek out of the window. Parked cars seemed to be in jeopardy as Loretta hugged the edge of the street, staying away from the centerline in case a vehicle came along.

Glancing in the side mirror, he checked to see if they were being followed. There was no sign of anyone tailing them, and he began to breathe easier. Strangely, by attracting attention instead of avoiding it, they had managed to avert suspicion. Twitch couldn't have missed their departure. But since no one in his right mind would expect a serious escape attempt to occur like an episode of *World's Worst Driver*, he had probably laughingly dismissed it. Turner could imagine Twitch rolling his eyes before turning his attention back to maintaining a perimeter around the motel.

They drove two miles before Loretta was able to pull over. Fortunately, her brake foot overrode her gas pedal foot. "I think I'm starting to get the hang of this," she said, as the tires screeched to a stop.

Neither Cassandra nor Turner offered words of encouragement.

Turner drove the rest of the way to Mary Sweet's place, while Loretta talked about taking the Buick out for more regular spins every Sunday after dinner. With Turner along as the driving instructor! Her suggestion threatened to permanently spoil his appetite.

chapter 14

URING THE DRIVE to Colorado Springs, Loretta talked about Mary Sweet. As Cassandra listened from the backseat, she instinctively held Justin close as he sang his sleepy song and finally fell asleep. She stroked his head gently, wistfully, as Loretta's voice blended hypnotically with the rhythm of the tires.

Mary Sweet was born in Pittsburgh's Hill District, a predominantly black neighborhood, sometime in the fifties. Raised in a dilapidated apartment, she was abused by several of her mother's boyfriends and seemed destined to mirror her mother's life. But she managed to escape and find employment in a steel plant. There she met and married a young man, and they moved to Chicago. Mary eventually discovered her husband was a gambler. When she confronted him about it, he became angry, and so began a pattern of abuse that ended with her fleeing to a women's shelter. She moved from one place to another until she finally found employment at a women's shelter in Denver. But when she was attacked by a knife-wielding, crazed woman, she left and began an outreach program from her home.

Cassandra fought back tears as they drove in silence the rest of the way. Mary's story of abuse was reminiscent of another story she knew. All too well.

As they entered Colorado Springs, Turner slowed down and took the approaching exit. Cassandra touched her eyes, hoping they weren't puffy, and breathed in and out deeply several times in an effort to dispel the sadness.

Ten minutes later they arrived at their destination. Turner pulled into the driveway and turned off the engine, checking to make certain they hadn't been followed. Then he helped Cassandra carry Justin up to the house.

Mary Sweet met them at the door. She was a diminutive black woman who exuded boundless energy, and Cassandra liked her immediately. In size and shape Mary contrasted sharply to Loretta. Mary was thin, almost bony, and was a head shorter than her friend. Her smile was genuine, but there was an urgency about her that suggested they would not be discussing the weather, the tabloids, or the latest fashion trends.

"Come in, come in," she said, glancing up and down the street before ushering them inside and closing and locking the front door. She hugged the four of them in turn.

Justin had woken up when Turner carried him up to the house. Mary Sweet fussed over him and ran a hand through his curly blond hair. "Well, hello there, little child," she said.

Justin smiled and then rolled his eyes tiredly, stuck his thumb in his mouth, and promptly fell back asleep.

"Bring him into the bedroom," Mary directed, guiding them down a short hallway. "You and your son will sleep here." She indicated the second door on the right, and Cassandra felt an overwhelming sense of gratitude for the hospitality. She sensed in Mary a kindred spirit.

Mary smiled at Turner and indicated the door next to it. "This is your room."

Turner followed Cassandra into the first bedroom and lay Justin on the bed. Cassandra tucked her son in and kissed him on the cheek before accompanying Turner into the living room. The front curtains were drawn tight, and she noticed Mary peek through them once before motioning for everyone to sit on the couch.

As they got situated, Mary went into the kitchen and returned a few moments later with three glasses of lemonade on a tray. "I know you're probably exhausted," she said, handing them each a glass, "but we need to talk." She slid a chair close to the couch and sat down so they were practically knee to knee. "Loretta has told me about your situation. Let me make sure I understand the facts." She recounted what Loretta had told her on the phone.

Cassandra nodded solemnly to confirm the accuracy of the account.

Mary reached out and took her hand. "So, baby girl, you won't go to the police. What *are* you planning to do?" Her eyes suddenly narrowed. "You're not thinking of going back to your husband!"

Shaking her head vigorously, Cassandra said, "I want to go as far away as possible where my husband will never be able to find us."

"Live with relatives?"

"No. Brad knows them. He'd track me down."

"So you realize he's dangerous. Many wives try to make excuses for their abusive husbands. I'm glad you're not hung up on that."

Cassandra slumped in her seat. "I used to be. I'd tell myself that his abuse was somehow my fault. If I could only look better, keep the house tidier, and spend less money then he'd stop yelling at me."

"Mental abuse is just as hurtful as physical abuse," Mary sighed.

"I used to think it was the bad economy and the pressures of his business," Cassandra continued. "I thought that the stress was to blame for his bad temper. And I felt guilty because I was part of his stress. After all, he was trying to provide for Justin and me."

"But now you know better, don't you?" Loretta said, unable to keep her disgust for Brad out of her voice.

Cassandra nodded and wiped away a tear.

Mary leaned closer in her chair. "Over two hundred thousand women are physically abused by their husbands or significant others every year in America. Can you imagine? That's more than six hundred women every day!"

"So many," Loretta muttered, genuinely shocked.

"And it's actually more than that," Mary added. "A large number of incidents are never reported. A medical friend told me that less than 20 percent of battered women ever seek medical help. Wives make excuses for their husbands, and many others won't report abuse because they think the police won't do anything about it."

More tears formed in Cassandra's eyes.

Mary rubbed the back of Cassandra's hand compassionately. "I can't say I agree with your decision not to go to the police. It's important to get the facts on record, to document the nature and instances of the abuse, and start a file that can and will be used one day to see that justice is served. But I realize you're not ready yet, and I won't pressure you. I'm just glad you had the courage to leave. Children who are exposed to family violence can suffer symptoms of post-traumatic stress disorder."

"Post-traumatic stress disorder?" Loretta asked.

Up to this point Turner hadn't contributed to the conversation. Now he said, "Post-traumatic stress disorder involves the symptoms that appear after a stressful event, like a natural disaster or an accident."

Or living with an abusive father, Cassandra thought bitterly.

"Well, listen to you," Mary said, arching an eyebrow at Turner.

"Symptoms can include things like bed-wetting or

nightmares," he continued. "Kids who witness abuse can have medical problems, such as stomachaches and headaches and even depression."

Cassandra winced at the mention of *depression*. Was it possible her four-year-old son was susceptible to it?

Mary took both of Cassandra's hands in hers. "Leaving was the best thing you could do for your little son, bless his heart." She paused and studied Cassandra momentarily. "I said I wouldn't pressure you to go to the police, and I won't. You're under enough stress as it is, baby girl. You look exhausted. What you need to do is go somewhere safe where you can have time to think and relax and sort things out."

"Where would that be?" Cassandra asked wearily.

"A former client of mine owns a small cabin outside of Silverthorne. For years she's been trying to talk me into making use of it, but I've never taken her up on it. Matter of fact, she called again just the other day, so I know the cabin is available. I'll call her and tell her I've decided to accept her offer. It's an ideal place—private and secluded. I'll give you the directions in the morning, and you can leave...after you get some rest. Agreed?"

"Agreed," Loretta said before Cassandra could reply.

chapter 15

*T*URNER WAS AWAKENED in the middle of the night by a cry. He lay in bed, staring into the darkness, listening. Muffled voices were coming from Cassandra's bedroom, next door. At first he couldn't make out what was being said, and he wondered if he was having a high-school-related nightmare.

A voice rose in pitch, and he heard, "Scary, Mommy. The man was scary."

Moments later a shadow crossed the threshold of his door, and he quickly sat up, completely awake now. He heard another voice, a woman's. Since Loretta's niece had picked her up earlier, he knew the voice belonged to Mary. She was speaking in hushed tones to Cassandra, who was answering back, although he still couldn't make out what they were saying.

His bedroom door slowly opened and a dark figure stood silhouetted in the doorway, backlit by the light from the streetlamp on the corner. "Turner, are you awake?" It was Mary.

"Yeah."

"Get up quickly."

He was on his feet in an instant, struggling into his pants. It may have been dark, but he wasn't going to parade around in his boxers. Even if they were clean.

Mary led the way into Cassandra's bedroom. Justin was whimpering softly and Cassandra was trying to console him.

"Turner," Mary said, lowering her voice to a whisper. "Someone's outside."

He stared at Mary in disbelief. During their drive to Colorado Springs, he had repeatedly checked to make sure they weren't being followed. They had spent the late evening talking and then had called Loretta's niece, visiting until she arrived and drove Loretta home. Then they had said goodnight and headed for separate bedrooms. Everything had been in order, and their plans were proceeding smoothly. Now this.

"Are you sure?" he whispered hoarsely.

"Justin had to go to the bathroom," Cassandra replied, her voice equally hoarse. "When I was tucking him back in bed, he said he saw a man at the window. When I looked up, there was no one there."

"The man was scary," Justin said, his voice quivering.

"Were you having a bad dream, little child?" Mary asked, stroking his head.

"I saw him," Justin insisted.

"There's only one way to find out," Turner said. "I'm going to slip outside and have a look around." He realized nothing less would ease minds and alleviate fears. And there was no sense calling the police. If Slick or his cohort *were* out there, they would simply disappear when the police arrived, and Mary would be left to explain things to the disgruntled officer who answered the false alarm. And once the police left, the intruder would return and be *really* scary this time.

Mary slipped something cold and metallic into his hand. "Take this."

Turner didn't need to hold it up to the window to know that she had given him a handgun. He hesitated to take it. He had never had any experience or training with weapons, unless you counted the archery lessons he gave at Camp Kopawanee. He might end up accidentally shooting himself in the foot. "Thanks, ma'am," he said, returning the handgun. "I'll be fine without it."

"If someone is out there, *he* may have one," she whispered.

That may be true, Turner thought, and the intruder may not have any compunction about shooting *him*. But Turner felt safer relying on his experience for a guide and his wits for a weapon. "You keep it," he said, implying that if the man outside got by him, she was the last line of defense. He glanced around the dark room. "I'll slip out a side window. Is there one near some tall shrubs?"

"Use the den window. The cedars along the side of the house will give you cover."

"Be careful," Cassandra whispered.

Turner nodded, intending to be *very* careful. If men were out there skulking in the yard, he didn't want to wander in and catch them off guard. Surprise a wild animal on the trail and there was no telling what might happen. Same principle with dangerous men. "Keep as quiet as possible," he said, giving obvious advice. "I'll be back in a minute."

Mary guided him into the den. He carefully opened the window and poked his head out, listening for any telltale noises. A dog barked in the distance, and the sound of traffic on the freeway hummed steadily in the night air, but otherwise it was still.

A three-quarter moon hung in the sky, casting a silver sheen over the yard. There were no visible signs that the area had been violated, and no indication that anyone still lingered. Still, a perfunctory glance wasn't sufficient to draw any final conclusions.

Turner climbed through the window and eased himself to the ground, careful not to betray his presence by stepping on a twig or brushing a branch against the side of the house. He ducked low and left the security of the bushes, scampering across the lawn and heading for the darkest recesses of the yard. Pressing against a tree to catch his breath, he listened above the sound of the blood pounding in his ears. A noise could mean anything...or nothing. The dog had stopped barking, but the steady sounds of the distant traffic continued. He hoped the white noise would cover any sound he made as he began the slow process of circling around to the back of the house.

He couldn't help wondering if he was walking into a trap. Slick and Twitch could be waiting to twist his arm into giving up Cassandra and Justin. And he didn't doubt for a minute the men's powers of persuasion. The trick was to avoid them altogether, verify their presence or lack thereof, and do it without revealing *his* presence and getting himself captured. Or...something worse.

As he crept through the row of fragrant cedars that bordered the yard, Turner prayed his foot didn't land on a dry twig or on the tail of a sleeping cat. One errant sound and his presence would be announced as surely as if he pulled out a trumpet and played a cavalry charge.

The matted leaves provided a soft bed, and he was able to reach the backyard without incident. As he peered around the trunk of a large tree, he froze. A figure was huddled in the shadows at the back of the yard, near a small shed. Turner saw a red glow and realized the man was smoking. He tested the air and decided it was a sweeter blend than the cigarette variety. Undoubtedly it was something illegal and equally unhealthy.

In the moonlight he recognized Twitch. How the man had found them, Turner couldn't guess. Turner had been careful to ensure they hadn't been tailed. But despite his precautions and care, here was Twitch, casing the place and waiting.

Justin *had* seen a face at the window. His non-nightmare had just become Turner's real nightmare.

Turner crept closer through the foliage. The pinprick of red light grew brighter, followed by a puff of white smoke, and he could hear muffled talking. Were there two men? It was then he realized Twitch was talking on his cell phone.

"What now?" Twitch inquired. There was a long pause and then he said, "Are you sure? I say I sneak in right now, knock out the doofus, and nab her.

Another pause. "Okay, okay. I'll wait. Just hurry up."

Turner had heard enough. His blood was now the temperature of a refrigerated beverage.

He made his way back to the house and climbed in cautiously through the den window. "It's me," he whispered, warning Mary so she didn't shoot him by mistake.

"What did you find out?" she asked anxiously.

"There's a man in the backyard," Turner replied, closing the window and following Mary into Cassandra's bedroom.

Cassandra listened to Turner's report and then asked, "What are we going to do?"

"We've got to get out of here," Turner said, remembering Twitch's suggestion about knocking out the *doofus*.

"But what about the guy outside?" Cassandra asked anxiously.

"We'll have to scare him off," Mary said. "Give you a head start."

"How?" Turner and Cassandra both asked at the same time.

Mary wagged a finger in the air. "This calls for a lesson from the Good Book."

"With all due respect, ma'am, there isn't time for Sunday school," Turner said.

"It's not a *talking* lesson, it's an *activity* lesson," she replied. "When Gideon and his army were sent against the Midianites, he used a plan that tipped the scales in his favor. It's time for Operation Gideon...and help from the good Lord Himself. Turner, you and Cassandra get the child and your belongings and wait at the front door. On my signal, head for the car and drive away like fury."

"Where to?"

"There's a motel just off I-25, along East Pikes Peak. One of the women I counsel runs it. Tell her I sent you." She scribbled down the information and handed it to Turner.

"What about you?" Cassandra asked.

"I'll go to the Johnson's, two doors down, and call the police. I'll stay there until they arrive. That will give you time to get away. The police don't need to be the wiser that you were ever here. I'll leave you out of my statement."

"But, ma'am—"

"Just trust me on this. I'll call you in the morning with directions to the cabin. Now get moving."

She had an air of authority reminiscent of Loretta. They obeyed.

Mary joined them at the front door moments later, carrying a boom box. "I'm going to open the back door a crack and put this in the gap," she said. "Then I'm going to turn on the back porch light, which is a floodlight, and illuminate the entire backyard. When the light comes on and the music starts blaring, that's the signal."

"I hate to leave you here," Cassandra said.

"I'll be okay at the Johnson's. I'm just sorry we didn't have a chance to talk more. But you've got to get away." She glanced heavenward as if uttering a prayer and then headed for the back door, carrying the boom box.

Turner and Cassandra waited.

An eternity passed before the back porch light flashed on, accompanied by a sudden blast of gospel music. To anyone in the backyard, it must have sounded as though the Second Coming had arrived.

Turner flung the front door open and grabbed the suitcases.

Cassandra picked up Justin and followed Turner out to the car. Turner threw the luggage in the backseat as Cassandra climbed in the front, holding Justin against her. Turner climbed behind the wheel, cranked the engine, and in honor of Mary's request, drove away like fury.

As they cleared the neighborhood, Turner glanced in the rearview mirror in time to see a set of headlights bearing down on them. As they grew in intensity, he realized they belonged to a black Mercedes, and he didn't need two guesses to know who was sitting behind the wheel. Obviously Slick was closer than Turner expected and had arrived in time to witness their departure. The chase was now on.

Cassandra noticed Turner's reaction and whirled around, following his line of vision.

"It's him," Turner said.

She clutched Justin closer in a gesture that conveyed what they both felt. Panic.

"Hang on!" Turner said, glancing over at Justin, who was pressed against his mother. The little boy's large, sleepy, blue eyes were filled with trust. Turner tried to smile at him to let him know that everything was going to be okay, but it was hard to smile a lie.

Turner gunned the engine and the Buick responded with surprising enthusiasm.

As they raced down the street, Turner peered wildly ahead, looking for an exit. The Buick was in great condition, a classic combination of tin and chrome, but it was no match for the thoroughbred that Slick was driving. The Buick would never be able to outrun the Mercedes.

When a side street came up suddenly, Turner cranked the wheel at the last minute. The car took the corner in a maneuver that would have impressed any Hollywood stunt driver.

But it didn't impress Cassandra. "Take it easy!" she gasped, looking at him like he was determined to kill them and save their pursuer the trouble.

Slick overshot the exit, and Turner saw the tires of the Mercedes smoke as the brake lights glowed blood red. The backup lights flashed on an instant later.

Turner's maneuver bought them a few extra seconds, and he took advantage of them. He roared down the street and turned into a residential area, taking each corner in turn—a right, a left, and another right—as he zigzagged through the sleeping neighborhood. Deciding not to earn more of Cassandra's disapproval, he kept all four tires on the ground.

"Where are we going?" she asked, hugging Justin desperately.

"Anywhere," Turner replied.

"The guy will expect us to try and outrun him. Let's pull in somewhere and sit tight."

Careful not to let the brake lights betray their location, Turner let the car coast down the street. A paved alley appeared up ahead, and he turned into it, noticing a large, metal trash bin that providentially jutted into the alleyway. He flipped around in a rear driveway and pulled up behind the bin, facing the direction they had come. A flick of a finger extinguished the headlights; a turn of the wrist killed the engine. Unrolling the window, he listened for the sounds of an approaching vehicle.

Rap music drifted from a house farther down the alley, and a marauding cat leaped from the top of the fence and landed lightly on the trash bin. Otherwise the alley was quiet and deserted.

Clouds hovered overhead, blocking the moonlight. Only the occasional pinprick of starlight jabbed through a gap in the clouds. There were no streetlights in the alley, so the headlights of an approaching vehicle would announce its presence before the tires did.

"Do you think we lost him?" Cassandra whispered, as though their pursuer would hear her if she spoke any louder.

"I don't know," Turner replied. "I took the corner pretty fast and drove like a mad man through the neighborhood."

"I noticed."

"It was fun," Justin said.

Turner smiled sheepishly at Cassandra and held his hand poised above the ignition key, waiting to fire up the Buick at a moment's notice. They sat in the darkness, glancing around and listening for the slightest indication of an approaching vehicle.

The trash bin screened them somewhat from the front. But what Turner hadn't counted on was Slick stumbling on to them from the rear. A beam of light suddenly appeared at the far end of the alley, followed by the screech of tires.

Turner's first instinct was to twist the key, wrestle the transmission into gear, and roar away in a cloud of smoking rubber. Cassandra's sudden grip on his arm told him she shared the same sentiment.

But he hesitated, studying the car in the rearview mirror. Did Slick recognize their vehicle? For all Slick knew, it could be a car that normally parked there, the occupant comfortably inside the house, in bed. From what Turner had observed of the neighborhood, a car like theirs was not out of place. The condition of the houses and fences told him that many residents probably hung on to anything that still ran, no matter how old of a model it was.

Slick began to move ahead but then stopped again. Turner could almost feel Slick's eyes studying the contours of the Buick, peering into the interior, searching for recognition. And then there it was!

The Mercedes spun into the alley and bore down on the Buick with the speed of a pizza deliveryman about to have his wages deducted for arriving late. As Slick raced down the alley, Turner cranked the engine and raced out, motor revving, tires squealing. Several back porch lights blinked on, and the marauding cat, lazily crossing the alley, disappeared beneath the wheels of the Mercedes.

Exiting the alley on two tires again—without any criticism from Cassandra this time—Turner cranked the wheel sharply and roared away. Ahead, the street wound its way up a steep hill, disappearing into a thick swatch of bushes and trees that covered the slope.

This was his intended destination. But instead of driving directly there, he continued his serpentine pattern, taking corners in a random order so Slick wouldn't figure it out, skip ahead, and beat them to the next intersection. Sometimes Turner took two lefts in a row, sometimes two rights.

The Mercedes stuck with them for most of it, however. Turner caught glimpses of the headlights in his rearview mirror. On one occasion they disappeared and Turner thought he had ditched his pursuer. But then the headlights suddenly reappeared, and the Mercedes bore down in hot pursuit.

And it *was* hot.

Perspiration stung Turner's eyes, and he wiped his face with the back of his hand. Cassandra's hair clung to her forehead and her cheeks were flushed.

As co-navigator, Cassandra continually glanced over her shoulder to give Turner moment-by-moment updates on the Mercedes's location...which seemed to be drawing closer.

Turner noticed a semitrailer pull out of a service station ahead and lumber into the street in a wide arc. Swerving around it in one fluid motion—which resulted in a gasp of shock from Cassandra and a shriek of excitement from Justin— he turned at the intersection just ahead and shot down the side street before pulling behind a sign that advertised State

Farm Insurance. Thick brush grew at the base of the sign like a bushy beard, hiding the Buick completely.

He flicked off the headlights and watched as the Mercedes went roaring by. But he knew it wouldn't take Slick long to realize that they were no longer ahead of him. They had to move on.

Keeping the headlights off, he eased the car out from behind the sign and headed in the opposite direction. They drove for ten minutes without any sign of the Mercedes.

"I think we lost him," Cassandra said, brushing the hair from her forehead.

"Losing someone like that's about as easy as losing thirty pounds," Turner replied.

Cassandra forced a smile. "So what now?"

He glanced in the rearview mirror out of habit. "Let's head for a motel. We need to get some rest and wait for Mary's call."

"She said there was a motel just off I-25 and Pikes Peak Avenue. Should we go there?"

"Better not, just in case the men planted a listening device or something. Someone could be waiting there for us."

Cassandra motioned toward the dashboard. "Too bad this old girl doesn't have a GPS unit. Where will we find a motel?"

"I work at one, remember? I have a pretty good idea where they're usually located."

Inside of ten minutes they found a motel on a quiet street, with a tree-lined alley where they could discreetly park. Checking in as *Mr. and Mrs. Jones*, they carried Justin and the luggage into the room, drew the curtains, locked the door, engaged the safety chain, used the facilities, and collapsed on the double beds.

chapter 17

*C*ASSANDRA SLEPT FITFULLY. Her dreams were invaded by random images of a black Mercedes bearing down on them, Brad's face contorted in anger, and a wall safe that was now missing a large envelope. Adding to her poor night's sleep was the fact that Justin was a bed hog. He kneed and elbowed her repeatedly as he tossed and turned, and at one point he ended up with his feet in her face.

She was finally dozing off when Justin suddenly jumped on her and chirped, "Good morning, Mommy."

"Morning, sweetie," she whispered, glancing across at Turner, hoping not to awaken him. It felt strangely natural to have him in the room with Justin and her. And comforting. "Did you have a good sleep?"

"Yeah," he said, jumping on her again.

She was in the middle of wrestling him down so she could hug him when she heard a buzzing sound, distant and soft. Glancing sideways, she noticed Turner's cell phone vibrating enthusiastically on the nightstand that sat between the two double beds.

"Wake Turner up," she said to Justin.

His eyes widened in anticipation. After climbing down, he hurried to Turner's bed and jumped on him. "Good morning, Turner. Time to wake up."

Turner came up out of bed with a sudden jerk and looked around in confusion.

"It's your cell phone," Cassandra said, pointing at it.

"Good morning, little man," Turner said, ruffling Justin's

hair and reaching for the cell phone. Propping himself up on one elbow, he pressed the talk button and stifled a yawn. "Hello?" There was a brief pause. "Yes, good morning, Mary."

"Put it on speaker," Cassandra mouthed to him.

Turner complied. "I've got you on speaker phone, Mary."

"Good morning to you too, Cassandra," came Mary's cheerful response. "How's that cute little child doing?"

"I'm good," Justin answered, reaching up to grab the phone.

"Everyone's fine," Cassandra replied, smiling as her son attempted to wrestle the phone away from Turner. "Thanks to you."

"How about you, ma'am?" Turner asked, holding the phone out of Justin's reach.

"I'm in my car, heading up I-25 as we speak."

"You're driving?"

"North."

Cassandra exchanged a worried look with Turner. "They're not after you, are they?" she asked.

"I hope so."

Turner shook his head as if to clear his foggy brain. "I don't understand."

Mary chuckled. "If anyone's trying to find you by following me, they're headed in the wrong direction."

"But what if they catch up to you?"

"I'm headed to the police station to follow up on the phone call I made last night. I don't think those guys will stick around too long."

Cassandra sighed in relief. "No, I don't suppose they will."

"Listen, I'm going to tell you the directions to the cabin. You all could use some serious R and R."

"I agree," Turner said.

"You probably won't have cell phone service once you reach the cabin, so call me from Silverthorne in a couple of days, and

I'll update you on things here. And Cassandra, please think about going to the police and filing a report. You shouldn't try to do this on your own."

"I'll think about it, Mary," Cassandra said. "Thanks for your concern."

Turner grabbed a paper and pencil and hurriedly wrote down the directions Mary provided. Then he thanked her and said good-bye.

Cassandra went to the window and parted the curtains slightly. "Do you think it's safe to leave?"

Turner joined her at the window. "I don't see a black Mercedes sitting in the parking lot, so I think we're good to go."

"You could sound more convincing."

"Those guys have tracked us every step of the way, Cassandra. But we lost them this time. There's no way they know where we are now."

"That's better." She wished she felt as confident as she tried to sound. "I'll get ready and we can grab a bite to eat before we hit the road."

"Sounds good," Turner said, opening the door slightly. "Everything's quiet out there."

"That sounds good too," she replied, smiling at him.

Twenty minutes later, they were in the car, driving in search of a fast-food joint. They found a McDonald's in less than five minutes and ordered at the drive-through window. Then Turner turned on to Highway 24 and drove north to intercept I-70, which would take them west to Silverthorne.

Cityscape to suburbia, suburbia to countryside, the tires sang of freedom and relief. In the distance, jagged peaks pierced the morning sky, making the horizon resemble the bottom half of a cracked eggshell. Cassandra should have felt relieved, even relaxed. But this morning something else was bothering her.

She glanced at Turner. Following high school, she never thought she would see him again. But he had come back into her life unexpectedly. For him to be working at the very motel she decided to check into was beyond coincidence. Her prayers had been heard and answered. But why... Turner? Who was he really? And why was he so willing to put himself in danger for her?

Choosing her words carefully, she said, "Everyone was so mean to you in high school, Turner."

He glanced at her. "Not everyone."

"I wasn't any better than the rest." She grimaced. "I didn't do enough to try and *stop* it."

Giving her a thin smile, he said, "Why should you have?"

"Because it was wrong. Like the time you were invited to Jen's party just so you could walk the dog."

"That wasn't your fault."

"But I could have talked her out of it. She would have listened to me, but I didn't say anything. I guess I was worried about—"

"Being teased like me?" he said, finishing the sentence for her.

She dropped her gaze guiltily. "Something like that."

Turner was silent for a moment. "I'll be honest, Cassandra. Seeing you again has been hard. Not because of anything you did personally. It's just that you brought back a lot of memories. I thought I had gotten over them, that enough time had passed that I could leave them behind. But I found out differently. And then seeing Brad again was a double—make that a triple—whammy."

"He always got his fun at other people's expense. Frequently yours." She reached across and placed a hand on his arm. "But for all the mean things that were done to you, you never retaliated. You never went out of your way to get even. You just took it. How did you manage?"

Turner shrugged. "I didn't have much choice. I took it because I didn't know what else to do. I couldn't stand up to Brad and the other guys or they'd have made mincemeat out of me. But don't imagine I didn't *think* about getting even. I'd have paid Brad and the others back in spades if I'd only known how to do it."

Cassandra sighed heavily. "To think of everything you went through—much of it in my presence—and now to think of what you're doing to help Justin and me. I feel so bad."

"Don't, Cassandra. Let it go."

"Look who's talking," she said, forcing a smile.

Turner grinned. "Actually I *am* getting even with Brad right now."

Cassandra felt a chill run down her spine. What did Turner mean? Was he getting even with Brad by...helping her? By taking her away from him—something Turner could not have done in high school—and doing it as payback? Was that his true motivation?

She fell silent and stared out of the window. She felt a flush of anger as she thought about being used as a pawn in a game of revenge. But then she remembered her conviction that she had been led to Turner. There had to be more to it than fate granting him a chance to have the last laugh. He had done so much for her already.

As if reading her thoughts, Turner said, "I hope my comment didn't upset you. This isn't about getting even by trying to settle an old score. It's about standing up to Brad and not giving him power over you anymore."

Cassandra's heart softened. Turner's concern for her was touching. "Thank you, Turner, for caring about how I feel.

That's something Brad never did. The only feelings ever up for consideration were his. In that way you're far ahead of him."

"Yeah, right."

She looked at him in earnest. "It's true, even in smaller ways. You fixed the safety chain for me. That's something he never would have gotten around to doing."

"Brad can throw a football farther, run the track better, and punch a bag harder than me. But I can fix a safety chain faster." He smiled grimly. "So that's the true measure of manhood?"

She tapped Turner on the chest, over his heart. "No, but what you have in there is. Brad worked to build other people's houses but neglected to build a *home* with Justin and me. And he always complained that he was too tired to do chores or jobs around the house." She pursed her lips sadly. "For me the only way he was handy was with his fists."

Turner didn't respond.

After a moment she said, "Thanks for being there for me, Turner." She nodded toward the backseat. "Thanks for being there for *us*."

"You're welcome," he said, reaching over and patting her hand. "Why don't you try and get some rest now?"

"You okay to keep driving?"

Turner nodded.

She leaned back against the headrest. "Thanks, I think I will. If you get sleepy, please wake me up."

"Sure."

Her restless night's sleep had caught up with her. The last thing she remembered was Justin singing a tuneless song to the monkey.

Turner watched as she breathed slowly, her profile outlined against the car window. And he contemplated the dramatic turn his life had taken.

Three days ago he had been living a quiet life as a student at Red Rocks Community College and handyman at the Mountain View Motel. Homework assignments and handyman tasks had been his primary focus. But they had been displaced by the arrival of Cassandra and Justin, whose safety was now his primary focus.

A husband—a very angry husband—existed. Brad Duncan was a force to be reckoned with. And so were the other two men. They posed a serious threat to Turner's life as a handyman and college student. But they posed more of a threat to Cassandra and Justin, and armed with that knowledge he drove on.

Highway 24 intersected with I-70, and Turner took the exit, west. In order to keep the car at a constant speed, he pushed harder on the accelerator as the landscape tilted heavenward. The sky became overcast, hiding the sun, and the highway stretched ahead like silvery-black wire uncoiling in the distance before disappearing over the next rise.

He glanced into the backseat to check on Justin.

The little boy had a thumb stuck in his mouth and was playing with the monkey's tail. Turner was glad he'd come across the stuffed toy in the maintenance room. Whatever child had left it behind had done Justin a great service.

Turner kept an eye on the gas gauge, which registered three-quarters of a tank. He was familiar with I-70 and knew that service stations were spaced conveniently along the route, but he was reluctant to stop for fear of waking Cassandra, and so he drove on.

His cell phone vibrated a short time later. He pulled it out of his pocket and checked the display. Maybe it was Loretta calling to see how they were doing. Or perhaps it was Mary calling to give him an update.

It wasn't.

A deep male voice said, "You lied to me."

It took him a moment to recognize Brad's voice.

Glancing over at Cassandra to make sure she was still asleep, he murmured, "What do you mean?"

"You know exactly what I mean."

Turner felt his heart rate quicken.

"You disappoint me, Pancake."

"It's not the first time, and I'm sure it won't be the last," Turner replied, straining to keep his voice steady.

"We'll see about that. Think you can get away with this? You were a loser in high school, and you're still a loser. And when I get my hands on you..." He left the thought dangling, like the end of a broken finger or a partially severed ear.

Turner's bravado flickered. He *had been* a loser in high school. And Brad had done some cruel things to him. He glanced over at Cassandra again and remembered the bruises on her back and arms. They bore testimony of what Brad's hands were capable of doing. And Turner could only imagine what *he'd* look like after Brad got through with him.

"It's kidnapping now, Pancake. Taking my son and running was a big mistake."

At the thought of Justin, Turner squeezed the steering wheel hard. This wasn't high school now, and he wasn't going to be bullied by Brad anymore. "You left us no choice," he replied.

"*Us,*" Brad hissed, hurting Turner's ear with the force of his reply. "So you bought in to her story? Well, you've left *me* no choice, either. You're a dead man. You hear me? A dead man."

"We'll see about that," Turner snapped and ended the call.

He seethed as they drove deeper into the mountains. It felt good to stand up to Brad, even though he had the luxury of doing it long distance. But as his anger began to cool, it was replaced by a gnawing sensation in the pit of his stomach. And the words *dead man* began to echo in his head.

*A*LTHOUGH RELUCTANT TO stop, Turner was forced to pull over to answer the call of nature. His conversation with Brad and the large Coke he'd consumed had finally caught up to him.

He slowed like a plane approaching the runway. Easing the Buick off to the side of the road, he hoped to coast to a stop, relieve himself, and taxi back onto the road again without disturbing Cassandra.

The sun peeked through the cloud cover, lifting the dullness like a thick curtain being pulled open. The world was reborn before his eyes, and the trees cast elongated shadows in celebration.

As he braked to a stop and put the car in park, Justin leaned over the front seat and tapped him on the shoulder. "I want a drink," he said, cradling the monkey under his arm.

Turner rummaged through the sack of food they had brought with them from his apartment. His fingers brushed a water bottle, and he pulled it out. He undid the top with a single twist and handed it to Justin. The little boy nestled back in his seat and guzzled the water.

Turner peered at Cassandra. She was still asleep, her head against the window, her hair pulled back around an ear as delicate as a rose blossom. The remnants of a relaxed smile graced the corners of her mouth.

"I've got to go to the bathroom, little man," he whispered. "Do you?"

The slurping sounds stopped long enough for Justin to say, "Nope."

Turner quietly opened his door. "Stay here," he whispered. "I'll be right back."

He left the door slightly ajar and headed for a group of trees—nature's outhouse. His eyes burned and he yawned deeply. The thought of curling up in a warm, comfortable bed was overpowering. He couldn't wait to reach the cabin and head for the couch, or with luck, to an extra bed in a spare room.

Before making his way back to the car, he paused to draw in a deep breath. This was the moment he had longed for, to be able to savor mountain air, fresh and tranquil. It contrasted with the heavy atmosphere that had settled over the motel, like an ominous cloud preceding a storm. The lush vegetation and the mountain solitude was a pleasant change from the cityscape of the greater Denver area.

The serenity and tranquility vanished, however, the instant he returned to the car and discovered the back door wide open. A quick glance revealed that Justin was not in the backseat.

As Turner scanned the area, he opened his mouth to call Justin's name but thought better of it. That would awaken Cassandra.

The clouds closed in and obscured the sun again, and the setting became eerily quiet and foreboding. Dropping to one knee, he examined the ground carefully. No footprints were visible, but there were some scuff marks as though Justin had fallen when he climbed out of the car. Because it was overcast, Turner had difficulty observing any indentations in the forest floor. But the displacement of pine needles, the occasional broken twig, and some compressed grass the size of a small footprint led away from the car.

Resorting to a tracking technique he'd learned at Camp

Kopawanee, he poked a stick in the ground to mark the last disturbance in the pine needles. Then he walked in a circle around the stick until he picked up the trail again. He started off once more, following the signs that led toward an outcrop of rocks. A rotted tree stump stood nearby, and he took his bearings off it. He had to be careful not to concentrate so much on following the trail that he got lost himself.

When the trail disappeared in the rocky landscape, he tried another tracking technique. He asked himself where he would go if he were the little boy. What object or formation might be interesting enough to investigate? What sounds might be enticing enough to explore?

His eye caught a flash of movement, and he noticed a squirrel vault from one tree branch to another. A giggle came from an opening in the bushes ahead, and Turner hurried toward it.

As he broke into a small clearing, he saw Justin standing at the base of a tree, gazing upward. Turner rushed forward and scooped him up in one motion.

"I saw a funny squirrel," the little boy said. "It jumped on the car and then ran away."

A squirrel had lured him from the car! If something that small could result in something this heart stopping, what protection was there against the truly big things? Turner didn't pause to contemplate the thought that suddenly flashed through his mind: *divine* protection.

"It ran up the tree," Justin said, pointing to a spot overhead.

Turner resisted the urge to scold him. "Don't follow squirrels without your mommy or me with you, okay?" He kept the sharpness out of his voice. The last thing he needed was for Justin to burst into tears.

"It had a bushy tail, Turner."

"Yeah, bushy tail," Turner muttered as he carried Justin back to the car and got him situated in the backseat. Then Turner climbed behind the wheel and put the car in gear.

As he pulled back onto the road, he hit a rock on the shoulder and the car bounced, jolting Cassandra awake.

"Are you still doing okay?" she said, rubbing her neck.

"Great," he replied. "Just had to make a pit stop."

"Mommy, I saw a squirrel," Justin said excitedly. "It ran up a tree."

Turner began planning his explanation, but Cassandra just yawned and smiled back at her son. "That's nice, sweetie," she said.

Exhaling slowly, Turner drove on in silence, chastened. He had let his guard down for only a moment, but that's all it had taken for Justin to slip out of the car. He grimaced and his grip tightened on the steering wheel. The experience was a wake-up call, and he promised himself not to make that mistake again. As long as that little boy was awake, he'd never let him out of sight. Ever.

chapter 19

 Y THE TIME they reached Silverthorne, the gas gauge registered half a tank. The sun rode high above the mountain peaks that surrounded the community as Turner pulled into a 7-Eleven.

Cassandra took Justin to the bathroom while Turner filled up the car and bought some groceries for their stay at the cabin. Along with the groceries, he also purchased a notepad and some colored markers. If they were going to batten down the hatches for a few days at the cabin, they would need something to entertain Justin beyond the textbooks and study notes Turner had brought with him. The food items would sustain life; the notepad and markers would maintain sanity.

Turner used cash for the gasoline and the store items, not wanting to leave a paper trail that Slick and Twitch could follow. He was well aware of their ability to track them. The two men were undoubtedly graduates of the Academy of Thugs, Goons, and Wise Guys, perhaps with a minor in clairvoyance and divination. They had traced Cassandra to the Mountain View Motel and to Mary's house. It was an intense game of cat and mouse, and there was no question in Turner's mind about who was who.

While waiting for Cassandra and Justin, he picked up a local newspaper and absentmindedly thumbed through it. He could imagine the front page screaming: *Boy Kidnapped by Mother and Handyman*. Of course it was too soon for news of their escape to make the headlines, but it might only be a matter of time if Brad chose to turn the matter into a media frenzy. But then Brad might not want an investigation, which would turn up the skeletons in *his* closet.

"You want the newspaper too?" the clerk asked, glancing at a sign that said *Please Do Not Read the Magazines.*

"No, I was just checking the weather."

"Continuing daylight, with a chance of darkness by nightfall," the clerk said dryly.

"Thanks," Turner remarked. "Good meteorologists are so hard to find these days."

Cassandra emerged with Justin in tow. Turner headed for the car, with Cassandra right behind, holding tightly to her son's hand.

Turner felt a sense of accomplishment in getting this far. They had a full tank of gas, several bags of groceries, and breathing room. He hadn't completely handled things with the skills worthy of an experienced camp counselor, but at least the threat was behind them.

The good feeling suddenly disappeared like yesterday's bank rates.

A police cruiser appeared and his throat went dry. He kept his smile frozen in place, doing his best to look like a happily married father and husband, which required some serious playacting, since he had no personal experience in this area.

Cassandra seemed on edge too, and Turner could tell she was staring at the patrol vehicle, despite her attempts to act casually.

"Keep walking," he said, talking through clenched teeth, as if the officer might be able to read lips.

The police officer drove by without giving them a backward glance.

Turner looked around to see if anyone eyed them suspiciously. But the customers went about their business, oblivious to them.

They climbed in the car, and he started the engine. After easing away from the pumps, he pulled onto the road, remaining a respectful distance behind the police cruiser. He didn't want to give the officer a good look at their car in case an alert had been issued regarding a *stolen* silver 1992 Buick Century. Turner had no idea what tricks Slick might pull out of his bag.

They turned at the next intersection, parting ways with the police cruiser. Turner began breathing easier as it disappeared behind a row of storefronts. The trees on either side of the road thickened, adding to his sense of security.

"How can stopping at a gas station be such a hairy experience?" Cassandra said. "I felt like everyone was staring at us. And the police officer! Where did he come from?"

"He just happened to be driving by, minding his own business. No harm done."

She reached across and took Turner's hand. Her skin felt cold, and he realized how tense they both were. He kept his hand stationary, wondering how long she would hold it. If holding hands comforted her, he was willing to oblige, even though she was a married woman. But he cautioned himself not to read too much into her simple gesture. Making a romantic mountain out of a platonic molehill would only complicate things further.

The moment ended when she finally slipped her hand out of his and picked up the paper containing the directions to the cabin. "Take the next left," she said.

He slowed and turned left onto a narrow, gravel road that wound through an uphill slope. Tree branches brushed against the sides of the car, and he hoped the paint job didn't get scratched. Otherwise Loretta might never cook for him again. He hugged the center of the roadway as though driving on a precipitous ledge intended only for mountain goats and Sherpa guides.

They traveled for what seemed like miles. Then Turner made another left turn and the road leveled out. Soon a clearing appeared ahead, and Cassandra caught her breath as they entered it.

"It's like looking through the peephole of an enchanted door," she said.

Justin said it more simply. "Wow!"

Nestled in amongst the pine trees sat a quaint cabin. The cedar siding appeared to have been recently painted, and the brown tin roof looked relatively new. A covered porch with wooden railings extended across the front of the cabin, where two rocking chairs sat side by side.

A lake was visible through a gap in the trees. A path led from the cabin and descended the gentle slope, ending at a small dock. Several craggy mountain peaks jutted above the tree line, and the blue sky accentuated the peace and tranquility of the setting.

Turner parked in front of the cabin.

"It looks to be in better condition than I had expected," Cassandra said as they climbed out of the car. "I had visions of the cabin being run-down, with cobwebs and overgrown shrubs. But it looks so cozy."

A thick carpet of pine needles led to the porch, where a welcome mat sat cheerily in front of the door. The curtains were closed; and a broom, a dustpan, and a shovel hung on the wall.

Two wooden pots, filled with artificial flowers, sat on either side of the front door. Under the container on the left was a key to the cabin. Relieved that the key was truly there—Cassandra had expressed a concern that it *wouldn't* be, necessitating a break-and-enter scenario—he unlocked the door.

The hinges creaked as the door swung open, and a musty smell greeted them. Cassandra went directly into the living room, parted the curtains, and opened the windows. A gentle cross breeze filtered through the room, displacing the stuffy air. Justin ran from room to room, exploring.

The cabin was fully furnished, as a quick tour of their new accommodations proved. The living room had a couch and an easy chair, with a TV-DVD combo centered between the windows. A wood-burning fireplace, with a natural rock front, occupied the far wall. An oak table and four matching chairs were in the adjoining dining room. The kitchen cupboards were stocked with cookware, although the fridge was empty, except for several bottles, the contents of which were suspect enough to cause no interest. Two bedrooms, each containing a queen-sized bed, were on the right side of a narrow hallway. A bathroom, a small laundry room, and a third bedroom were on the left. In every respect the cabin offered more room and amenities than did Turner's apartment. They had just been upgraded to the penthouse suite, complete with authentic images of nature, visible through the windows.

Turner selected the bedroom closest to the front door. His rationale was that if anyone arrived unheralded in the night, they would have to get by him first.

He set his suitcase next to the bed and lay down on the mattress to test its firmness. His eyes were on fire, but he forced himself back out to the car for the groceries. There were several items that needed refrigeration.

As he walked from the car back to the cabin, he surveyed the yard. Because the cabin was set back in the trees, he realized someone could approach on foot without detection. He wouldn't have minded a couple of Doberman pinschers staked at either end of the cabin, with enough slack in the rope to

121

run off any trespasser, whether it be hired goon or former high school football hero turned wife abuser. Because of the dense foliage, he would have to keep his guard up even more.

When they were settled in, he and Cassandra gravitated to the rocking chairs on the front porch, while Justin distracted himself by chasing a dragonfly that happened to whisk by. The little boy tirelessly pursued it around the clearing but finally gave up when the insect flew away. Then he sat down in the pine needles and raked a pile together as though building a sand castle on the beach.

Turner thought about the markers and paper he'd purchased. Nature offered an infinite variety of stimulating playthings, all free. He would reserve the art projects for the evenings, when Justin was forced to come inside for the night.

Cassandra and Turner rocked back and forth in their chairs, and Turner heard her sigh of relief. This was probably the first time she'd felt safe in days, if not months. What would it be like to live in constant fear like that? Never knowing when the next blow might land?

He grimaced inwardly. He knew something of what it was like. The constant dread. The eternal tiptoeing around and trying to make yourself invisible. If you weren't noticed, you couldn't be a target. So you slunk around, always watching, always waiting. Yes, he could relate to her situation.

But to think that Cassandra Todd, cheerleader, homecoming queen, class beauty had become a victim too! He'd always thought the victims were the ugly ones, the untalented ones, the losers. How could someone like her have turned into someone like he used to be?

He let his gaze wander past Justin, across the front yard and down the trail that led to the lake. The sky had cleared and was a cloudless sapphire, and the lake a jewel of equal beauty, reflecting the tranquility that permeated the surroundings. It was a quaint, pastoral setting—a Hallmark moment worthy of a postcard from heaven. So why did he feel a nagging combination of uncertainty and dread unlike anything he'd felt since high school?

ASSANDRA MADE BREAKFAST the following morning while Turner and Justin went on an *adventure* down to the lake. They had spent yesterday afternoon settling in, then napping and had barely had a chance to explore their surroundings. She laughed to herself to think how excited Justin was to have the whole outdoors as his playground. It contrasted with the postage-stamp-size backyard of their Las Vegas home that held only a tiny sandbox and swing set.

A momentary sadness came over her as she thought about her former home and life. But she quickly blocked the memories and focused on the beautiful setting in which she now found herself.

It felt familiar to be in the kitchen, cooking breakfast and setting the table. But for the first time in months she wasn't worried about how the meal would be received. Turner, she knew, wouldn't criticize her if the toast was slightly burned or the eggs undercooked. It was enjoyable preparing a meal that would be appreciated.

When things were ready, she went to the door and called, "Hey, you two! Breakfast time!"

Justin rushed into the clearing a moment later, giggling so much he could hardly stay on his feet. Turner appeared right behind him, arms extended, fingers bent like claws, voice roaring deeply.

"The bear's gonna get me!" Justin laughed, falling down in the soft mat of pine needles. "Save me, Mommy!"

Turner roared again, and Justin scrambled to his feet,

rushing toward Cassandra, who held out her arms and cheered him on. Justin reached her at the same time Turner did, and the three of them briefly collided, sharing a group hug as they steadied one another and laughed.

"You're safe," Cassandra said. "The bear won't get you now."

Turner gave one more growl, and Justin squealed and twisted out of Cassandra's arms and ran into the bedroom, laughing harder.

"Whew, maybe that will keep him occupied for a few minutes," Turner said, collapsing in a kitchen chair and eyeing the table setting.

"He has a lot of energy, doesn't he?"

"That's for sure."

She poured three glasses of juice naturally and efficiently, as though they had been coming to the cabin for years. Then she coaxed Justin out of the bedroom, promising not to let the bear get him. Justin peeked around the kitchen doorway and eyed Turner warily, making a wide circle around him as he climbed up to the table.

"Breakfast looks and smells delicious," Turner said, reaching for a slice of toast.

"Would it be all right if we said grace first?" Cassandra asked. "There's so much to be thankful for."

"Sure," Turner said, withdrawing his hand.

"Dear Lord," Cassandra began, "we're thankful for this food. Please bless it to nourish and strengthen us so that we may do Your will. Thank You for your guidance and help, and for wonderful friends like Loretta and Mary and especially Turner. Amen."

Turner looked at her and their eyes locked momentarily. Then he dropped his gaze and reached for a slice of toast and two strips of bacon.

As they ate, they made small talk. Justin told Cassandra

about their walk down to the lake and the pretty dragonflies he'd seen skimming over the water. Turner told how Justin had tried to catch a dragonfly and had nearly ended up in the lake.

"You have to be careful around the water, sweetie," Cassandra cautioned.

"Don't worry. We had a little talk on water safety," Turner explained. He speared a third strip of bacon with his fork and smiled at Cassandra. "You sleep okay last night?"

Cassandra glanced in pretended disapproval at her son. "I did until Mister Buster woke me up. But it gave me a chance to lie there and feel the sunshine streaming through my window. It reminded me of the times as a little girl I'd wake up to its warmth on my face and listen to the birds chirping in the trees. It's been years since I didn't jump out of bed and start doing a dozen things at once."

"I understand. Not having Harvey's list waiting for me felt great too."

Cassandra wiped a piece of egg from Justin's chin. "Thanks for keeping Justin entertained while I got things ready."

"No problem," Turner replied, between mouthfuls. "It's a beautiful day. I thought we could go for a canoe ride on the lake."

"A canoe ride?"

"Yeah. I found some lifejackets and paddles in the closet."

She hesitated. "I haven't been canoeing before. Brad wasn't into that kind of thing."

"That's okay. There's nothing to it." He puffed out his chest dramatically. "Besides, you're looking at a certified canoe instructor."

She looked at him in surprise. "Really?"

"Four years at Camp Kopawanee."

"I wouldn't have taken you for the outdoorsy type."

127

"Camp Counselor Turner Caldwell at your service, ma'am." He gave her a mock salute. "With credentials to prove it."

She laughed. "In that case I'll make a picnic lunch."

"Sounds great. I'll get the gear and haul it down to the dock. Want to help me, little man?"

"Sure, Turner," Justin replied, hopping down from the table.

A short time later Cassandra arrived at the dock with the picnic lunch. She felt a rush of excitement as the lake unfolded itself like a jewel set against a forest-green backdrop. The sound of cars honking had been replaced by the chirping of birds, and the odors of exhaust and industrial emissions had given way to fresh, mountain air. The hustle and bustle of people on their way to work had been supplanted by solitude and tranquility. This was a world she could get used to.

A fiberglass canoe sat on the dock.

"A boat, Mommy!" Justin cried excitedly.

"Canoe, sweetie," Cassandra said, correcting him.

"Let's go in the boat, Mommy."

Turner put the smallest lifejacket on Justin and snapped the buckles in place. As he helped Cassandra into hers, she noticed how efficiently he adjusted the straps and fastened the buckles.

Once the three of them were properly outfitted, Cassandra helped Turner slide the canoe over the edge of the dock. As the craft settled on the water, Justin clapped his hands excitedly.

"So how do we climb in without tipping over?" Cassandra asked.

"I'll climb in first and steady it while you hand me Justin. Then lay your paddle across the canoe and gently slide from the dock into the bow by grabbing the near side with one hand and placing a foot in the center of the canoe. Crouch low and grab the far side with the other hand as you put your other foot in the canoe. Get yourself balanced and then sit on the bow seat."

"You *do* know about canoeing. When did you first get interested? Did you go camping as a family when you were young?"

"We went once," Turner laughed.

"Only once?"

"At my insistence, my parents and I went camping when I was eight. That was before they separated for a while. The outing was a disaster. Between the canoe springing a leak, the tent blowing down in a rainstorm, and my dad splitting the toe of his boot with an ax, the adventure was the last we ever undertook in the great outdoors. From that day on our family 'camping' trips consisted of Holiday Inns and fast-food restaurants."

"That's too bad," she said, looking at the surrounding vista. "You missed all *this*."

"Not actually. After that outing, my parents enrolled me in the Scouting program, mostly so I'd stop bugging them about going camping and hiking again. I started as a Tenderfoot and worked hard on my merit badges, becoming an Eagle Scout when I was sixteen. I was the youngest boy in my troop to earn it. As a result I got to attend an international Scout jamboree in Alberta, Canada."

"So you really are a Boy Scout."

Turner laughed and climbed into the canoe. He took Justin from her and showed him how to hang onto the center yoke. Then Turner put the lunch in the bottom of the canoe, beside the plastic bailing bucket, and steadied the canoe while she climbed in.

"That wasn't so bad," she said, as she got settled on the bow seat.

"Ready to shove off, me hearties?" Turner asked.

"Aye, aye, Captain," she replied.

"Aye, aye, Captain," Justin mimicked.

With a gentle thrust, the canoe moved away from the dock.

"Which side do you want to paddle on?" Turner asked.

"Does it matter?"

"I'll show you. Start paddling."

Cassandra dipped her paddle into the water on the right side. She noticed Turner do the same. They paddled in a large circle and came right back to the dock.

"Fast trip," she said.

"Can we go for another ride, Mommy?" Justin begged.

"Sure," Turner said, laughing. "Now that we have our sea legs under us, I think we're ready to face the ocean deep."

They pushed off once more.

"So which side should I paddle on?" Cassandra asked.

"The right. I'll take the left."

"Do we have to paddle in unison, or what?"

"Just paddle evenly, smoothly. I'll match your pace. And keep your paddle as vertical as you can."

"Okay."

"Full speed ahead," Turner said. "Hang on to your hat, little man."

Justin felt the top of his head. "I'm not wearing one."

Cassandra chuckled and dug in with her paddle. The canoe cut a straight line away from the dock. The only sounds were the rhythm of the paddles slicing into the water, lifting, and sending droplets back to their source.

They slowly navigated toward the middle of the lake. The water became a kaleidoscope of refracted rays as the canoe disturbed the glassy surface.

At length they stopped to rest, allowing the canoe to glide to a stop. Utter silence prevailed—a stillness deeper than the lake bottom itself.

Cassandra glanced over the edge of the craft and marveled

at how clear the water was. The lake bottom was visible, where trunks of ancient trees lay crisscrossed at various angles like giant Pick-Up Sticks. Jagged rocks thrust toward the surface, but the canoe floated above them with the ease of a bird gliding overhead.

Green slopes, frilly with conifers, ran down to the lake from all directions. On one of the rounded peaks to the south stood an old ranger station, a lookout tower on cross-braced stilts. It appeared to be abandoned but was within walking distance.

She pointed out the ranger station to Turner and commented on what an excellent view it would afford, adding reverently, "Everything is so beautiful. This is nature's house and the décor is amazing." She looked around appreciatively until Justin's attention span expired.

"Let's go," the little boy said. "Paddle fast."

Cassandra twisted around to look at Turner. "Is the motor ready in the back?"

"Ready," Turner said, thrusting his paddle into the water.

"Faster, faster!" Justin said, sounding like a coxswain coordinating the rhythm.

Cassandra paddled until her arms burned and her fingers cramped. She was definitely out of shape, but she kept it up so as not to disappoint the little coxswain. Turner matched her, stroke for stroke, and the canoe maintained a straight course.

They reached the far side of the lake just as her arms went up in flames. Perspiration stung her eyes and dripped off the end of her chin.

"Let's cool off," Turner said, slapping his paddle against the water and sending a cascade toward Justin and her.

Cassandra screamed in protest and replied in kind, and soon the water churned as though they were inside a giant blender. Even Justin got in on the action, laughing in delight as he reached over the side and flipped water in both directions.

As Cassandra attempted to turn around to improve the angle of her attack, the canoe listed. She quickly leaned in the opposite direction, and the canoe began rocking. Turner tried to counterbalance the canoe by leaning in the other direction. But they ended up leaning in the same direction, and the canoe rolled like a log in a lumberjack logrolling competition, pitching them into the lake headfirst.

Cassandra came up sputtering and gasping. "The water's freezing!"

She and Turner grabbed Justin at the same time and got their arms tangled around one another. Justin bobbed between them, squealing in delight. The lunch, which fortunately Cassandra had put in an airtight plastic bag, floated nearby.

After getting their arms undone, Cassandra pulled Justin to her and wiped his face. Wading ashore, she undid their lifejackets.

Turner grabbed the floating lunch and then beached the canoe. He undid his lifejacket and hurried to join them. They lay on the warm pebbles, enjoying the sunshine.

Glancing across at him, Cassandra noticed how Turner's wet clothing revealed his physique. Although he lacked Brad's large, muscular build, he was not the skinny kid he'd been in high school. He had filled out, and his chest and arms were sinewy and cut. And in his expression she saw an inner strength and confidence she had not noticed before. He was obviously in his element.

At this moment she felt completely safe. And as she looked at the surrounding beauty of this mountain setting, she couldn't imagine being anywhere else, with anyone else.

"I'm hungry, Mommy," Justin said, poking her with a finger.

Cassandra smiled and sat up. "Who's ready for some lunch?"

"Me!" Justin and Turner said at the same time.

Cassandra unpacked the lunch, which consisted of sandwiches, juice boxes, apples, and cookies.

"Food always tastes better in the fresh air," Turner said, biting into a sandwich. "Nature adds a seasoning all its own."

"It does, doesn't it?" Cassandra replied, munching a piece of apple.

Justin finished quickly and went to play in the pebbles, completely entertained by his surroundings. Cassandra was grateful there was no need for television, video games, or coloring books.

Later the three of them had a rock-skipping contest. With the right angle and trajectory, the rocks, worn smooth over time, skipped across the water in a merry dance before sinking out of sight. Cassandra's arms still felt rubbery from the paddling, but she put everything she had into each throw to make an impression. She didn't want Turner to tell her that she threw like a girl!

Justin's initial throws chumped into the water, creating a single splash. But when he managed to skip a rock twice, he jumped up and down and cheered.

Turner launched a rock and counted, " ...five, six, seven."

"Good throw, Turner," said Justin. "Watch me."

The little boy wound up and threw with all his might, almost pitching forward into the lake. Turner caught him in time to watch the rock skip three times. They all cheered.

When that game ended, Turner found a piece of driftwood and tossed it out into the water. They then took turns throwing rocks at it.

Cassandra bounced a pebble off the driftwood on her fourth throw. Raising her arms in celebration, she danced in a circle.

Justin joined in and danced with her. "Come on, Turner," he said, holding out his hand. "Let's dance."

They joined hands and danced in a circle. This led to a new game, and soon they were playing Ring-Around-the-Rosy.

"Ring around the rosy, a pocket full of posies; ashes, ashes, we all fall down," they sang.

They played the game over and over, falling down repeatedly, which caused Justin to laugh hysterically. Cassandra finally came to the rescue by distracting him with a collection of pretty rocks. Soon his pockets were filled, and he began piling more in the canoe.

"I think we'd better get back before the canoe gets too heavy," she said.

Turner helped them into their lifejackets and then nosed the canoe into the water, steadying it while she and Justin climbed aboard. He joined them and they started their return journey.

Cassandra wondered if Justin would want to go faster, but he was busy examining his rock collection. She and Turner were able to paddle leisurely across the lake, keeping in time with each other and maintaining a straight course.

Once, she turned back and smiled at Turner. "I think we're a good team."

"Yes, we are," he replied softly.

There was a subtext in his comment—a meaning that went beyond his spoken words. And she tried to read between the lines and interpret the meaning. Or was it just that she hoped there was something deeper?

When they finally reached the dock, Turner steadied the canoe while she climbed out. Then he lifted Justin to her and picked up the little boy's treasures from the bottom of the canoe. Justin busied himself with the rocks while Cassandra extended her hand to Turner.

He took a firm hold and climbed up beside her.

"Thanks for today," she said, continuing to hold his hand. "It's been a long time since I've had a day like this."

They stood side by side, holding hands, looking across to the far shore. If she had been a teenager, his hand in hers would have sent her into shivers of delight. But she had gone through too much. Holding Turner's hand was not based on infatuation or attraction or seduction. It just felt right.

"It's so peaceful here," she said. "I wish it could..." She let her voice trail off.

An eagle soared overhead just then, its cry echoing across the clearing. She watched the graceful bird arc upward, climbing until it was a mere dot. A beauty mark on the face of heaven.

A fish jumped near the dock, causing ripples that gradually widened until the entire lake seemed to shimmer. A slight breeze, scented with pine, descended from the west, whispering through the trees.

"You know, this is the first day in a long while I haven't found myself watching the time and dreading five o'clock coming," she said, brushing a strand of hair from her eyes.

"Five o'clock?"

"The time Brad would get home from work."

"Oh."

She turned and looked up into Turner's face. "Today has been a gift, Turner. I've felt a sense of peace I haven't had in a long time."

Turner squeezed her hand and then released it.

Cassandra lingered as a warm feeling spread through her body like the rings rippling across the lake. She watched as Turner laid the lifejackets on the dock to dry and then knelt beside Justin to admire the rock collection. She wondered how Turner could seem so much like a father to Justin in so short a time. If she had known what kind of father Brad would be... She shook her head sadly and then crouched next to Justin and Turner, helping them scoop the rocks into the bag that had carried their lunch.

When the task was completed, she took Justin by the hand and led him off the dock. "Come on, Turner," he called, looking back as Turner paused to secure the canoe and paddles.

Smiling, Turner hurried to catch up, taking the bag of rocks from Cassandra and grabbing hold of Justin's other hand.

"Swing me," Justin cried, his eyes sparkling in anticipation.

Cassandra laughed when he squealed excitedly as she and Turner swung him between them on their way back to the cabin. It had been too long since she'd felt this happy.

chapter 21

*T*URNER SPENT THE rest of the afternoon outside with Justin, letting him explore to his heart's content. This gave Cassandra a break. Plus he hoped the fresh air and activity would wear Justin out so he would sleep in longer the next morning.

Their wanderings took them into some bushes between the lake and the cabin. There was an old log, half-decomposed, lying lengthways in a small clearing. Turner brushed away a chunk of bark and sat down to catch his breath. A wasp rose from underneath the log and hovered in front of him, compound eye to human eyeball. Moments later it was joined by another, and then a third.

"Look at the pretty flies," Justin said, as a fourth and fifth wasp appeared.

The decision to leave was as easy as falling off a log. Literally. Turner flipped over backward and rolled to his feet. Tucking Justin under one arm, he raced back into the front yard. When he was certain they hadn't been pursued, he put Justin down. "We can't go back there, little man. The pretty flies will sting us."

"But I want to play with them."

"They don't want to play with us."

Justin squirmed, determined to go back and investigate, so Turner tried to distract him. "Let's go this way. I think I just saw a squirrel."

Justin grew excited. "A squirrel? Let's go see."

"We have to be very quiet or we'll scare it away."

Watching Justin tiptoe across the carpet of pine needles made Turner chuckle. Their safari progressed from tracking squirrels to stalking tigers...then to hunting elephants...and finally to seeking dragons. Keeping up with Justin and making sure he was safe was a full-time job. But he hadn't had this much fun in years. Not since Camp Kopawanee. It was a delight to watch Justin explore and learn and grow. He delighted in the little boy's...delight.

After dinner and a game of impromptu hide-and-seek, that coveted time arrived that parents everywhere look forward to: children's bedtime. Cassandra put Justin in bed, gave him several drinks, and told him two bedtime stories. Justin remained wide-eyed and alert.

Turner came in and told a bedtime story his mother used to relate to him when he was a little boy. Justin still wouldn't go to sleep. The plan to wear Justin out had clearly backfired.

Although Turner wanted some downtime to put his feet up and do some studying before going to bed, he could tell it wasn't possible yet. Ruffling Justin's hair, he said, "Hey, little man, I hear you're pretty tough."

"I'm strong," Justin said, flexing his arms to show his muscles.

"Wanna have a pillow fight?"

Justin's eyes glowed like sparklers.

"I don't think that will help him calm down," Cassandra said, doubt registering in her expression.

"We've got to do something to burn off more of his energy," Turner replied. "There are some extra pillows in the closet. I'll get them."

"Are you sure about this?" Cassandra said.

"No," Turner replied. "But it's worth a shot."

He pulled down two large pillows from the top shelf in the closet and held one out to Justin. As the little boy reached for it, Turner snatched it away and hit him with it, almost bowling the little boy over.

Justin laughed and made a grab for it. Turner let Justin wrestle it away from him, putting on a good show for effect. Justin hit him with the pillow, and Turner flopped on the bed, pretending to be dazed and disoriented.

Laughing louder, Justin hit him again. Turner fell off the bed and landed on the floor, gasping for air like a fish flopping around on the dock. Justin was on him in an instant, and they rolled around, grunting and groaning.

Cassandra clapped her hands when Justin pinned Turner to the floor and raised his arms in celebration. Turner gave him a moment to appreciate the victory and then lifted him bodily, tossing him onto the bed. Justin landed on the mattress like a stuffed teddy bear.

As the little boy scrambled to recover, Turner tossed a pillow at him and knocked him back down. Then he threw the bed sheet over Justin and said, "Where's Justin? Where did he go?"

"Under here," came the muffled response.

"Mommy," Turner said, addressing Cassandra. "Have you seen Justin?"

"I'm under here," Justin repeated, giggling.

Turner let him wiggle free.

Justin grabbed the sheet and buried Turner beneath it. "Where's Turner?" he asked. "Where did Turner go?"

"I'm under here," Turner replied, thrashing about as though unable to escape.

Justin pulled the sheet off him and said, "There you are."

Turner grabbed him, and they wrestled around a while longer. He threw Justin back on the bed and picked up a pillow. But instead of hitting him with it, Turner swung around and hit Cassandra.

Her mouth gaped open in surprise. When he hit her again,

she laughed and reached for the other pillow, swinging wildly at him.

He ducked and hit her again, causing her to momentarily retreat.

"Get him, Mommy," Justin cried excitedly. "Get Turner!"

Cassandra hesitated briefly and then moved in for the attack. She hit him firmly, causing Justin to squeal in delight. Turner hit her in return, causing the little boy to squeal even more.

She swung the pillow at Turner in a wide arc but missed him. Her follow-through put her off balance, and when he hit her from behind, she fell onto the bed. Before she could recover, he placed the pillow in front of him and jumped on top of her, pinning her down.

The play fight ended abruptly when he looked into her face and saw genuine panic. A cry rumbled in her throat, and she flailed her arms and legs in an effort to escape. He scrambled to his feet and clutched the pillow awkwardly, picking at a feather that poked through the pillowcase. "I'm sorry," he said. "I didn't mean to—"

"It's all right," she replied, sitting up and breathing rapidly. "I just freaked out for a minute." She picked up Justin. "That's enough for tonight."

"I'm sorry," Turner said again.

She looked at him apologetically. "I'm sorry too."

An awkward silence followed.

Justin squirmed in his mother's arms. "Let's fight some more, Mommy. It was fun."

"Not tonight," she said, her voice breaking slightly.

"It's bedtime, little man," Turner added, reaching over and smoothing down Justin's hair. "But we'll do some more fun stuff tomorrow, okay?"

Justin considered the offer and said, "Okay."

Turner gathered up the pillows and put them away. Glancing at Cassandra, he said, "I'll be out on the front porch."

He left the bedroom and sat in the rocking chair on the porch, reflecting on what had just occurred. He chastised himself for spoiling this perfect day. He should have known that jumping on Cassandra and pinning her down was the wrong thing to do. It reminded her of Brad, and it had terrified her. He had seen it in her face...again.

He continued to rock back and forth in the chair, his mind far away.

A while later he was surprised to see Cassandra standing beside him, her hands folded in front of her. "Justin asleep?" he asked.

"Finally," she replied, joining him in the other chair and looking out across the yard.

The night deepened, enveloping the surrounding trees and the lake like spilled ink, leaving Turner with a peaceful sense of isolation.

Clearing her throat, Cassandra said, "I'm sorry about how I reacted, Turner. I—"

"I'm the one who needs to apologize. I got too rough."

She forced a smile. "I can see we aren't going to agree on who should apologize to whom."

"Let's say the apologies cancel each other. Deal?"

"Deal," she replied, reaching over and shaking his hand.

"But I'm the one who's more sorry," he whispered.

Cassandra broke their clasp in mock exasperation and was silent a moment. At length she said, "When we were back in high school, did you ever think we'd end up here?"

"I didn't even know this place existed back then."

She looked at him narrowly. "You know what I mean, wise guy. I'm talking about ending up in this *situation*. We had our whole future ahead of us. I had such dreams, such plans."

"Life doesn't usually turn out the way we expect it to."

Cassandra sighed. "It started out promising enough. Even my marriage to Brad began like a storybook tale."

Turner looked at her dubiously.

"It's true," she persisted. "Because he was the captain of the football team and I was head cheerleader, everyone assumed we were meant for each other. The peer pressure was immense. Plus he was charismatic and persuasive, and he promised me he'd settle down."

"So he changed?" Turner asked in surprise.

"At first, yes. Following graduation, he started working for his dad in construction. He had such enthusiasm and was ready to set the world on fire. He kept talking about the future and what an exciting life we could have together."

"So eventually you agreed to marry him," Turner said, more as a comment than a question.

"Yes. And it was the biggest mistake I ever made. But of course I didn't know it at the time." She stared off into the darkness before continuing. "Our wedding was special. It was outside at a country club, like I wanted, and most of our high school friends were there. My dad came from New York to give me away, and my mom even showed up sober. Everyone gave us such a wonderful send-off."

"How did you end up in Las Vegas?"

"Brad's dad had some contacts there in construction. They offered Brad a job contracting million-dollar homes. We did great for a few years. I started taking some college classes in interior design. Eventually we had hoped that Brad could build spec houses, which I would then design—you know, pick paint colors and carpeting and fixtures."

"Interior design?" Turner made a face. "My apartment must have driven you crazy."

"Now that you mention it, there are one or two things I could have done to it."

"Only one or two?"

"Or ten or twenty," she said, hiding a smile. And then her expression grew serious. "We had the perfect home in the perfect neighborhood. Then the Great Recession started and projects dried up. Brad got moody and depressed. And it didn't help that I got pregnant soon after business went bad." She sighed, remembering. "The morning sickness was so terrible that I was practically bedridden and had to drop out of college. Brad was furious. He blamed me for being careless and even refused to get me any medication for nausea."

She toyed with her hands briefly and then said, "Despite my condition, Brad expected me to carry my full load of responsibilities, especially now that I was home all the time. If his shirts weren't ironed, he got upset. If his dinner wasn't ready on time, he got more upset." She grimaced. "And when I lost my figure, he became restless. He began going out in the evenings with his buddies from work and coming home at all hours, drunk and disoriented."

Turner frowned. "Not exactly husband of the year."

Murmuring in agreement, Cassandra continued. "Following Justin's birth, Brad became jealous of the attention I gave our son. It became a strange game of who-do-you-love-more? If Justin cried, I wasn't allowed to check on him until I first prepared Brad's meal. Ironically, the longer Justin cried, the more upset Brad became, but he seemed to enjoy watching me squirm."

"That's the Brad I remember."

"Sometimes he'd apologize afterward and ask my forgiveness. But then he'd turn right around the next time and be controlling again."

Turner muttered to himself

"The only thing that got me through was God. I turned to Him and started to attend church, and I read from the Bible and prayed constantly. My earnest hope was to find a way to save our marriage."

Arching an eyebrow, Turner asked, "So how did that work out for you?"

Cassandra made a face at him. "I know you think my prayers weren't answered because our marriage failed. But I was blessed in other ways. I found the courage to leave." She wet her lips and continued. "I was prepared to stay for the sake of our son and endure it. I was ready to do almost anything to make our marriage succeed. And frankly the thought of leaving Brad terrified me. I had worked so hard for what we had. Our home was lovely, and I didn't want to give it up. I prayed to know what to do. And then on the night when Brad got angry and punched me because of the trophies, I *knew* what I had to do, and I found the strength to do it."

Turner stared down at the porch floor.

"You may not believe that God loves us and helps us in our time of need, but you have to realize that *I* believe it, Turner."

"I do, Cassandra. And I only wish I had your faith."

"Give it time," she said. "You may have given up on God, but I don't believe He has given up on you."

Wishing to change the subject, Turner asked, "Have you decided what you're going to do and where you're going to go?"

She shrugged apologetically. "Whatever I decide, Turner, I won't tell you. It's best if you don't know. That way, if Brad hassles you again, you won't be able to tell him anything, and he'll leave you alone."

Turner wondered if she really believed that or whether in her desperation she was clinging to a naïve hope. If Brad had tormented him in high school over minor matters such as the social pecking order, how much more would he harass Turner in an effort to find Cassandra and Justin?

They fell silent as the evening breeze wafted across the porch and tantalized the air with fragrances of spruce and rich earth. The moon peered above the treetops, bathing the yard in a silver glow, and an owl hooted from somewhere in the distance.

"It's so peaceful here," she said at length. "I'm going to hate to leave, but I can't stay here forever. I've got to go to the bank and finish my business. And you've got classes to attend."

Turner considered their return. It was going to be problematic, all right. Cassandra would have to slip through the net that Slick and Twitch had undoubtedly drawn around the bank, conduct her business over a period of a day or two, and then make good her escape. He, on the other hand, was going to show up at the motel and his college classes and be a sitting duck for Slick to pick up and hand over to Brad, who had already told him he was a dead man. And he knew that no matter how much he professed his ignorance concerning Cassandra's ultimate whereabouts, Brad would never believe him. And the condition he would be in when Brad finally came to that realization might make death seem welcome.

There was no way he could simply drop back into his former life. And Cassandra's former life was gone forever. He could see no alternative but for them to go to the police, as Loretta and Mary had suggested, and ask for protection.

The challenge was to convince Cassandra. But first he had to prepare a rebuttal to her argument that Brad would simply march through a restraining order, storm the castle, overpower the sentry, and carry away the occupants.

But without police protection, they had no protection at all, not even a castle wall to deter the imminent invasion and give them time to slip out the back. But he knew Cassandra wasn't ready to accept this line of reasoning yet.

The statement she had just made—give it time—applied to her, as well. She needed more time before she was ready to see the truth in what Loretta and Mary had told her. She needed to go to the police for help, and it was up to Turner to convince her.

He decided to go into town in a couple of days to pick up a few grocery items and call Loretta and Mary, to get a sense of where things stood. That would give him time to work on his line of reasoning with Cassandra...time for her to relax and enjoy their surroundings...time for clearer heads to prevail.

"I wish I knew how things were going to turn out," she said, looking up into the night sky as if searching for an answer.

As he followed her gaze, an idea suddenly occurred to him—one that hopefully would help her relax and provide a pleasant distraction while he worked on his rebuttal. "Let's make tomorrow another special day," he said.

She sat up in her chair. "Sure. What do you have in mind?"

"I have a great idea. But I'm going to keep you in suspense."

She groaned in protest and stood up. "On that note, I'm going to go to bed and hope my curiosity doesn't keep me awake." Placing a hand on his shoulder, she squeezed gently and added, "Thanks for all you're doing, Turner. I really appreciate it. Good night."

"Good night," he said, patting her hand. "And sweet dreams."

The warmth of her touch on his shoulder lingered long after she went inside, leaving him alone with his thoughts. And plans.

chapter 22

ASSANDRA WOKE THE following morning feeling more rested than she had in ages. She showered and then went into the kitchen to start breakfast. But Turner was already at the stove, making scrambled eggs and helping Justin spread jam on a piece of toast.

"I slept in," she said. "And it felt good."

"There's no such thing as sleeping in when you're on vacation," Turner replied, turning the eggs over in the frying pan. "The day begins when we say it begins."

"Or when Mister Buster here says it begins," she said, kissing Justin on the head. "Morning, sweetie. How did you sleep last night?"

"I dreamed a bear was chasing me," Justin answered.

Turner winced guiltily and focused on the eggs.

Cassandra came over and stood beside him. "So what's on the itinerary today?" she asked, nudging him with her elbow.

"What's itinerary?" Justin asked, licking the jam off his fingers.

"Something fun," Turner said. "We're going on a hike."

"Yeah!" Justin yelled, spilling jam down the front of his shirt.

Cassandra imitated him in fun, waving her arms in the air. It felt good to be this carefree and not have to worry about meeting expectations...or else!

Turner smiled. "I'm glad to see so much enthusiasm."

"Actually, a hike sounds fun," she said. "Let's eat breakfast and then I'll pack a lunch. We can find a nice place to picnic."

They sat down to breakfast and talked as if they had been

doing it for years. Cassandra noticed how easy it was to converse with Turner about...everything. She could discuss the weather with him as easily as she could her favorite movie. There was so much to talk about. And this time none of it involved high school or other references to the past.

When he finished eating, Justin jumped down from the table and headed for the door, wiping his sticky fingers on his pants.

Cassandra opened her mouth to order him back, but Turner said, "No sense making him clean up now. He's only going to get dirtier."

She nodded in resignation and continued eating while Turner went outside to keep an eye on Justin. She appreciated how careful Turner was to not leave Justin unattended. He watched her son like a hawk, and the gesture touched her deeply and made her feel safe. She knew this respite couldn't last, but for now she pushed aside her worries concerning the future in order to enjoy the present.

When everything was ready, she appeared on the porch with the sack lunch. "Who wants to go on a hike?" she called.

"Me!" Justin called, grabbing Turner's hand and hurrying toward the cabin.

"So where's the trail?" she asked, coming down the steps to join them.

"Right this way," Turner said, pointing to the far side of the clearing. "It heads up the slope to the west and should give us a great view of the lake."

"Let's go," she said, falling in behind Turner and Justin.

The sun peered over the treetops, warming the air. It had cooled down considerably during the night, but now the chill was gone. The day promised to be another vacationer's delight. The sky was cloudless and looked like a deep blue fabric stretched tightly across the surrounding mountain peaks.

148

The trail ran across the face of the terrain like an ancient scar. It was lined with wildflowers in various stages of bloom. Thick bushes threatened to overgrow the trail, but the packed, damp soil of the path resisted intrusion.

"What are these flowers called?" Cassandra asked, pointing to a stand of reddish-purple flowers growing along a dried-out creek bed near the trail.

"Those are Mountain Fireweed," Turner replied.

"They're beautiful."

"They're one of the first plants to reappear after a forest fire. When the leaves are young, they can be eaten like vegetable greens, but when they get older—like these—they taste tough and bitter. The stems can be peeled and eaten raw and are a good source of vitamin C."

"Well, thank you for the lesson, Professor Caldwell," she said. It felt good to banter with someone and not have to measure every word she said.

"Let's pick some," Justin said, taking a step toward them.

"Stay on the trail, little man," Turner said. "See those tall plants beside them, with the little, round, greenish-white flowers? That's stinging nettle."

"Can we pick them too?"

"They're owie," Turner said. "They'll hurt you."

Justin's eyes grew large, and he stepped back onto the trail.

Farther ahead the path ran into a stand of evergreens before disappearing around a large outcropping of weathered granite that protruded from the ground like petrified fingers.

The trail showed evidence of hikers and other outdoor enthusiasts, although it looked long forgotten and neglected. Just where it led, Cassandra couldn't guess. But that only added to the excitement of the hike.

"Can we see a bear today, Mommy?" Justin asked, stopping to examine a gnarled twig that lay on the trail.

She shook her head and said, "I hope not." Then turning toward Turner, she asked, "Do you know any safety tips? Like what to do if you come across a bear?"

"Sure. Leave."

She rolled her eyes and scanned the trail ahead. "I hope our approach doesn't sound like a dinner bell to some hungry b-e-a-r, lying in wait with a napkin tied around its neck."

"Attacks are rare. And we're making enough noise to give anything ahead advance notice."

"I think you're supposed to play dead if one attacks you."

"It will usually stop its attack once it no longer feels threatened. If you remain quiet and motionless for as long as possible, there's a chance it will lose interest and leave."

"Just a *chance*?"

"Actually a good chance. But I'll tell you my idea of survival. Make sure you can outrun the person you're with."

Cassandra picked up a pinecone and threw it at him. "Very funny."

The trail stopped at the face of a steep embankment, about ten feet high. Turner scaled the incline, demonstrating rock-climbing experience, and then reached down for Justin's hand. Cassandra lifted her son so Turner could grab him around the wrists and pull him up. Then he extended his hand to her.

After clasping his hand firmly, Cassandra went up the face with surprising ease. She was aware of the strength in his arms, and she felt secure in his grip.

Before continuing the hike, they paused to enjoy the vista. The far end of the lake was visible through the treetops, and the lookout tower she had noticed the day before stood on its perch to the south. The mountain peaks were framed dramatically against the blue sky.

From here the trail picked up again, leveling off so walking became easier. But it was obvious to Cassandra that they weren't going to set any land speed records. Justin stopped to examine every flower, explore every bush, and investigate every tree. She smiled at his delight in the little things: an insect climbing up the stalk of a flower, furry lichen growing on an exposed boulder, and a piece of rotted wood lying along the edge of the path. Everything was exciting to him, and she watched him in fascination. His joy in experiencing the surroundings was infectious, and she was glad to let him take his time. She noticed how patient Turner was about it too, and she appreciated it for her son's sake. This was such a rare opportunity for a little boy raised in the city.

At one point Justin stumbled and fell over a rock. The trail was spongy with pine needles and other plant matter, and he was back on his feet in an instant. He wiped his hands on his shirt, putting twin smudges down either side.

Turner grinned and looked at Cassandra as if to say, *Told you so.*

She stuck out her tongue at him and pulled a face before she could stop herself, suddenly embarrassed by her actions. It was so...teenager-like. But Turner only laughed and brushed a few pine needles off Justin's shirt.

Hurrying over to examine a stand of tall flowers with graceful yellow petals, Justin stared at them but didn't touch them. "See the flowers, Mommy."

"Globeflower," Turner said. "A member of the buttercup family. You can pick them, little man. But just don't eat them."

"Are they poisonous?" Cassandra asked.

"They contain a chemical that works like a laxative."

"What's laxative?" Justin asked.

"It helps you go to the bathroom."

"I don't have to go to the bathroom."

Cassandra chuckled and knelt beside her son while he

plucked a flower and stuck it in her hair. She looked over at Turner and smiled.

Turner eyed her intently before suddenly dropping his gaze. "W–we should keep going," he said.

Cassandra smiled to herself. Had Turner just blushed? She was used to men looking at her, longingly, lustfully. But Turner's reaction lifted her spirits in a way that leering glances and open invitations never could.

They continued along the trail, which rose in elevation, forcing them to go even slower. It led to an outcropping of rock that overlooked the lake far below. To Cassandra the scene was postcard worthy.

"Let's picnic here," she said, setting the lunch sack down. "Justin, honey, don't get too close to the edge."

"I'll keep an eye on him," Turner said.

Cassandra spread out a lunch similar to yesterday's fare, and the three of them ate as they viewed the vista that presented itself in all its rugged beauty. She thought how the fresh air added the right ambience to the food. Fine wine and gourmet cheese couldn't have tasted better than their humble offerings, considering the beauty and tranquility of the setting.

Justin, to whom the scenery was something to be explored rather than viewed, inhaled his sandwich and got to his feet, ready to proceed. Cassandra packed the remainder away, and they set out again. She didn't dare let Justin take a step on his own for fear he'd wander too close to the edge of the cliff. It was better to keep moving with him safely wedged between Turner and her.

The trail wound through a thick growth of trees and gradually rose again. So far they hadn't seen any animals. She was hoping to spot a deer or an elk in the distance to add to Justin's memory book, but only the occasional bird flitted by.

At length Justin pointed ahead and said, "See the big hole, Mommy. "

Cassandra had been walking with her head down, watching her footing. She looked up to see a jagged hole in the side of a vertical shaft of rock, where the mountain took a sudden upturn. It was a perfect cave for a napping bear or lurking mountain lion.

"Let's go see it," he said.

"Is it safe?" she asked, glancing uncertainly at Turner.

He studied the opening. "I don't see any signs of an occupant. No droppings or remnants of fur and bones or uprooted plants. But better to be safe than sorry." He picked up a rock and threw it into the opening.

Cassandra got ready to scoop up Justin and make a break for it should an angry carnivore, sporting a fresh goose egg, come charging out. But only the sounds of the rock careening off the walls echoed back. Nothing grunted in protest and no enraged animal emerged to defend its territory.

Turner peeked inside the cave and sniffed the air. "No animal odor," he noted.

"Let's go inside, Mommy," Justin said, darting ahead.

Turner grabbed him by the arm. "Hold on, little man," he said, negotiating his way over some strewn boulders and jagged pieces of granite as he entered the cave. "I'll go first."

Cassandra followed with Justin. When her eyes adjusted to the dimness, she saw that the narrow opening gave way to a spacious room. The decor would not win an interior design award, but it was intriguing nonetheless. The floor rose gradually toward the back of the cave, where several small ledges sat like benches. The inner recesses of the cave remained in the shadows, but for the most part the interior was well lit.

Justin climbed up on a rock bench and sat dangling his legs back and forth, looking proud of himself. Cassandra took advantage of the lull to sit down on a large boulder, waiting for her son to declare an end to the rest and relaxation.

A trickle of water oozed between layers of rock in the side of the wall. Turner put his finger up to it and collected a single water droplet. Applying it to the tip of his tongue, he nodded in approval.

Cassandra tasted it and found that it was as fresh as spring water.

"It has been filtered as it seeped through the layers of rock and sediment to reach this outlet," Turner explained. "And look here." He pointed to a ring-shaped mineral deposit on the floor at the base of the wall. "That's called a soda straw. When the water evaporates, it leaves minerals behind. Over time the deposit gets bigger and forms a hollow formation that looks just like—"

"A soda straw," Cassandra said.

"Let me see it," Justin said, rushing forward.

"Be careful," Turner cautioned. "It's very—"

Justin grabbed it and it crumbled between his fingers.

"—fragile," Turner said.

Justin's lip began to tremble and his eyes clouded over.

"It's okay, little man," Turner said, comforting him. "It'll form again. No harm done."

Justin sniffed back tears and went to investigate a colorful rock that caught his attention.

As Cassandra watched her son, she became aware of a cool draft of air. Peering into the dimness, she noticed the outline of a narrow tunnel, leading off into the blackness beyond. It probably surfaced farther up the mountain, she decided, drawing fresh air down into the cave.

The moderate temperature and deep silence beckoned: relax…drift…sleep. And she could feel herself further disconnecting from her former life as the stress continued to dissipate like morning dew. It was hard to believe that her marriage and life in Las Vegas hadn't been a dream—a nightmare actually—because in many ways it seemed so long ago. It was easier and far more pleasant to imagine that being with Turner and Justin was her real life. Self-delusional, true. But for now all she wanted to do was sit back and enjoy the moment.

chapter 23

JUSTIN EXPLORED THE interior of the cave, finding wonders that captivated his four-year-old imagination. Several stalactites hung from a low section of the ceiling. They were several inches in length and resembled grayish icicles. He studied them with fascination before turning his attention to a small growth of yellowish-brown lichens nearby. He touched the fuzzy plants and giggled, saying they tickled him.

After exploring the interior of the cave for twenty minutes, his attention span maxed out, and he raced for the entrance. "Let's go outside!" he said.

Cassandra came out of her reverie in time to see Justin flash by her. Instinctively she leaped to her feet and attempted to grab him so he didn't get away. In the process, she stumbled over a rock and her ankle twisted sideways. She cried in agony and fell to the ground.

"Mommy!" Justin yelled, rushing back to her.

She felt nauseous with pain and began shaking uncontrollably. Perspiration beaded on her forehead, and she fought the urge to vomit.

Turner was beside her in an instant, cradling her head and wiping a smudge of dirt from her cheek.

"Stupid me!" she moaned through clenched teeth.

"Are you okay, Mommy?" Justin asked, starting to cry.

"Mommy's okay," she said, wiping his tears and grimacing as she pushed herself up into a sitting position. "Let me try to stand up."

"Rest for a minute," Turner said, dabbing her forehead with the bottom of his shirt. "I need to look at your ankle."

She winced as Turner gently lifted the leg of her pants and rolled down her sock. The initial wave of nausea began to pass, and she found herself breathing a little easier. "How does it look?" she asked.

"It's starting to swell. I'm going to leave your shoe on to keep compression on your ankle. Now I just have to find a way to immobilize it."

"Got any splints in your back pocket?" she said, as a tremor shook her body again.

"No, but I can find something."

While Justin cuddled up in her arms, Turner left for a minute. He returned carrying a small log. "It's rotted in the middle so this should work," he said.

She watched as he broke off two curved pieces, about the length from her ankle to her knee. He put them on either side of her leg and had her hold them in place. Then he removed his T-shirt and tore it into strips, which he used to tie the two pieces in place.

As he worked, she noticed the way his muscles flexed like strands of steel wire as he tied the strips at intervals around the splint. There was confidence in his expression and certainty in his eyes. "Pretty creative," she said, wincing at the sudden pressure around her leg.

"I'm a handyman, remember?" he said, tying the last strip in place. "Ready to give it a try?"

She exhaled sharply and nodded. "Talk about giving me the shirt off your back."

"I've got a dozen more just like it in my closet at home. Now let's get you back to the cabin and ice your ankle."

"Let me help you, Mommy."

Justin was more hindrance than help, but Cassandra didn't

have the heart to discourage his efforts. Together he and Turner managed to get her to her feet.

"I'll piggyback you for a ways," Turner said.

"I'm too heavy," she protested, feeling an increased sense of helplessness.

"My toolbox at work, now that's heavy. I'm used to lugging it around."

"So now I'm a toolbox?"

"Only much cuter," he said, and Cassandra was certain she saw his cheeks redden at the comment.

She tried to take a step on her own, but the pain was too severe. Reluctantly agreeing to Turner's offer, she gingerly climbed onto his back and wrapped her arms around his neck. His skin felt warm and firm, and she felt his muscles respond to the extra burden. She seemed to be suddenly floating as Turner beckoned to Justin and then started down the trail.

They reached the embankment a short time later, and Turner put her down to assess the descent. Cassandra could see that the loose rocks and dirt posed a problem, especially to someone in her condition.

"What about over there?" she asked, pointing to a grassy slope on the far side of the embankment that was freckled with exposed tree roots and smooth, weathered rocks.

Turner went over and examined the grassy slope. "It should work," he called to her. Returning, he helped her over to the place he had selected for their descent. "I'll get Justin down first," he said. Then holding onto Justin firmly, he started down, using the tree roots as toe and finger holds to cautiously pick his way along.

"Let's go faster, Turner," Justin said, his eyes dancing.

"Not now, little man."

When they reached the bottom, Turner looked up the slope

at Cassandra and nodded in encouragement. "You can do this," he said.

He instructed Justin to remain there and then climbed up beside Cassandra to provide assistance. She set her jaw determinedly and started down, stabilizing herself with her arms and keeping her injured ankle slightly elevated so she didn't snag it on a tree root or a rock. Turner helped steady her, but the surface was uneven and every time she slid over a bump, it jarred her. She gritted her teeth and did her best to hide the pain, knowing it would upset Justin to have her cry out in agony.

When she reached the bottom, Turner helped her stand up. She leaned against him for support, her muscles trembling from the strain.

When they were ready to continue, Turner had her climb on his back again. With Justin in front so he could keep his eye on him, they started out once more.

The return journey lasted less than half the time, and Turner kept up a steady pace. With each step he took, her leg jolted slightly, and she tried to keep her mind off the pain by keeping a watchful eye on Justin.

Cassandra could feel Turner perspiring and hear his breathing growing heavier. She suggested he stop and rest, but he refused to slow the pace or let her down. He kept encouraging Justin to walk faster, and several times he took Justin by the hand and walked him along when the little boy wanted to stop and explore.

When they finally reached the cabin, Turner carried Cassandra into the living room and helped her into an easy chair. He placed a pillow on top of the footstool and slid it under her leg, to elevate her ankle. Then he got a plastic grocery bag and filled it with ice cubes from the refrigerator.

Cassandra winced as he removed the splint and her shoe.

Placing the cold compress on her swollen ankle, he said, "I saw a bottle of aspirin in the cupboard. I'll get you a couple of tablets for pain."

"Thanks," she replied, shifting in her chair to make herself comfortable.

Turner came back into the living room with a glass of water and the medication. She popped the tablets into her mouth, raised the glass to her lips, and swallowed them in one gulp.

"They'll kick in soon," he said, leaving the room momentarily.

Justin climbed into her arms to console her. He stroked her hair and said, "Poor Mommy."

Cassandra cuddled him in the realization that his love and attention complemented the pain medication.

"Looks like you're in good hands," Turner said, putting on a clean T-shirt as he came back into the living room.

"The best," she replied, kissing Justin on the cheek.

Turner sat beside her on the arm of the chair. "How you holding up?"

She hesitated before answering. "It's funny how you take things for granted, isn't it?" she said, painfully readjusting her ankle on the pillow. "We walk or run and never give it a second thought. And then something like this happens, and it sure makes you appreciate the simple things."

"Can I get you anything more?"

"Do you have any spare ankles with you by any chance?"

Turner pretended to look in his toolbox. "Let me see. I've got an extra toilet kit, a safety chain, some duct tape, a pack of chewing gum, and a bunch of tools. But no spare ankles. Sorry."

"And you call yourself a handyman."

"I didn't say I was a *good* one."

She laughed. "Actually you're a great one. The splint really helped. I'm sorry about your shirt though. But you can have it back when I'm done with it." She crinkled her eyes as she smiled.

"Sure. I can always use rags at work."

She laughed louder but stopped when she moved her ankle accidentally. "I'll buy you a nice shirt when this is all over, I promise."

"The old ones make better rags. Nobody steals them."

She paused and looked at him curiously. "Were you this funny in high school?"

"What do you mean?"

"You have a great sense of humor. Anybody ever tell you that?"

"My fashion designer and hair stylist mention it all the time."

She laughed again, careful to keep her ankle steady.

They talked for a while longer, reminiscing about the day's adventures. At length Turner nudged her and said, "Looks like the Energizer Bunny's batteries finally ran down."

Justin had fallen asleep in her arms, his chin drooping against his chest.

"Would you mind carrying him into the bedroom?" Cassandra asked.

"No problem." Turner cradled him carefully in his arms and made his way into the far bedroom. When he returned, Cassandra held out her arms to him.

"I think I'd like to go lie down on the bed myself," she said. "This chair is hurting my back."

Turner took her by the hands. "Should we do it piggyback style or carry-the-bride-over-the-threshold style?"

She smiled wryly. "The piggyback thing worked better."

He crouched down, and she put her arms around his neck. When he stood back up, Cassandra felt no sign of strain from him due to the added weight. She held on tight as he carried her into her bedroom and set her gently on the bed. As he helped her lie down, their faces were inches apart, and she could feel his breath on her cheek. She looked into his eyes and saw something she hadn't noticed before. It was a reflection of growing feelings and desire. And she wondered if he saw the same expression in her eyes.

A question raced through her mind. Was he going to kiss her? She was uncertain of what her reaction would be if he did. She *was* a married woman, after all. At least according to the letter of the law. But as far as the spirit of the law went...

She had her answer the next instant when he suddenly straightened up and reached for a pillow. "I'll put this under your leg, to keep your ankle elevated," he said, breaking eye contact. "You going to be okay?"

"Uh-huh. Thanks, again."

He walked to the door and turned and looked at her. "I'll make dinner in a while. You get some rest."

She nodded and settled back in the bed, trying to sort through her emotions. She had only been away from Brad for a few days, and in the meantime she had met someone who amazed her. Turner Caldwell had blossomed from a high school dweeb into this extraordinary person. Her head spun as she considered the transformation. And, yet, she wondered if the transformation was really that dramatic after all. True, he had grown taller, but perhaps he had always been this interesting and talented and kind in high school but no one had taken the time to notice. Perhaps Turner was simply a victim of being...a victim. Whatever the answer, she knew she and Justin had been led to the right person. She liked Turner Caldwell. But more than that she needed him.

chapter 24

ORNING DAWNED ACCORDING to the clock but not in the manner to which Turner had become accustomed based on his brief experience at the cabin. Sunshine didn't cheerily peer in around the edges of the curtains. Light didn't skip across the surface of the lake like water nymphs dancing in celebration. Instead darkness clung determinedly to the mountain peaks and to the valley below.

Clouds had rolled in, hanging like thick layers of soiled cotton batting. The air was heavy and solemn, promising rain. But for the moment the clouds greedily retained the water vapor and continued to move in from the west, amassing in silent formation.

Cassandra had spent a restless night and was still in a great deal of pain. The aspirins weren't cutting it. Turner decided to drive into Silverthorne and get something stronger. And because it was shaping up to be an inside day, he decided to look for a Redbox kiosk and pick up a couple of DVDs. Also, he'd call Loretta and Mary to make sure they were all right and to see how things were going.

Justin accompanied him out onto the front step and waved vigorously as Turner drove away. Turner watched him in the rearview mirror and wondered how many times Justin had done the same thing to his daddy as Brad left for work.

The cabin disappeared quickly in the overgrowth. It became easy to imagine that nothing existed past the point of Turner's vision, that his time with Cassandra and Justin was only an illusion.

As he drove toward the main road, he considered how Cassandra's accident might actually be a blessing in disguise. With her ankle now swollen to three times its normal size, and turning the color of a Concord grape, she was in no shape to walk, let alone continue her run from Brad. Perhaps now she'd agree to go to the police and file a report. Maybe this was the clinching argument to the rebuttal Turner had been seeking.

A strange feeling came over him as he reached the main road and headed south toward Silverthorne. Two people had unexpectedly become part of his life, and they were counting on him. But he was just a handyman and college student, single and unattached. What did he know about the roles of husband and father, abdicated by Brad?

He wondered if Brad had any idea what he was losing. Did he know what a great little kid his son was? Or how exquisite his wife was? Did he comprehend what he had lost by forcing the most important people in his life to flee?

His loss is my gain, Turner thought. But then he caught himself. Was the gain really his? In a few days, once the coast was clear and Cassandra could walk again, she would finish her business at the bank. Then she and Justin would disappear from his life for good. Something tugged at his heart, and he shook his head to clear his brain. No matter how it turned out in the end, Cassandra and Justin were part of his life for *now*. And that was what he needed to focus on.

No rain had fallen as yet, but the clouds continued to roll in, blotting out even a hint of sunshine. The air became cooler, and a soft rumble of thunder echoed through the mountain valley.

When he reached Silverthorne, he drove up Blue River Parkway, looking for a pharmacy. The first order of business was to get some medical supplies—an actual splint, an elastic bandage to secure it in place and provide compression, something stronger than aspirin for the pain, and a gel pack that would contour around her ankle and be more comfortable than the lumpy bag of ice cubes currently being used.

Moments later a police cruiser passed by and his heart rate doubled. Was there an APB out on Cassandra and him? He kept his eyes straight ahead, appearing casual and relaxed, although he felt anything but. The officer glanced in his direction and then looked away. Turner watched him intently in the rearview mirror. The officer didn't wheel around and give chase, lights flashing, siren blaring. He merely continued to the end of the street and turned right.

Turner found a pharmacy across from an outlet mall on Blue River Parkway and pulled in. After checking to make certain the police officer hadn't doubled back, Turner climbed out of the car and went in search of the pharmacist. He wanted to get an opinion on the best medical supplies to buy for Cassandra.

The pharmacist, a thin woman wearing the traditional white jacket, stepped from behind the counter and led him to the correct aisle. She showed him several options, expressing her opinion on each, which Turner readily accepted. His arms were soon loaded with enough medical supplies to start his own clinic. He thanked her for her assistance and proceeded to the front counter. Two people were in line ahead of him, so while he waited he scanned the headlines of the local newspaper sitting on the counter. Nothing screamed *Child Kidnapped*. And though he couldn't see the inside pages, he doubted if there was anything about the three of them either. Obviously Brad hadn't leaked anything to the press. Yet.

When it was his turn, he returned the clerk's smile and paid for the items in cash. Then he headed to the exit, feeling comfortable enough to pause and hold the door open for an elderly woman with a cane.

Intending to call Loretta and Mary next, he came across a food mart near the edge of town and decided to do the grocery shopping first. He'd call on his cell phone later, if he could get service, or from a pay phone at a gas station if he couldn't.

He made his way up and down the aisles, throwing items indiscriminately into the shopping cart. The good mood made him more frivolous in his selections. He picked several items just so he could see Justin's eyes light up when he discovered the sugary treasures. Turner hoped Cassandra would be equally satisfied with the healthy choices of vegetables and fruits he added for her.

He ended up buying more than he intended, considering he didn't know how much longer they were going to be at the cabin. But they would take the excess with them anyway, he decided.

With the shopping cart significantly filled, he went through the checkout counter, again paying in cash. He noticed that the money Loretta had given him was almost gone. He needed to find an ATM before leaving Silverthorne.

Pushing the cart out to the Buick, he put the grocery bags in the trunk and decided to call Loretta and Mary before he went in search of a Redbox and an ATM. He wondered what news the two women would have to tell him.

As much as he wanted the matter resolved, thoughts of having to reenter the real world created a strange sensation in the pit of his stomach. A cold, empty feeling came over him as he thought about waking up one morning soon and finding Cassandra and Justin gone. In a few days his entire world, which had been turned upside down, would be righted again. Could he live with it restored to its former order?

The phone calls to Loretta and Mary could change everything.

We've found a counseling clinic where Cassandra and Justin can stay while things are being worked out. Take them there ASAP.

Turner would become a solitary man again.

They're going to go into something like a witness protection program.

Life for him would return to normal.

They'll have new names, new identities, and be moved to a distant city.

His heart would become an empty chamber once more.

There won't be any contact number. You'll never see them again.

A sense of loss overcame him, and he almost decided not to call. At least not today. He needed more time to adjust to the winds of change that were about to sweep everything away. He could make up an excuse by telling the truth about Cassandra's injury and how she wasn't able to travel. Then the three of them could snuggle indoors and let the rain descend, watching DVDs and remaining cozy and warm while nature cleansed herself.

But that would only be delaying the inevitable. They were going to have to return to the real world sooner or later. It wasn't fair to keep Cassandra and Justin in limbo just so he could enjoy their company for another day or two.

He flipped his cell phone open and punched in Loretta's number. He couldn't get cell reception, however, and he experienced a degree of relief. But it was fleeting because he couldn't delay making the call. He'd have to find a pay phone.

As he drove down Blue River Parkway and approached a gas station, checking for a pay phone, he spotted a black Mercedes. Quickly, he skidded to a stop and pulled off to the side of the road.

Blinking rapidly, he stared at the stocky man standing beside the Mercedes at the gas pump, talking to the attendant who was fueling the car. A second man sat in the car, in the passenger seat. The stocky man was turned away so Turner couldn't see his face, but he recognized him nonetheless.

It was Slick.

The attendant was pointing north, in the direction of the cabin. Turner could see the attendant sweep his arm to the left, as though describing the turn-off. He motioned left again. Turner could understand the directions as clearly as if he was standing beside them, listening in.

Slick slipped the attendant some cash and went to the outside pay phone.

Turner didn't linger to mentally eavesdrop. Being careful not to squeal the tires, he backed up a short distance so a stand of trees blocked him from Slick's view. Cranking the wheel, he turned the car around and drove to the next street and turned north. It was vital that Slick not see him because he would recognize the Buick. One glimpse of it and Slick would appear in Turner's rearview mirror in seconds, following in his wake.

As he neared the edge of town, he tromped on the gas pedal. The Buick responded. Turner hoped that the police officer had pulled into a doughnut shop for coffee and wouldn't notice the silver blur streaking north.

Turner reached the open road and watched the speedometer register triple digits. Still, the five-mile drive to the turnoff seemed to last forever.

Anxiety filled his heart as he considered what Slick's arrival meant. Had the oily-haired man taken Mary by surprise and forced the information of Cassandra's whereabouts from her? Had Slick and Twitch threatened Loretta and Harvey? Were one or all of them being held captive somewhere, trussed up and gagged...or worse?

The possibilities were awful to consider.

chapter 25

CASSANDRA SMILED AS she watched Justin. He was sitting on the carpet near her, coloring a picture and humming under his breath. His tongue worked from side to side as he tried to stay between the lines, and his expression was a study in concentration.

"Look at my picture, Mommy," he said, holding it up for her to see.

"It's nice, sweetie," she said, trying to ignore the incessant throbbing of her ankle. She was unable to sit comfortably for any length of time.

When Justin returned to his coloring, she tried to distract herself by thinking about the day they had spent at the lake, canoeing and having the water fight and skipping rocks. She had never felt more relaxed in her life. Even the hike was enjoyable...at least the first half. And since arriving at the cabin, she had found a deep, personal level of tranquility. She wondered if she'd ever be able to recapture it once they left.

She also wondered if she'd ever again meet someone like Turner. He continued to impress her. His outdoor skills, first aid knowledge, and familiarity with the flora and fauna of the area were encyclopedic. But more than that, he was kind to her and so good with Justin. It was a blessing to be with him. How could she have ever known back in high school the important role he would eventually play in her life?

She was also surprised at how little she had thought of Brad during her time here. And Justin hadn't spoken of him since the night they left. Did he also feel safer without Brad around? Her heart broke at the thought.

As she shifted in her chair to get comfortable, she heard car tires skid in the front yard. This was followed by the sound of a car door slamming and footsteps thudding on the front porch seconds later. The front door opened, and Turner came rushing into the room.

"They found us!" he said.

Cassandra put a hand to her throat and glanced at Justin, who smiled at Turner and then returned to his coloring. Her son's innocence and vulnerability tore at her insides, twisting them into knots. "How?" she stammered. The tranquility she had experienced moments earlier was shattered by those three words. *They found us!*

"I don't know," Turner replied. "But we've got to get out of here. Now." He scooped up Justin in his arms. "Come on, little man," he said. "We've got to go."

"But I want to color my picture."

"I know. But right now, we're going on an adventure."

Justin relented and clutched Turner around the neck as they disappeared out the door.

Cassandra waited, heart pounding. Then a new terror gripped her heart. Loretta and Mary! Had something happened to them?

Turner returned. Wordlessly he put his back to her, and she climbed on.

"Loretta and Mary are the only ones who know where we are," she said.

She felt Turner's back muscles stiffen. "That's what worries me too," he replied.

"You don't think those guys got to them, do you? They're all right, aren't they?"

Turner didn't reply. Instead he ducked as he went through

the door and said, "We've got to leave. If those guys reach the main road turnoff before we do, we're hooped. They'll block the road."

At the car, Turner eased her to the ground and Cassandra stood up, balancing on her good foot. She understood the urgency of the situation. If their escape route was cut off, they'd be captured and handed over to Brad, who would repay Turner back tenfold for his role in helping her. And she didn't even want to consider what wages her sins would net her.

Turner got her situated in the car and then rushed back for their luggage.

Cassandra unrolled the window and listened for sounds of an approaching car. Nothing. Nor could she see telltale signs of dust rising above the trees, kicked up as if the Tasmanian Devil—Justin's favorite cartoon character—had leaped from the television and was now tearing down the road, drooling as he came.

"When are we going on our adventure?" Justin asked.

"Just as soon as Turner comes back, sweetie." She tried to keep the terror out of her voice as she glanced anxiously toward the cabin.

Justin knelt up in the backseat and looked out the side window. "I like going on adventures with Turner."

Cassandra felt a weight press against her heart. Justin's comment was so innocent, so natural. It was as if his life in Las Vegas with Brad and her never existed. And maybe to Justin it no longer did.

Turner emerged from the cabin with his arms filled with luggage and bags. He used his foot to close the door, not stopping to lock the cabin, and raced for the car.

"Did you remember to get the monkey?" she called to him. It seemed ridiculous even to her to worry about the monkey at a time like this, but Turner didn't hesitate to respond.

"Got it!" He opened the trunk and tossed everything inside. Then he climbed in behind the wheel and reached for the keys.

"Let's go, Turner," Justin said.

"Good advice, little man."

As Turner inserted the key in the ignition, Cassandra heard a roaring in the distance, born of rubber urgently traversing gravel. A cloud of dust rose above the treetops, in the direction of the main road. She glanced at Turner and knew he heard it too. And she didn't need two guesses to know what that meant.

The Tasmanian Devil had arrived.

chapter 16

*T*URNER'S IDEALISTIC SELF considered making an attempt to talk things over with Slick, mano a mano. But his rational self laughed him to scorn. Slick would never trust him now because Turner had lied to him. And Turner would never be able to convince the oily-haired man that he was willing to cooperate, or at least strike a deal.

Slick and Twitch didn't seem like the compassionate and understanding types, and Turner knew it would be useless to try and talk his way out of the situation.

After ramming the car in gear, he drove across the yard and plunged into a growth of silverberry bushes. He winced as the branches scratched their way down the length of the Buick like gnarled fingernails, as saw-toothed as car keys. The screech of wood against metal set his teeth on edge.

"What are you doing?" Cassandra gasped, grabbing the dashboard and looking at him as if he'd just lost his mind.

"Hopefully, buying us a few extra minutes. He slammed on the brakes and lurched to a stop. Loretta was *not* going to be pleased with the new designs on her car. But since Slick was going to hand him over to Brad so he could rearrange his— Turner's—dental work before killing him, he wouldn't have to worry about losing Sunday dinner privileges with the Joneses.

"Can we go for another ride?" Justin asked excitedly.

"Sorry, little man," Turner said, glancing up at the storm clouds. "We're going to have to go on foot." Reaching back, he lifted Justin into the front seat and held him tight. Then he pushed the door open, straining against the resistance of the compacted undergrowth. "They'll be here any minute," he said, as the sounds of the approaching car grew louder.

"Who?" Justin asked.

"Just some guys." He set Justin down and looked at him earnestly. "Do you want to play a game of hide-and-seek, little man?"

"Yeah!"

"Okay, we're going to go hide. But you have to be very quiet so no one finds us. Promise?"

"Promise."

Turner helped Cassandra out of the car and bent over so she could climb on his back. Then he gripped Justin's hand and led the way through the bushes, determined to put as much distance between themselves and the car as possible.

He headed for the trail they had taken yesterday. There was an outcrop of rock partway up, overlooking the cabin. From that vantage point and using the bushes as cover, he could watch the men's moves. They would undoubtedly search the cabin, find it vacant, and hopefully wander down to the lake to search there. At this point he could sneak back down the trail with Cassandra and Justin and disable their car. Then they could make their escape in the newly pinstriped Buick. He'd call Loretta and Mary at the first opportunity to check on them, and then keep driving. In some distant town they'd go to the police and file a report.

For the moment it was important that Justin not see the men. He might call out to them, giving away Turner and Cassandra's position. Then they would be caught for certain since the men were carrying nothing heavier than handguns and grudges, while Turner was loaded for bear, with a four-year-old in tow.

They ascended the trail much faster than they had the day before. Turner continually reminded Justin about the game of hide-and-seek they were playing and that there was no time to stop and look at bugs or flowers. At one point he had to take Justin by the hand and encourage him along when a squirrel scurried in front of them and disappeared up a tree.

By the time they reached the outcrop, Turner was out of breath. He set Cassandra down and had Justin remain with her. Then he crawled onto the outcrop of rock and peered down on the cabin below.

He saw the two men cautiously approach the front door and try the handle. The door swung open but they hesitated before entering, perhaps sensing a trap. They peered through the front window and then conversed for a moment. Leaving Twitch to guard the front door, Slick went around to the side window and cupped his hands against the glass.

He circled the cabin completely and came back to the front door, shaking his head at Twitch. The two men pulled hand-guns from their belts and gripped them assault style as they disappeared inside the cabin.

Turner could hear the men shouting for the fugitives to give themselves up. This was followed by the sounds of furniture being overturned and doors being slammed. The men were trashing the place, and Turner wondered how he would explain the damage to Mary and her friend who owned the cabin.

A short time later Slick emerged, followed closely by Twitch. Turner watched to see which direction they continued their search. Not surprisingly they didn't have the courtesy to close the front door and call a house-cleaning company before moving into the front yard and scanning the area, slowly turning in a complete circle.

When the plane of their view intersected with his, Turner ducked behind the camouflage. After waiting a minute, he dared another peek. The men were nowhere to be seen.

He scanned the trail, wondering if they had somehow caught sight of him or perhaps had heard his heart beating. From the corner of his eye, he saw a flash of movement and flinched involuntarily. But it was only a swallow flying overhead, its shadow racing across the ground in an effort to keep pace.

He glanced back at Cassandra, planning an escape route should the men make their way up the trail. She was busy trying to distract Justin by pointing out a caterpillar that was inching its way up the stalk of a purple flower.

When he turned back, he saw the men moving down toward to the lake. He felt a rush of relief because they were going the wrong way. This would give him the chance to carry Cassandra back down the trail, disable the men's car, and escape in the Buick. Just a few more yards and the men would be completely obscured by the foliage.

His relief quickly faded as he saw Slick leave the trail and head toward a thick growth of silverberry bushes. He watched as Slick tore at the protruding branches, exposing the Buick. The oily-haired man called to Twitch, and Turner could almost see an evil smile spread across Slick's face at the discovery.

"I know you're here somewhere," Slick shouted, his voice echoing menacingly.

Turner prayed Justin wouldn't call out: "Here we are!"

Fortunately he didn't. But Turner felt the cold realization that now it *was* a game of hide-and-seek, and the stakes had increased significantly. And depending on which direction the men continued their search, the game would either end in a hurry or endure for an eternity.

Turner watched as they rustled around in the bushes. He heard metallic sounds and guessed they were searching the Buick's interior. Surely they didn't think the three fugitives were slumped down in the seats, hoping no one would think to look there.

The men emerged from the bushes a short time later, and Turner readied himself to collect Cassandra and Justin and flee farther up the trail if need be. But the men headed for the path that led down to the lake and disappeared in the foliage.

Crawling back to Cassandra and Justin, he whispered, "Let's go."

Cassandra climbed onto his back, and together they made their way back down the trail. Several times Turner's feet slipped in the loose earth and pine needles that carpeted the path, but he managed to maintain his balance.

When they reached the bottom of the trail, Turner put Cassandra down. "Stay here while I make sure the coast is clear," he whispered.

There was always the chance the men had doubled back. If that was the case, he didn't want the three of them to be taken all at once. Cassandra would still have an opportunity to climb into a hiding place with Justin and wait until dark, while Slick and Twitch tried to worm information out of Turner using a variety of tried and tested techniques meant to inspire cooperation.

"I wanna come too," Justin said.

Cassandra leaned down and whispered, "You stay here and protect Mommy from bears."

Justin sucked in his breath excitedly and began scanning the trees for any sign of them.

Turner left Cassandra there, sitting in the shade of some bushes. Justin stood beside her with a stick in his hand, wielding it like a sword.

After scurrying across the clearing, Turner darted into the thick vegetation and ducked behind a rotted tree stump. He could hardly hear above the sound of blood pounding in his ears. It was a staccato drumbeat, gradually increasing in tempo, heightening the suspense.

He waited to make sure his presence was still undetected and then followed the Buick's entrance into the bushes. It was now a matter of starting the car and backing up into the clearing to pick up Cassandra and Justin. Then he would slash the tires on Slick's car and be gone in one palpitating heartbeat.

As he hurried to the driver's door, he noticed that the hood of the Buick was ajar. Perhaps the latch had been sprung during their frantic plunge into the bushes. He wondered how he could close the hood without attracting attention. Deciding not to risk it, he climbed in the car, inserted the key, and turned it.

Nothing.

He turned the key again.

Still nothing.

The truth struck him with force. Slick had turned the tables on him and incapacitated the Buick instead. That explained the hood being partially open. Nobody would be leaving by Buick.

He slipped into the clearing and approached the black Mercedes, hoping the keys were still in the ignition. They weren't. And the blinking red light on the dashboard told him that if he as much as touched the door handle, the alarm would sound and the men would come running.

He hurried back to Cassandra to explain the situation and work out a plan.

She took the news hard but stoically. "We've got to find a place to hide until we can figure out what to do."

"Let's go to the cave," Justin said.

Turner stared at him in surprise and then looked at Cassandra. How much of their situation did the little boy actually comprehend? Something told him he had underestimated Justin.

Glancing up the trail, Turner tried to visualize their journey. It would not be easy, but the cave was a better idea than anything he could come up with. The clouds continued to roll ominously overhead, and he hoped the three of them would get there ahead of the rain. A deluge now would make the steep part of the trail difficult to negotiate, and the rocky embankment, impossible.

Patting Justin on the head, he asked, "Think we can make it, little man?"

Justin's big, blue eyes looked directly at him. "Sure, Turner."

Inspired by Justin's implicit confidence and trust, Turner turned to Cassandra. "It won't be much of a home, I'm afraid. But it will be shelter." Once more his gaze swept the sky. "We'll need your pain medication and a few other things from the car," he said. "I'll be right back."

He returned to the car and was about to open the trunk when he heard a twig snap nearby. Ducking down, he peeked around the rear fender and saw Twitch making his way back up the trail. In seconds his pursuer would come into plain view, and it would be too late to make an escape.

Abandoning the car, Turner crouched down and scurried back to Cassandra. "Someone's coming," he whispered. "We've got to go right now."

She nodded resolutely and reached around his neck. He lifted her into position, grabbed Justin by the hand, and headed up the trail, moving quickly toward the thicker vegetation that lined the path a short distance ahead.

When they reached the denser foliage, Turner slowed down, being careful to pace himself because there was still a long hike ahead.

"Do you think anyone spotted us?" Cassandra asked anxiously.

"I don't think so," he replied, aware of the tension in her arms.

Justin slipped out of Turner's hand and walked ahead. "Come on," he said.

"Right behind you, little man," Turner said as they continued up the trail, *homeward* bound.

chapter 27

THE HIKE TO the cave the first time had been an enjoyable outing for Turner, graced by alpine scenery nestled beneath a robin's-egg blue sky. The pace had been relaxing, and he'd enjoyed watching Justin stop and examine rocks, flowers, and trees along the way.

The second trip was anything but relaxing. The scenery went unnoticed and the fresh air unsavored. There was no loitering so Justin could investigate the flora and fauna. Instead Turner kept them moving at a frantic pace, afraid the sky might open up and complicate their predicament, and even more afraid the men might catch a glimpse of them and give chase.

By bending forward, he found he could support Cassandra more easily. But eventually that strategy began to take its toll. His legs and back burned as though carpenter ants were boring holes in his muscles, releasing a painful acid in the process.

His lower back was threatening to go into spasms, but he kept moving. It was either that or get caught in the impending deluge. Or, worse, face two unhappy men who were scouring the area, guns in hand, the bullets of which *would* bore holes in his muscles. The choice was simple, and so he kept putting one foot in front of the other, willing himself forward.

He pushed himself until he was convinced he couldn't take another step. Mercifully, and problematically, they arrived at the steep, rocky embankment. Scaling it yesterday had been an adventure. Today it loomed like the sheer walls of a cathedral, mocking any intentions to ascend them.

Cassandra echoed his thoughts. "You can't carry me up that."

She slid off his back and leaned against the face of the rock, while Turner discreetly massaged his knotted muscles and considered their dilemma.

"Let's slide up the hill, Mommy," Justin said.

Once more Turner found himself looking at Justin in wonder.

Yesterday they had slid down the hill. Perhaps today they could inch their way *up* the grassy slope. It certainly was less daunting than attempting to scale the rocky face. But Cassandra's injured ankle posed a problem, and he wondered if she'd be able to negotiate the slope in her condition. Normally, landing on soft mountain grasses would be less consequential than careening down weathered granite, which was as abrasive as coarse sandpaper. But if she slipped or put pressure on her injured ankle, despite the soft grass, it would compound the injury.

Draping Cassandra's arm around his neck, Turner helped her over to the grassy slope. It was long and steep, more inviting for descents than for what they intended, but they were running out of options. He surveyed the route, trying to decide how best to make their attempt. Nearby was a section where the grass gave way to thicker vegetation. "The trees form a diagonal ladder of sorts," he noted. "By moving from one exposed tree root to another, we can crawl up the slope."

"What about Justin?" Cassandra asked.

"I'll help you up to the top first, and then come back for him." He looked at Justin and placed a hand on the little boy's head. "Will you wait right here while I help your mommy?"

"Uh-huh," Justin replied, becoming fascinated by a spider dangling from a silken thread attached to the branch of a gnarled shrub.

Taking a deep breath, Cassandra began carefully crawling up the slope. Turner followed right behind, using protruding roots and rocks to anchor himself so he could support her good foot and help her proceed. She slipped once but he caught her, clinging desperately to an exposed tree root so they both didn't tumble to the bottom. He managed to steady her, but she bumped her injured ankle in the process and sucked in her breath to fight the pain.

"Are you okay?" he asked.

"Yeah," she exhaled sharply in reply. "Let's keep going."

With sustained effort they managed to reach the top without further incident. Cassandra lay on the slope, nursing her throbbing ankle.

Turner paused to catch his breath and looked at her. Her hair was matted, her clothes grass stained, and her hands soiled with earth. She noticed his perusal and forced a smile. "I'll be okay," she said. "Just go get Justin."

Turner quickly descended the slope and knelt beside the little boy. "I want you to hang on around my neck and not let go, okay?"

Justin nodded and climbed onto Turner's back, locking his arms securely around Turner's neck. Choosing his foot and toeholds carefully, Turner ascended the grassy slope. Cassandra grabbed Justin when his head appeared above the crest of hill, and she pulled him to her.

A sudden flash of lightning, followed by a rolling clap of thunder, caused Justin to curl into a ball and cover his ears. The sound echoed down the mountain valley and finally faded in the distance, seeming to shake the trees as it passed.

"Time to go," Turner said, as the first droplet arrived as a harbinger of more to follow.

He got Cassandra situated on his back as another blast of

185

thunder rumbled overhead. Justin clung to Turner's leg and wouldn't let go.

"It's okay, little man," Turner said. "Your mommy and I are right here."

Justin grabbed Turner's hand, and they continued up the trail. Their progress was slow and at times unsteady, but once the trail leveled off, Turner was able to walk more easily.

As they proceeded, Cassandra's hair brushed against his neck, and the touch of her breath warmed his cheek. He was also aware of her occasional soft groans, and he knew she was hurting.

The aspirin tablets she had taken this morning were still working but the effects would wear off soon. And the medication was back in the trunk of the car. He would return later to retrieve the painkillers, some food, and anything else he could carry.

They reached the cave before the rain descended in earnest. He was grateful they had managed to remain dry. At this elevation and with the drop in temperature, mild hypothermia was a serious threat. Especially for Justin. And Turner wouldn't be able to make a fire because the smoke would betray their location.

Dehydration was another concern. It weakened the body and dulled the mind, causing a person to overlook important survival information. And although there was a trickle of water that oozed between layers of rock inside the cave, it was not a sufficient quantity to keep the three of them hydrated. He got Cassandra situated on one of the natural rock benches and elevated her ankle to make her as comfortable as possible. Then he hurried outside and found a fallen log nearby. He ripped off a piece of chunky bark and quickly retraced his steps, pausing briefly at the mouth of the cave to dig a hole in the ground with the back of his heel.

Rain droplets began dancing at the cave entrance, becoming a frenzy of splash and splatter. With Justin wedged between them on the rock bench, they watched the deluge, mesmerized by its intensity. It was as though they were tucked in a cleft behind a waterfall. The rocky floor sloped toward the opening so the water didn't flow inside. But the sounds of Mother Nature venting herself filled the cave, and Justin clung to Turner, burying his face against Turner's chest with each peal of thunder.

"I wish we could have brought some food," Turner said. "But at least we can keep ourselves hydrated. The hole I made will capture rainwater once the ground becomes saturated enough. But for now, the bark will have to do."

He went to the entrance and held the curved piece of bark out far enough to capture some rain. Then holding it like an oblong cup, he gave Justin a drink. He repeated the procedure several times until the three of them were refreshed.

They sat together and watched the raindrops until fatigue overcame Turner, and his eyelids gave in to the law of gravity.

"Get some rest," Cassandra said, as Turner's head bobbed. "I'll keep an eye on things."

"Maybe just for a few minutes," he murmured. If he was going to make a return trip to the car for food and medication, in muddy conditions, he was going to need to recoup his strength. He closed his eyes and in a matter of minutes, he could no longer hear the rain.

He slept for a while and then suddenly flinched awake, shaking his head in an attempt to clear his brain. Staring vacantly at the interior of the cave, he realized how cold and uncomfortable he was. The temperature had dropped several degrees, and the rocks had not become any softer. The humidity added a bite to the air, and a chill had crept into his bones.

Cassandra reached over and squeezed his arm, but it was not to welcome him back from dreamland. There was a message there. She was in pain and needed more pain medication, and Justin was whimpering about being hungry.

Turner rose stiffly to his feet. He gritted his teeth, refusing to allow misgivings to creep into his brain about his ability to do what needed to be done. He was going to have to rely on his instincts and training because two special people were counting on him to succeed. There was no margin for error. The stakes were too high.

chapter 18

URNER EMERGED FROM the cave, grateful that the rain had stopped. Still, the trail was muddy and puddles had formed in low spots. He was forced to walk along the edge of the path as he headed toward his first major obstacle: the embankment. Because of the slippery conditions, he was afraid of descending the grassy slope like a one-man bobsledder determined to set an Olympic record.

Fortunately the same exposed tree roots that had aided his and Cassandra's ascent now prevented his breaking any records. But it did not come without a price. Several times he lost his grip and slid over protruding roots as unforgiving as a bare-knuckle fighter's gnarled fists, slowing his descent enough that he could grab a root or branch and regain control.

He realized that a return ascent this way would be impossible, due to the wet and slippery conditions. The rocky face of the embankment would offer better finger grips and toeholds. But that was only if he could successfully negotiate his way to the car, retrieve the necessary items from the trunk, and make his exit without Slick or Twitch inconveniencing him by placing a gun to his head and giving him an ultimatum.

The prospect of the two men lying in wait was both real and sobering. Not only might it mean his demise, but Cassandra's and Justin's as well. They would be left alone to face the elements, unaware of his fate, while nature exacted an ultimate toll for their daring to venture into her domain.

The remainder of the journey was a mental blur until he reached the outcropping of rock that overlooked the cabin.

His senses, dull and damp, suddenly heightened with the realization that the moment of truth had arrived.

Crouching behind a bush, he tried to determine the best way to approach the Buick. The threat of Slick and Twitch's presence lurked in every shadow, cowered behind every rock, and skulked beside every tree. It was omnipresent and omniscient, as though the men were anticipating his every move and outsmarting his best-laid plans.

He swept his apprehensions aside. Every second he delayed added to Cassandra and Justin's misery, and he needed his full powers of concentration if he was going to succeed.

Bolstered by a new determination, he left the rock outcropping and headed down the trail. When he reached the edge of the clearing, he paused to catch his breath and do what reconnaissance he could. He didn't dare walk into the open, so he began a circuitous route, working his way around to the car. With every step, he wondered if there would be a sudden blast of gunfire from behind a tree, dropping him in his tracks. But the area remained locked in nature's unsettled embrace. There were no incongruous sounds, such as a bullet sliding into the chamber of a gun or the trigger being gently squeezed. No chuckle from Twitch, anticipating impending triumph. Just the intermittent sound of raindrops dripping from trees and the soft moan of the wind, accompanied by the beating of his heart, as audible in his ears as the bass drum in a college marching band.

His first journey to the car had seemed long. This one seemed longer. His skin tingled in dreadful anticipation of the sound of gunfire delivering a bullet with his name on it. And because the occasional raindrop wouldn't deflect the bullet, he knew the next thing he'd hear would be the sound of his body thudding to the ground in a bedraggled, wounded heap.

But no whisper. No gunfire. No bullet.

Surely Slick hadn't come all this way only to give up. He and Twitch had to be here somewhere, waiting, watching.

He made it around the clearing and followed the Buick's path into the bushes. Peering into the back window, he checked to make sure his adversaries weren't sitting patiently inside, guns ready.

He quietly opened the door and pushed the button to open the trunk, pausing to allow his heart rate to slow from a gallop to a walk. Moving cautiously, he inched the trunk lid open, ready to dive for cover if the hinges creaked, tattling on him. At the halfway point, and with still no sound, he was able to peek inside.

A small electronic device sat on top of the luggage. A tiny red light on the device flashed, and Turner instinctively flinched. It was a motion-activated sensor, and he expected it to emit a piercing sound or blow up in his face. But neither occurred. Still, he knew that his presence had been detected and a signal had just been sent somewhere.

Flinging the lid open, he grabbed the device and threw it into the bushes. Then he began rifling desperately through the trunk, realizing he was tempting fate by the delay. But he was so close to getting what he needed, he granted himself the luxury of fifteen more seconds.

An old leather jacket lay in one corner of the trunk. He had noticed it earlier when he had loaded the car but had not given it much thought. Now, it seemed like a gift from heaven. He slipped it on, and even though it was oversized and smelled musty, it provided immediate warmth.

He stuffed a grocery bag full of necessities, including the painkillers, and lowered the lid, leaving it ajar so the click of the latch wouldn't give him away.

Turning to leave, he came face to face with Twitch, who held up a small electronic receiver. And a gun. "Thought you'd be showing up, sooner or later," he said, his head twitching in triumph. "Where are the woman and the kid?"

Obviously the fifteen seconds Turner had allowed himself were too generous. He drew in a deep breath to untangle his raveled nerves and glanced around for an avenue of escape.

"Don't do anything stupid," Twitch warned, waving the gun. "Put the bag back in the trunk and let's go inside. We'll talk in there." An evil grin of anticipation accompanied the word *talk*.

A feeling of helplessness and dread overcame Turner as he thought of Cassandra and Justin huddled in the cave, waiting expectantly. And since he was the *doofus* that Twitch was anxious to incapacitate, Cassandra and Justin would be waiting a long time.

Twitch glanced at the receiver in his hand, a puzzled expression on his face. "The device has been moved. What did you do with it?"

Turner glanced toward a thick stand of stinging nettle, growing nearby. The nettles were tall, with large pointed leaves growing in pairs opposite each other on the stems. Greenish-white flowers dangled in clusters where the stem and the leaves joined, and the bristly, stinging hairs protruded like three-day-old stubble. "Threw it in the weeds," he said, hoping his reference to the nettles as *weeds*, which technically they were, would deceive Twitch as to their noxious and painful potential.

"Get it," Twitch ordered, motioning toward the stand. "And don't try anything cute. I'll be right behind you every step of the way."

That's what I'm counting on, Turner thought.

Discreetly slipping his hands into the pockets of the leather jacket so there was no exposed skin, Turner began walking through the stinging nettle as if looking for the device, being careful not to let the bristly hairs touch his neck and face. When the sharp, pointed hairs penetrated the skin, they broke off and released chemicals, which formed a painful rash. He'd had one experience with stinging nettle during his first summer at Camp Kopawanee, and that was one time too many.

As Twitch followed closely behind, the tall nettles brushed across his face and hands. Turner watched to see how he reacted. The more exposure Twitch received, the more severe the rash would be.

Twitch began to scratch his hands and arms, unconsciously at first. White welts appeared on his face where the nettles touched him, but he doggedly kept the gun trained on Turner. "Hurry up, hurry up!" he barked impatiently, doing his best to remain watchful while digging at his arms and scratching his face.

"I'm hurrying," Turner replied, as he continued to weave his way around.

He stepped on a stick about the size of a baseball bat lying on the ground and glanced back to see if Twitch had noticed it. He hadn't. Turner readied himself to pick it up and catch his opponent by surprise with a blow to the side of the head. Hopefully, the stick wouldn't explode in a cloud of decomposed wood fragments, causing Twitch to shoot him in the leg for exercising bad judgment.

But Turner never had a chance to determine the stick's condition. Twitch suddenly cried out and began to dig furiously at his arms and face. He momentarily dropped the gun. Turner rushed out of the nettles and ducked behind a tree, listening as Twitch thrashed about and shouted threats.

Turner wracked his brain for an idea. He knew that Twitch would be in a vengeful mood when he emerged from the nettles. The situation called for decisive action. He remembered a game called Evasion they used to play at Camp Kopawanee. A group would begin with a head start and leave clues for the other group to follow—broken branches, scuffmarks on the forest floor, rocks piled to create markings—all the while trying to keep ahead of the pursuing group. The purpose of the game was to see how long the lead group could evade their pursuers, while leaving more and more obvious clues behind. If the pursuing group hadn't caught them after two or three hours, the game usually ended with the lead group creating a smoke signal or blowing on a whistle and waiting to be caught.

It was time for Evasion, only Turner had no intention of allowing himself to be caught. He wondered if Twitch was nature savvy enough to read and follow the clues Turner intended to leave.

He wasn't.

The broken branches and the deep scuffmarks leading away from the car were lost on him. Clearly Twitch was more at home in darkened alleys and abandoned warehouses at midnight. The forest and the surrounding mountains were a foreign world to him.

To get his attention, Turner snapped a dry twig and allowed himself to be seen through a gap in the trees. Twitch did a double take and started toward him.

Turner let him draw closer but kept several tall trees between them so Twitch wouldn't have a direct shot. Then Turner began leading him deeper into the forest, ducking behind trees before reappearing briefly and darting through bushes but allowing Twitch to catch glimpses of him at regular intervals.

Turner also left signs for his own benefit so he would be able to find his way back to the cabin. But they meant nothing to Twitch, who continued to bulldog his way forward in angry pursuit.

The forest became a maze of trees and shrubs as he led Twitch farther from the cabin. The moss growing on the north side of the trees allowed Turner to keep his bearings as he continued east, pushing deeper into the dense growth. There were no landmarks visible now, no mountain peaks or foothills to provide bearings. Twitch would never be able to find his way back to the cabin in this lifetime.

The Survival Rules of Three says that a person can survive three minutes without air, three hours without shelter, three days without water, three weeks without food, and three months without hope. Turner wasn't worried about the three months without hope rule. By the end of three days without water, Twitch would be totally devoid of hope.

At one point Twitch stopped his pursuit. Turner watched through a gap in the shrubs as the man stood indecisively, looking around in an attempt to get his bearings. Turner could tell by his pursuer's expression that Twitch knew he was lost.

Turner stepped into the open briefly and then darted behind a tree as Twitch fired in his direction. The bullet passed through some overhanging pine boughs and thudded into a nearby tree trunk. Bark chips scattered, and Turner caught the scent of fresh pine gum.

He heard footsteps rustling toward him and knew the chase was back on.

Quickly, he ducked into the undergrowth and gained some distance between them. Then he burrowed into a pile of deadfall and lay absolutely still, taking long, slow breaths. He heard Twitch race by. When he was certain his pursuer was ahead of him, Turner emerged from his camouflage, brushed off his hair, and followed in pursuit.

If he appeared *behind* Twitch, it would further confuse the man. By doing this several times, appearing from a different angle on each occasion, Twitch would become totally disoriented.

As Turner crept forward, he noticed his quarry up ahead, peering into a fallen log. Perhaps Twitch thought Turner was tired and had decided to seek shelter. A squirrel suddenly darted out of the log, startling Twitch so badly that he fired several shots, missing it completely.

Turner decided to lead Twitch even further into the forest so the gunshots wouldn't be heard back at the cabin. He didn't want the two men to be able to get their bearings on one another by firing shots into the air. "Nice shooting," he called sarcastically, leaping behind a tree just before a bullet tore into the bark.

He slipped away and circled around Twitch, climbing a tree and hiding in the thick foliage. He peered through a small opening so he could determine his pursuer's whereabouts.

Twitch entered the clearing a short time later and wildly scanned the perimeter. "Where are you?" he cried, uttering a string of dark promises while he reloaded his gun.

Turner waited for him to pass and then climbed down, circling farther to his left. "Here!" he called, jumping behind a boulder perched at the top of a ravine. Twitch turned and fired in the direction of the sound. Turner cried out as though he had been hit and quickly climbed down into the ravine. He took cover behind a tree and groaned loudly to lure the armed man onward.

Twitch appeared on the crest of the ravine and paused to study the terrain. When it looked as though he might remain on the rim to maintain the visual advantage, Turner cried out in pretended pain and watched as Twitch made his way down the slope in search of his wounded quarry.

Turner picked up a piece of rotted wood and tossed it into some nearby bushes. Twitch fired a round into them and moved in that direction. Turner threw another piece of wood into a farther stand of bushes and, once again, Twitch fired. In this way Turner led his adversary deeper into the ravine, which splintered off in several directions in a series of twists and turns, filled with dense foliage.

When he had led Twitch far enough, Turner cut a wide berth around him and doubled back. Taking his bearings, he scrambled out of the ravine and paused at the top to listen. In the distance he could hear Twitch crashing through the foliage and occasionally calling out taunts.

After peeling off the jacket, Turner turned it inside out and used it like a rag to remove the venomous hairs from his clothing. Then he tossed the jacket aside—an unfortunate but necessary loss—and headed for the cabin, following the signs that he'd left for himself. Signs Twitch would never see.

chapter 19

ASSANDRA WRAPPED JUSTIN in her arms and snuggled against the chill of the cave. That it had come to this was impossible to have predicted. A week ago they had been living in a stylish home in Las Vegas, with a décor and furnishings she had personally selected. Now they were hiding in a small cavern—uncomfortable, cold, and hungry.

She entertained Justin to help pass the time and to keep her mind off the throbbing in her ankle. He loved stories, so she told ones usually reserved for his bedtime, and then retold them several times, adding slight variations to amuse him. When he became restless, she let him wander around the interior of the cave, but he soon became too cold and hungry to do anything but huddle in her arms and whimper.

She rested her chin against his head and sang softly to him, running through his favorite songs: "Jesus Loves the Little Children," "Old MacDonald Had a Farm," and the theme songs to several cartoon shows. She sang several hymns to buoy her own spirits too. But after a while she fell silent and simply cuddled Justin and prayed for Turner's arrival.

Without a wristwatch it was impossible to track time. She had no idea if Turner had been gone for one hour or five. But it seemed an eternity, and she fought her growing anxiety. In a situation like this it was easy to imagine the worst that could possibly happen and dwell repeatedly on the morbid details. Turner could be injured or captured or both. The possibilities were endless and frightening.

She remembered telling him that she was like the two people in the survey who wanted to know their futures in advance if they could. Now she wondered about it. If she could have known that she and Justin would end up shivering in a mountain cave, would she have left in the first place? Yes, she decided, because she still believed it was for the best. Despite everything she had lost, she had gained much too. And although it came at a high price, it was worth it.

The other night in Turner's apartment, she had awakened from a dream in which Brad was calling to her from afar, begging her to come home. She had lain there in the darkness and considered calling it quits, returning the envelope to him, and accepting the consequences. But she had already passed the point of no return, and it was impossible to go back now, not with everything that had transpired. The stakes had been raised immeasurably, and only a consequence of equal proportions would satisfy Brad. She had humiliated him by taking Justin, along with the envelope from the wall safe, and leaving. And adding to that humiliation was the fact that she had involved other people—good people—who now knew Brad for what he was. The skeletons had been released from his closet, and his ego would never be able to settle for anything less than *her* complete and utter humiliation. And perhaps she could endure such a fate, if she had a guarantee that Justin would be safe from Brad's future outbursts. But she didn't need to see the future to know how that would turn out.

"When's Turner coming back, Mommy?" Justin asked, calling her back to the moment.

"He should be here soon, sweetie." She stroked his head as her anxieties returned. "Should we pray for him?"

"Okay."

Cassandra closed her eyes and said, "Dear God, I know Turner has had a hard time believing in You and finding a need for You in his life. But he's a good man and has done so much for Justin and me. Please protect him and guide him safely back to us. Amen."

"Safely back to us. Amen," Justin echoed.

Clutching him against her, Cassandra stared at the forest beyond the cave opening. Turner was out there somewhere, putting his life on the line for Justin and her. Strong emotions swelled within her, and she closed her eyes in prayer once more, offering a silent and more personal petition on his behalf. And theirs.

chapter 30

URNER APPROACHED THE Buick from the dense foliage on the north side of the vehicle. The bushes glistened with water droplets, and he got soaked as he worked his way through them. But though he felt cold and tired, he basked in a sense of triumph over how things had turned out with Twitch. Dealing with him in this environment had been almost too easy.

In this moment of self-congratulations, he let his guard down and was taken by surprise when Slick emerged from the bushes and pointed his gun at him. "Where's Alec?" he demanded.

Turner flinched and then shrugged innocently.

"Alec, you out here?" Slick called, maintaining eye contact with Turner. When there was no answer, he narrowed his gaze. "I don't know what's become of him, but you're dealing with me now, my friend."

He solemnly motioned Turner to move away from the car, cautioning him to keep his hands visible. Turner complied, looking at him as calmly as a person can when staring certain death in the face.

"Brad had some important documents and financial records in his possession," Slick said. "But his wife took them from their safe." He clicked his teeth grimly. "There are some concerned people who would like to have them back."

Turner remembered the conversation in Harvey's office and how worried Brad had been about the documents Cassandra had taken. "I don't know where they are," he said truthfully.

"That may be true. But you know where *she* is."

Now Turner understood why he wasn't lying on the forest floor with a bullet in each kneecap.

"So it's rather simple," Slick continued. "You take me to her, she hands things over, and everybody leaves happy."

Wink, wink, nudge, nudge. Turner knew that once he handed over the documents and financial records, Cassandra and he were dead. Slick would leave their carcasses in the forest for the cougars and mountain lions to fight over. And Justin would be returned to his father's *loving* care and protection.

"So what's it going be?" Slick inquired coolly.

As Turner desperately attempted to assess his options, an idea suddenly occurred to him. "She and the boy are in an abandoned cabin at the base of the lookout tower," he said, remembering the tower Cassandra had pointed out the day they went canoeing. "We went hiking yesterday, and she sprained her ankle. We stayed overnight at the cabin, and I came back today to get some medical supplies. It's a bit of a hike from here, so we need to leave right now. She needs help."

Slick studied him for a moment and then nodded.

Turner grabbed his backpack and dumped the contents into the trunk. Rifling through Cassandra's suitcase, he picked out some clothes for her and Justin. He stuffed them into the backpack, along with the plastic bag he'd already filled with the painkillers and the food items.

Then he shrugged into his backpack and turned to face Slick. "I'm ready," he said.

"Good. Lead the way. I'm right behind you."

His gun was right behind Turner too. And Turner realized that once they reached their destination and Slick figured out it was a wild goose chase, the oily haired man would be making the return trip alone, one or two bullets lighter.

Turner thought of Cassandra and Justin, huddled in the

cave, awaiting his arrival. He had to come up with something fast because he only had the distance from the cabin to the tower in which to turn the tables on Slick. The span was a fixed distance, a giant ruler that gauged the length of the path leading to doomsday. And unless he formulated a plan and succeeded in implementing it, every inch they traversed meant one less inch of life remaining for him.

He adjusted the backpack and walked toward the trail that led to the lookout tower. Slick followed, holding the gun at Turner's back as a reminder not to try any "funny stuff," as he put it. Normally the warning would not have gone unheeded. But the battle of wits had begun, and unless Turner did try some funny stuff soon, he was a dead man. And that prospect was not funny at all.

Although the sun had emerged from behind the thinning clouds, a casual brush against the overhanging pine boughs doused them with water droplets as they walked. Slick's rumpled suit was already water-stained, and the hem of his pants became mud-rimmed within minutes. But he didn't seem to care. With bulldog determination he urged Turner forward, oblivious to the unpleasant conditions.

Slick's oily hair retained its style. The moisture from the branches ran off his head like water off a fisherman's rain hat, and he didn't look nearly as miserable as Turner was beginning to feel. Once Slick found out that this was a ruse, things were going to turn nasty. And Turner knew he would feel even more miserable...when Slick shot him.

The trail became steeper, making the footing more difficult. Slick lost his footing several times and almost went down because his patent leather shoes were not meant for walking in these conditions. And each time he lost his balance, he held the gun out as a warning for Turner to keep his distance. But Turner kept as close as possible, because if he was going to catch Slick off guard at some point, the tricky footing would give him the best opportunity.

"How much farther?" Slick asked, surveying the trail ahead.

"You'll see the lookout tower through the trees in a while. The cabin is right beside it."

Slick grunted under his breath and motioned for him to keep walking.

With difficulty they ascended a steep section to where a series of switchbacks weaved a stitch-work pattern across the mountain slope. Turner looked for an opportunity to catch his captor by surprise, but Slick seemed to anticipate his intentions and kept a wary eye on him.

Turner had hoped that Slick's flabby gut would slow the man down, or at least tire him out. But Slick matched him step for step, his jaw set determinedly. And every time Turner turned to look at him, Slick waved his gun impatiently.

According to Turner's estimation, they had covered a quarter of the distance to the lookout tower, and he still hadn't been able to make his move. The edge of the path was too steep to risk bolting into the thick foliage, and he couldn't turn and race back down the trail because Slick would shoot him before he took three steps.

Turner tried to think of a way to disarm him, but Slick maintained a sufficient distance between them. Turner couldn't get his hands on the gun without getting a face full of lead. And it was obvious he couldn't out-muscle him because Slick was half bulldog and half gorilla. His arms were thicker than Turner's legs, and he had at least sixty pounds on him. Turner was dead meat if he tried any funny stuff and dead meat if he didn't. It was a chilling dilemma to be sure.

But if he was going to go down, Turner decided to go down swinging. He just had to pick the right time and the right place. But each step he took reduced the opportunity, and the pressure began to mount.

He shifted the backpack to one shoulder so he could shed his load quickly. It would be easier to launch a counterattack without the bulky backpack hampering his efforts. It was now a matter of survival of the fittest. And with Cassandra and Justin counting on him, Turner had to ensure that *he* was the fittest.

The wind picked up slightly as they proceeded up the slope to the next switchback. Turner quickened the pace, hoping to increase distance between them, but Slick kept up.

On the next rise they came to a place where the trail had been washed out. Descending into the scar that had once been the pathway, Turner carefully picked his way across the exposed rocks and tree roots.

Slick waited until Turner was on the other side and then motioned him to stop. Then he began working his way across, keeping the gun trained on Turner, who watched and waited for an opportunity to strike.

When Slick looked down to check his footing, Turner decided to make his move. As he began to shrug out of the backpack, intending to pick up a rock and hurl it at him, Slick snapped his head back up, aware that he had momentarily let down his guard. Turner froze, his jaw set and his muscles tensed.

Slick shook his head in warning and made his way up to the other side. "For a moment there I thought you were going to try some funny stuff."

"Let's just hurry," Turner replied, shifting the backpack to his other shoulder. "Cassandra's waiting."

A heavy feeling settled over him as he realized that perhaps his last window of opportunity had just slammed shut.

He knew Slick would not let his guard down again. Staring sullenly ahead, Turner continued leading the way.

At a particularly steep section of the trail, Slick began to breathe heavily. Turner tried to push the pace discreetly, hoping he didn't wear himself out first. Carrying Cassandra to the cave had been extremely taxing, and his anxiousness over her and Justin was emotionally draining. The strain was beginning to take its toll.

They had arrived at a bend in the trail where the path flattened out momentarily before continuing its ascent. A small stream flowed down the rocky slope and pooled along the edge of the trail. At the lowest point in the path the water actually overflowed the trail, submerging it in several inches of runoff.

As Turner turned to face Slick, he noticed that the ground was spongy beneath his feet.

"I get the feeling you're leading me on a wild goose chase," Slick said, stepping menacingly toward him.

Instinctively Turner backed away, glancing around for some means of escape or, failing that, some form of self-defense. The ground became even softer, and he felt something shift underfoot. The trail was unstable where he was now standing in the ankle-deep water. "The cabin is just—"

"Give it up," Slick warned, leveling his gun at Turner.

Turner took a slow, deliberate step away, hoping to lure his adversary forward.

To maintain the distance of intimidation, Slick stepped closer. "I'm going to give you to the count of three to tell me where she is," he said. "Then I'm going to blow your right kneecap to smithereens."

"I told you, she's in a cabin near the lookout tower."

Slick's eyes narrowed. "One."

Turner backed farther away. "It's abandoned. She and the boy are waiting for me there."

"Two."

As Turner took another step back, Slick advanced and his foot sunk up to his ankle in the soft mud, causing him to momentarily look down.

Instantly Turner peeled off the backpack and launched himself forward. He managed to grasp the barrel of the gun and point it heavenward, where, for the first time in years, his silent plea for help was also ascending.

The gun went off, and in his shock Turner almost lost his grip. The two men struggled briefly, shifting their footing for better leverage. Turner was no match for his assailant, and he realized it was only a matter of seconds before Slick wrenched the gun free and blew off a kneecap... for starters.

But Slick never got control of the gun and neither did Turner. Without warning the trail suddenly gave way beneath them, slumping down the mountainside. The large pool of water rushed forcefully behind, lubricating the slope and turning it into a soupy torrent of sludge.

Turner found himself falling. He mingled with the mud and debris as though being pureed in a food processor.

Slick was several feet away, sliding out of control and flailing his arms and legs in an effort to regain his footing. He rammed into a protruding boulder and grunted loudly as the gun sailed into the air. Vainly attempting to fight the force of the current, he momentarily disappeared around the boulder.

Turner twisted sideways and barely managed to miss a sharp, broken tree stump that protruded from the mud and threatened to skewer him like a shish kabob. He sent a second plea heavenward when he realized the current was carrying him toward a cliff that dropped off into eternity. He saw himself going over the edge, and in that moment an image of

Cassandra and Justin, huddled together in the cave, came to him. But there was no time to process the sadness and regret because everything was happening too chaotically.

He tried to fight against the current but it was too powerful. Realizing he only had seconds to live, he twisted around so he was pointed headfirst down the slope. He began doing a variation of the breaststroke, pulling harder with his left arm than his right in order to angle his way toward the edge of the mudslide. The cliff was rapidly approaching, and he fought the urge to panic. Pulling even harder, he managed to work his way over far enough to grasp a scraggly bush that grew on the edge of the cliff. As he clung to it desperately, he felt like his arms were being pulled from their sockets. The extra weight of sediment added to his burden, but he managed to hold on. The mudslide continued on its way, careening over the cliff and disappearing into the emptiness below.

Glancing into the space that yawned beneath him, Turner frantically clung to the bush. He looked across as Slick came bobbing along in the murky flow, arms flailing, legs kicking, before disappearing over the cliff. Slick's scream lasted a long time.

The relief Turner experienced at being spared Slick's fate was quickly overshadowed by the reality of his situation. Maintaining his grip with numb, muddy fingers, while weighed down with multiple coats of mud, was becoming increasingly difficult.

Pleading for strength, he grabbed another section of the bush and pulled himself sideways, inching his way out of the current until, at last, he rolled onto dry ground and lay gasping for breath.

"Thank You," he said softly, addressing the sky. He began to tremble and tears filled his eyes. He wiped them with the back of his gritty hand and realized how much effort that took.

He was exhausted and craved sleep. But with Cassandra and Justin still waiting for him, he couldn't afford that luxury.

He forced himself to his feet and slowly climbed toward the trail, glancing frequently at the layer of mud and debris that remained from the death ride. Now that the pool had drained, the mudslide only oozed along, belying the deadly flow it had been. Gratitude filled his heart as he considered how lucky he was to be alive. He glanced heavenward in the realization that when the urgency of the situation was over, he was going to have to reevaluate certain things in his life.

When he reached the trail, he noticed that a little water remained in the pool. He took a drink and then washed himself off. Removing the layers of mud revealed several rips in his clothing and a few superficial cuts on his hands and arms. But considering what had happened to Slick, he wasn't going to complain.

Because the backpack had been swept away in the mudslide, he was going to have to return to the cabin and get more painkillers for Cassandra. It was important that she be able to help herself as much as possible on the trip down from the cave, considering the slippery footing. Hopefully he would only have to carry her when absolutely necessary. To lose his footing with her on his back would only spell more injury.

Taking one last look at the wounded trail, he turned and retraced his steps toward the cabin.

chapter 31

$\mathcal{A}$LTHOUGH THE PAIN in her ankle kept her from sleeping soundly, Cassandra dozed off and on. Justin remained in her arms, for warmth, and sucked his thumb.

Dreamlike images crept into her mind each time she closed her eyes. She saw herself in her home in Las Vegas, secretly packing a suitcase and hiding it in the trunk of her car. Then she was talking to the compassionate waitress in the diner. Next she was on the Greyhound bus, headed for Denver. And then she was desperately trying to rearrange Brad's trophies because Justin had disturbed them.

The images came rapidly, but not in chronological order. They zoomed in and out of focus like an old celluloid movie. But each one triggered an emotional response that was distinct and clear.

Another image swirled into her head, and she saw herself in the den, opening the wall safe. It was Brad's personal safe, and she had never been allowed access to it. But she had come across the combination one day when she was cleaning the den. It was written on the back of his business card and had dropped to the floor when he was putting things away. She memorized the code and then slipped the card in among a pile of papers on his desk. Now as she saw herself looking inside the safe in the hope of finding some cash, she discovered it contained only their passports, the mortgage agreement, several of Brad's sports medals, a handgun, and a large manila envelope that lay at the bottom of the pile. She picked up the mortgage agreement and glanced sadly around the den. Tears came as she considered the hope and promise the agreement had originally stood for but the disappointment and failure it now represented.

She saw herself replacing the document in the safe and then pocketing her passport. Next she reached for the manila envelope. Lifting the flap, she discovered it contained a small ledger and several business documents. She flipped through the ledger and saw it consisted of columns of numbers, listed under headings such as *Repairs* and *Maintenance Expenses*. There was even a column that read *Loans*. She knew the figures weren't household expenses because they were too large and detailed.

She remembered snippets of telephone conversations when Brad thought she wasn't listening, and the hushed voice he used whenever certain numbers came up on the call display. Occasionally a business associate would drop in, and Brad would hustle him into the den and close the door. Heated words were often exchanged, although they were too muffled for her to hear clearly. But in time there were enough clues so that she could begin to connect the dots. Her husband was involved in illegal business dealings.

The ledger was evidence of that. And by taking it with her, it would give her leverage if she needed to bargain with him. It was a trump card that she would play if she had to. And only after she and Justin were safely out of Brad's grasp for good would she tell him where she had hidden it. But should he find her first and do her any harm, the letter she had given to Loretta would be mailed to the police, outlining the nature of Brad's business dealings and indicating the location of the manila envelope. As she had told Loretta—the envelope represented justice.

She forced her eyes open and stared around the interior

of the cave. The images faded, and she tried to replace them with happier thoughts. She visualized the new life she wanted to make for Justin and herself. They would probably live in a nondescript apartment for a while, far from Las Vegas and the memories it held. She would find a job and do whatever it took to give her son a good education and every opportunity to succeed in life.

As she sat basking in the glow of these future aspirations, a troubling thought crossed her mind. What about Turner? What was to become of him... of them? At this very moment he was out there risking his life for them. When it was all over, could she simply walk away? Would it end with a parting handshake and "Thanks for everything, good-bye forever"?

There was no question she found him attractive. But it was his kind and gentle nature that was even more appealing. With him she did not have to measure her every word or keep Justin quiet so he wasn't disruptive. She was free to be herself—to laugh and joke and speak her mind without fear of reprisal. Turner listened to her concerns and validated her feelings. Being with him was everything her marriage was not, and the idea of their relationship ending was something she wasn't certain how to handle. It was not a simple matter of packing her suitcase and leaving in the middle of the night.

Shaking the troubling thought aside, she offered a silent prayer once more for Turner, her former classmate now transformed from boy to man, who had providentially come back into her life in her greatest hour of need.

chapter 32

*T*HE RETURN TRIP to the cabin took Turner only thirty minutes, but it was still late in the day when he arrived. There was no way he was going to be able to get Cassandra and Justin down from the cave before sunset. He simply didn't dare risk negotiating the trail in the darkness. They were going to have to spend the night in the cave.

That prospect didn't worry him personally because he had slept in caves and dugouts many times during his scouting and Camp Kopawanee years. But he was concerned about Cassandra and Justin. Sleeping on rocks and enduring the cool mountain air—not to mention Cassandra's injured ankle—would mean a sleepless night for them.

The sun peered through a crack in the clouds as he descended the last leg of the trail. He cautiously approached the cabin in case Twitch had miraculously found his way back. But there was no sign of him.

As he stepped onto the front porch, he made a mental inventory of the supplies he needed for the hike to the cave. He would use pillowcases as duffle bags and carry as many amenities as possible.

He grimaced when he saw the interior of the cabin. Furniture and other items lay strewn about, and he wished he had time to straighten things up. But that was too low of a priority on his to-do list.

Rummaging through the kitchen cupboards, he collected the bottle of aspirin, a small first aid kit, some matches, a flashlight, three water bottles, and a sharp knife. Then he searched through the closets and found an old backpack with a metal frame. Rejoicing in this discovery, he gathered up some blankets and three jackets that were hanging on a hook in the front closet. He put on one of the jackets, then stuffed the backpack full of blankets and tied the other jackets to the frame with some string he found in a drawer.

The backpack was bursting at the seams, and he wondered how he'd get the bulky load up the embankment. He remembered seeing a length of rope on a closet shelf and decided to bring it along. The rope would come in handy when he reached the vertical face.

He went to the Buick to get the few remaining food items and supplies he had purchased in town. He put them into a plastic shopping bag and tied it on top of the jackets. As he turned to leave, his eye caught the stuffed monkey. There really wasn't room for it, but when he thought about the privations Justin had already suffered, he picked it up and crammed it into a side pocket.

Then he slipped the backpack over both shoulders and headed for the trail that led to the cave. The clouds had thinned and the sun dipped toward the mountain peaks, and he calculated it would be dark in an hour.

As he proceeded up the trail, he shifted the backpack to keep it centered. It reminded him of the times he'd carried Cassandra. He could still feel her arms around his neck and the warmth of her body pressed against his. The memory was a stark contrast to the deadweight he felt now.

He passed the outcrop of rock that overlooked the cabin and continued on. As he rounded a curve in the trail, he startled a squirrel that was holding a pinecone in its paws. The squirrel dropped its bounty and scurried to the top of a nearby tree in an impossibly short amount of time, pausing long enough to scold Turner for the intrusion.

Turner smiled grimly and pressed on. The cave was still some distance ahead, and he longed to be able to travel with the squirrel's speed and agility.

Ahead, a small stream trickled down the hillside and crossed the path. It conjured up images of Slick being swept to his death and he—Turner—barely avoiding the same fate. He shuddered at the thought and struggled to repress the frightening images that were resurrected. Gritting his teeth determinedly, he continued toward the embankment.

The trail rose for a distance and then leveled out once more. A short time later he rounded a curve in the path and came to the embankment. He took off the backpack and studied the task ahead.

Scaling the rock face would be safer than attempting to climb the adjacent slope as they had done before because the grass was still too wet and slippery. He uncoiled the rope and tied one end to the backpack and the other end to a short length of stick. Then he tossed the stick to the top of the embankment. It caught in a crevice, and he tugged on the rope to make certain it was secure. Satisfied, he drew in several deep breaths and began the ascent, walking up the face, hand over hand.

He paused to catch his breath and then hauled the backpack to the top. After untying the rope and coiling it up, he shrugged into the shoulder straps and continued up the trail.

Ten minutes later he rounded a bend and saw the cave ahead. He called out a greeting so his arrival wouldn't startle Cassandra or Justin.

"Turner! Turner!" came the muffled reply.

Turner felt something stir within him when Justin appeared in the mouth of the cave and rushed toward him.

Cassandra tried to call him back, but Turner said, "I've got him." He hugged Justin against his leg. "Hello, little man. You take good care of your mommy?"

Justin nodded wearily.

Holding him by the hand, Turner stepped inside the cave. Cassandra was sitting on one of the natural rock benches. She looked tired and miserable, and pain registered in her eyes. But she immediately slid off the bench and stood up, holding out her arms toward him.

Turner dropped the backpack and stepped into her embrace. They held one another close and didn't speak for a moment. Justin joined them and turned it into a group hug.

"I—we—were so worried about you," Cassandra said at length. "What happened?"

Turner nodded toward Justin. "Not now. We'll talk later." He held her at arm's length and looked into her eyes. "How are you holding up?"

She embraced him once more and Turner could feel her body tremble. "We're okay," she replied. "Now that you're here."

"I brought some coats. Let's get you into them and warmed up." He removed the jackets from the backpack and handed them to her and Justin.

"Mine's big," Justin laughed, as Turner helped him put it on. The little boy looked small and vulnerable in the oversized coat.

"But it'll keep you snug and warm, little man."

Turner helped Cassandra into her coat and did up the buttons. He rubbed her arms lightly to help warm her up.

"That feels good," she said.

"I've got something that will help you feel even better." He fished the bottle of aspirin from the backpack and shook out three tablets. Then he handed them to her, along with a water bottle.

She accepted them gratefully and sat back on the bench, waiting for the aspirin to work.

"Now, let's eat," he said.

"Great. We're starved."

He reached for the plastic grocery bag and set out the food.

Justin grabbed a cookie and had it halfway to his mouth when Cassandra stopped him. "We need to say grace, sweetie." She looked across at Turner. "Especially today."

Turner nodded and waited respectfully until she finished.

She no sooner said, "Amen," than Justin bit into his cookie. "You should eat something more healthy first," she said. But as she watched him savoring every crumb, she added, "Those cookies do look good. Maybe I'll have one too."

They each had a cookie and then another. After the appetizer, they had crackers and cheese, veggies, fruit, and then another cookie each for dessert. When they had eaten their fill, Turner put the leftovers in the plastic grocery bag.

"I'm going to hang this in a tree for the night," he said. "We don't want any b-e-a-r-s snooping around."

"Do you think there are any in the area?"

"I haven't seen any signs of them, but you can never be too careful. I'll be right back."

He walked a short distance down the trail and hung the plastic bag high in a tree. On the way back he stopped at a fallen log. Rolling it over, he found some dry kindling and also some chunks of bark underneath. Carrying them back, he used the matches to start a fire just outside the mouth of the cave. The flames would discourage any bears or mountain lions from sniffing out the food and coming inside the cave for appetizers.

"Won't the smoke give away our location?" Cassandra asked.

"No one will bother us tonight." Turner replied.

Cassandra looked at him questioningly. "Are you going to tell me or what?"

"Let me check your ankle first."

She sighed impatiently as he carefully undid the wrapping and removed the splint. Her ankle was still swollen and had bruised noticeably. He got up and left the cave for a moment, returning with a clump of soft, green moss. He dipped it in the water that had collected in the hole he had dug earlier and then placed it on her ankle.

Cassandra sucked in her breath but didn't flinch. "That was smart of you to dig the hole," she said. "It collected enough rain water for us."

"And now it's helping me make a cold compress. We'll leave it on for fifteen minutes, and then I'll wrap your ankle for the night."

She reached up and touched some mud in his hair. "Turner, what happened?"

"It's a long story," he replied, sitting beside her.

She nudged him with her elbow. "I've got nothing but time. I need to know."

While Justin poked at the fire with a stick, Turner explained how he had led Twitch into the forest. Cassandra covered her mouth to hide a gasp when Turner recounted Slick's fate. She looked at Turner in horror. "I'm so sorry," she murmured. "I'm so terribly sorry. I never should have gotten you involved."

"And I knew I shouldn't have told you about it."

"Of course you should have. You could have been..." She left the word *killed* dangling in the air. Leaning her head on his shoulder, she nestled against him. "I'm so sorry," she said once more. "And I'm just so grateful you made it safely back to us."

Justin threw the stick into the fire and climbed into Turner's lap. The three of them snuggled together and fell silent, lost in their own thoughts.

As the interior of the cave grew dim, Turner stated the obvious. "We're going to have to stay the night. It would be foolish to try to return to the cabin in the dark."

"If the Flintstones can live in the Stone Age, so can we, right?"

He laughed. "I brought some blankets and matches, so we'll be okay. I just need to get some more firewood."

He went back outside and scoured around for some dry pieces of wood. Carrying several armfuls back to the cave, he stacked them inside in case it rained during the night. The natural draft from their quarters kept the smoke outside, but enough heat stayed in to make the interior warm and cozy.

It was dark now, so Turner retrieved the flashlight from the backpack and switched it on. He picked a section of the floor that was the least rocky and spread out the blankets. Returning to the backpack, he got Justin's attention and then pulled out the stuffed monkey. The little boy squeaked excitedly when he saw it. He clutched it to his chest and started to climb under the blankets.

"You need to peepee first," Cassandra said.

"Justin or the monkey?" Turner said, ducking a playful swat from Cassandra.

He took Justin outside and waited until the little boy had sufficiently watered a clump of mountain grass. Then he brought him in and tucked him under the covers. Justin snuggled with the stuffed monkey and did not ask for a bedtime story. He was asleep almost instantly.

Watching Justin sleep peacefully made Turner realize how tired he felt. But he needed to take care of Cassandra before he could give in to his exhaustion.

He rewrapped Cassandra's ankle and helped her climb under the blankets beside Justin.

"Turner, thanks so much for all you've done," she said, reaching up and pulling a chunk of dried mud from his hair. "You're amazing."

He took her hand and squeezed it. "You're pretty amazing yourself."

"I haven't done anything," she said in surprise.

"There are two people in this cave who would disagree with you."

She waved her hand dismissively and yawned. "Thanks, again, for everything Turner." Her eyes began to droop and she yawned again. "I'll never be able to—"

"Shh! No more talking," Turner said, pressing a finger to her lips. "You need to get some sleep."

"No, I'll stay awake...and talk to you...for...a...while..." Her eyes closed midsentence, and she began breathing slowly and steadily.

"Sleep tight," he said softly, pulling the blanket up tighter around her.

He watched her sleep for a few moments. Then he added a few more pieces of wood to the fire and lay down on the blanket beside her. The last thing he remembered was the flickering glow of the fire on the walls, lulling him sleep.

Nighttime landscape surrendered to dreamscape, which mercifully was barren of images of the day's dramatic events. He was simply too exhausted to dream.

chapter 33

*T*HE FIRE DIED out during the night, but it had served its purpose. No predators—animal or human—paid a visit. Turner knew because he checked the area for tracks at first light.

He retrieved the plastic bag from the tree and prepared a simple breakfast. They sat on the blankets and ate the remainder of the food. Cassandra took the last of the aspirins and washed them down with bottled water.

Justin was still hungry, and Turner noticed Cassandra slip him her last piece of apple, claiming that she was too full to finish it.

Turner put another cold compress of moss on her ankle before rewrapping it, making sure the splint was secure, but comfortable.

As he gathered up the blankets and jackets and stuffed them into the backpack, Cassandra said, "I fell asleep on you last night. Sorry about that."

"It's okay."

"And I'm even sorrier about what you had to go through with those men."

Justin was attempting to stuff a colorful rock into the backpack and so was pleasantly distracted. Turner looked at her and said, "The oily haired guy talked about some documents and financial records you took. He told me some concerned people wanted them back. Exactly what was he talking about?"

"Brad kept records of his business dealings. When the economy turned bad, he borrowed money to keep his business afloat. But he borrowed from the wrong kind of people. Interest was unreal. And illegal. The documents are proof of loansharking."

"So where are the records now?"

"In a locker at the Greyhound bus depot in Denver."

"And the key?"

"It's in your apartment, hidden in the hollow handle of the dustpan in the closet." She smiled wryly. "I figured it would be safe and undisturbed there." Then she grew serious. "If anything happens to me, Loretta is to send the letter I gave her to the police. It spells out everything."

Turner put on the backpack and shifted it to get it centered on his back. "Nothing is going to happen to you." He helped her up. "I promise."

She balanced herself on her good ankle and smiled at him appreciatively.

"I've got something for you," he said. "I made it this morning." He briefly stepped outside the cave and reappeared with a spruce branch, stripped of its needles and curved at one end.

"What is it?" she asked.

"Your crutch." He placed the curved end under her right armpit and assessed it for length. "Made to measure, I'd say."

She tested it out and found that she could hobble to the mouth of the cave if she was careful. "It's great," she said. "Thank you."

"My pleasure."

They looked at each other long and hard, and then Turner turned to check on Justin. The little boy was busy lapping at the tiny trickle of water that oozed from the side of the cave wall. He made contented slurping sounds and licked his lips repeatedly.

"Ready to go, little man?"

"Ready," Justin replied, wiping his chin and heading for the entrance. "Let's run."

"No running for Mommy," Cassandra replied, gingerly exiting the cave. "Let's just walk and see what fun things we notice, okay?"

"Okay," Justin replied. He headed for some stringy moss that hung from a nearby tree, resembling tattered shreds of cloth. Picking a piece off a branch, he held it up and stared at it in fascination. "Look, Mommy. The tree has funny hair."

"Old Man's Beard," Turner observed. "It's common up here."

"It does have funny hair, doesn't it?" Cassandra said, chuckling. Her amusement was cut short by a sharp pain when she put too much weight on her injured ankle.

"Lean on me," Turner said.

She paused to take several deep breaths. "You're not going to start singing that song, are you?" She managed a weak smile.

"You wouldn't want me to do that. You're in enough pain already."

"I'll be okay," she said. "Let me just take my time."

"Take all the time you need."

The pace was too slow for Justin, so he was allowed to run a short distance ahead and then run back, repeating the procedure until they eventually reached the grassy slope.

"Let's slide down it again," he said excitedly.

Because they had already negotiated the grassy slope, they were able to do it more easily this time. Turner clung to Justin, who seemed determined to take a running start, and made it safely to the bottom. The backpack made him top-heavy, which worked to his advantage. It snagged on the rocks and tree roots and slowed his progress.

He got Justin situated and then assisted Cassandra, who made sure she kept her injured ankle elevated during the descent. "That wasn't as bad as I thought it would be," she said.

"Can we do it again?" Justin asked excitedly.

"Sorry, little man," Turner said. "We need to get your mommy to the doctor. But how about you and I go for a canoe ride when she's all better?"

Justin cheered and pretended to paddle as they continued down the trail. Running ahead, he turned in a big circle and rushed back, making swishing noises.

Now that they were almost to the cabin, Turner felt a sense of relief. He would get Cassandra and Justin comfortably situated and then walk out to the main road, hitchhike to the police station, and arrange for Cassandra and Justin to be picked up. Then they would file a police report and deal with the inevitable investigation into Slick's death and the search and rescue efforts for Twitch. Afterward they'd go to the doctor so Cassandra's ankle could be X-rayed and wrapped properly.

As they descended the last section of the trail, Turner watched in amusement as Justin ran a few steps ahead and then turned and raced toward him, sounding like a motorboat. His excitement was infectious, and both Turner and Cassandra laughed at his antics.

When they entered the clearing, Turner halted abruptly and the laughter stopped. A Ford Explorer with a National car rental sticker on the bumper was parked beside the cabin. The front door of the cabin suddenly opened, and a figure stepped out onto the porch.

Cassandra came up behind Turner and grabbed hold of his arm. "I don't believe it," she gasped.

"Daddy!" cried Justin, running toward the cabin.

chapter 34

URNER SAW THE look of horror on Cassandra's face as Brad scooped up Justin and tossed him playfully in the air. She squeezed Turner's arm so hard that her fingernails left imprints. Then she released her grip and grimly stepped into the open.

"Look, Mommy," Justin chirped. "It's Daddy."

"Surprise," Brad said humorlessly. His expression hardened as he glared at them, and Turner saw accusation in Brad's countenance and a determination to fulfill the threat he had uttered on the phone. *You're a dead man!*

Despite his providential escapes, Turner could see no way out this time. Brad had them securely in his clutches. There was no avenue of retreat and nowhere to run.

But if Turner expected to see Cassandra cower apologetically, he was mistaken. Looking at her husband defiantly, she said, "I'm not going back with you, Brad."

Brad feigned offense. "Is that any way to greet your husband?"

"That's as good as it's going to get." She held out her hand to her son. "Come here, Justin."

Brad held Justin tighter and scanned the yard. "Where are the other guys?"

Images of the forest maze and coursing mud flashed through Turner's mind. "They're gone," he replied.

Brad looked puzzled, as if realizing he was now alone in this. He clenched his jaw and his eyes darted back and forth. His expression conveyed indecision but not sadness.

"Are you going to stay with us, Daddy?"

Brad looked at his son. "I need to talk to your mommy and this man."

Turner recognized Brad's contemptuousness in the reference to him as *this man*. And he realized he was still a nonentity to Brad, just as he had been in high school.

"Brad, put Justin down," Cassandra warned.

"All in good time."

She winced as she took a step closer. "Now!"

"Let me explain it to you this way, dear." He spat the word *dear*. There was no affection in his voice and none reflected in his countenance. "I have something you want, and you have something I want."

She wet her lips and maintained her composure. "Justin is not a bargaining chip."

Brad tossed Justin playfully in the air again. "Hey, tiger. Want to go for a ride with Daddy and get some ice cream?"

"Ice cream. Yeah!"

"Brad...no," Cassandra said, her façade cracking.

He looked triumphantly at her.

"Put him down, Brad," Turner said, squaring his shoulders.

Brad's false smile disappeared. Still holding Justin, he leaped off the porch in a burst of rage and pointed at Turner menacingly. "You stay out of this!" he screamed.

Justin's eyes widened in terror. "You're scaring me, Daddy."

"Brad, let him go," Cassandra pleaded.

Brad trembled convulsively and refocused his eyes as though suddenly remembering he was holding his son. Inhaling slowly, he recovered his smile and ruffled his son's hair, all the while glaring at Turner from the corner of his eye.

Turner had never stood up to Brad before—not in the tripping incident in the cafeteria or the dead-cat-in-the-locker stunt or any of the other countless incidents. But this time was different. Brad was bargaining with a little boy who meant something to Turner, and Turner wasn't going to allow Justin to be used as a pawn in this contest any longer. "I know where the documents are," he said evenly.

"Turner!" Cassandra gasped.

"You let Justin go, and I'll give them to you."

"Turner, no!" Cassandra cried. "Once he gets them, he'll take Justin anyway."

"He won't get them until you and Justin drive away in the Explorer. He won't be able to follow you."

"But what about you?"

Turner didn't answer.

Brad scowled. Obviously Cassandra's concern for someone else was a blow to his ego. It was a reversal of their high school roles, and it appeared to gall him. But because of Cassandra's wisdom in creating some bargaining leverage, Brad hesitated and considered the situation.

"What's it going to be, Brad?" Turner asked.

Brad stroked Justin's head as if he was holding a stuffed teddy bear, the prize at a carnival game. "You think you've got it all figured out, don't you, Pancake?" His voice turned icy. "You were no match for me in high school, and you're no match for me now." He lifted the edge of his shirt, revealing a gun tucked in his belt.

"Brad," Cassandra pleaded.

"Into the cabin," he said, ignoring her.

When Turner hesitated, Brad exploded again. "Now!"

Justin began to cry, and Cassandra made a move toward them, but Brad motioned her back. "Into the cabin!" he yelled. Then to Justin, he snarled, "Stop crying!"

The little boy cried even harder.

In an effort not to anger Brad further, Cassandra hobbled up the front steps and motioned Turner to follow.

Once inside Brad held Justin toward Cassandra. "Lock him in the bathroom."

"No, Brad. Not that."

"Do it!" he screamed, in a tone to match Justin's wail of despair.

She clenched her teeth defiantly. "If you think I'm going to—"

She never had a chance to finish. Brad pulled his gun and struck her over the head with it. Dazed, she fell to the floor.

Justin screamed in sheer terror. "Mommy!"

Turner lurched forward to try wrestling the gun away. But Brad pointed it in Turner's face and hissed, "One more step and you *are* a dead man."

Turner believed him. And he knew he would be in no position to help Cassandra or Justin if he was mortally wounded. "Let me make sure she's okay," he said.

"Stay away from her," Brad warned. "Now find something to wedge under the bathroom door so Justin can't open it. Do it!"

Turner slowly removed the backpack and went to the porch, returning moments later with a wedge-shaped piece of wood.

Brad nodded and said, "Down the hall, to the bathroom." Once there he shoved Justin inside and slammed the door. "Wedge it tight so he can't get out," he ordered.

The terrified boy pounded on the door and rattled the doorknob, but Brad held it closed tight. "Right now!" he commanded, leveling the gun at Turner.

Grimacing, Turner wedged the piece of wood under the door and backed away. He glared at Brad and trembled with anger as Justin's cries rose in intensity. And for the second time in as many days, he sent a silent petition for help heavenward.

Cassandra moaned, and Turner went to her side, ignoring Brad's injunction to stay away from her. There was a noticeable bump on the side of her head. When he gently touched it, she moaned again. "You didn't have to hit her, Brad," he said grimly.

"She had it coming."

Ignoring the muffled pounding from the bathroom, Brad stepped toward Turner and pointed the gun at Cassandra. "Are you going to tell me where the documents are, Pancake, or do I shoot her in the leg?"

"You wouldn't."

Brad took aim.

"Wait!" Turner cried, as an idea suddenly sprang into his head. "They're outside."

"Outside? I already searched your car."

"They're hidden under a log."

Brad studied Turner dubiously.

Justin continued pounding on the door, and Turner could hardly resist the urge to rush to his aid. But that would be foolhardy, he knew.

Checking to make sure Cassandra was breathing freely, he led Brad out onto the porch and pointed toward the bushes that he and Justin had explored two days earlier. "Over there," he said.

"Why under a log?"

"Cassandra was worried someone might search the cabin."

Brad grunted in disgust and waved the gun. "Get moving."

Turner proceeded toward the bushes. "How did your guys find us?" he asked, fearful that the information had been wrung from Loretta and Mary at great cost.

"Just keep moving," Brad directed.

Turner's heart rate quickened as they approached the log, which lay in a small clearing. "Lift that end," he said. "And I'll lift this one." He deliberately chose the end closest to the cabin.

Brad walked to the far end of the log and kicked it several

233

times as though testing its condition. The sound of winged activity came from within and Turner hoped Brad didn't hear it. Or if he did, that he didn't recognize it for what it was.

"I'll warn you right now," Turner said. "It's heavy."

Brad smirked. "Maybe for you."

Turner took his stance. "Lift on the count of three."

Brad balanced the gun in his left hand and took a firm grip on the other end of the log with his right hand. "Okay, one...two...three!"

On *three* Turner only pretended to lift, but Brad gave a mighty heave and the rotted log broke in two. A swarm of angry wasps came swirling out of the opening like a living dust devil and swarmed over the two men in an instant.

Even though Turner had anticipated the attack, he wasn't prepared for its intensity. He was stung on the face and arms several times before he could even blink. Brad dropped the gun and yelled and batted the air with both arms. Turner darted into the bushes, grateful for the cover the thick foliage provided. He heard Brad scream in pain, and he could tell by the fading sounds that Brad was headed for the lake at full speed.

Wincing from the wasps' venom, Turner raced for the cabin. He only had a short time to revive Cassandra and free Justin. If he failed, they were in *real* trouble because next time Brad would be far less forgiving than the wasps.

chapter 35

ASSANDRA REGAINED CONSCIOUSNESS as the water splashed on her face. She opened her eyes to see Turner standing over her, water bottle in hand.

"We've got to get out of here!" he said.

Her head felt like it was going to explode, and she tenderly rubbed the goose egg on her right temple. She made an effort to focus her eyes. "Justin...where is he? Where's Brad? Did you tell him where the documents are? What happened?"

"No time," Turner replied, helping her to her feet. "I'll explain later."

"Your face!" she said in surprise.

"Wasps."

She looked at Turner in confusion. He let go of her to see if she would remain steady. She wobbled slightly and then looked around in alarm. "Where's Justin?"

"Locked in the bathroom," he said, heading down the hallway.

She followed, limping painfully but determined to keep up. Inside the bathroom, Justin's desperate cries had softened to muted whimpers.

Turner pulled the wedge free and pushed the door open. Cassandra hobbled ahead of him and found Justin curled up in the bathtub in a fetal position, his thumb stuck in his mouth, his cheeks stained with tears. But what alarmed her the most was Justin's listlessness. His eyes were open but unseeing.

Stifling a sob, Cassandra picked him up and cradled him against her. "I'm so sorry, sweetie. I'm so sorry."

"We've got to hurry," Turner said, taking Justin from her.

She wiped back tears and limped toward the front door, following Turner.

"This way," he said. "We'll slip out the back window."

Cassandra looked at him questioningly.

"In case Brad has eluded the wasps and is on his way back," he explained. "We'll hide in the woods. Then I'll head for town tomorrow morning to get the police once I know Justin is stable."

Cassandra opened the window and took Justin from him so he could climb out. Then she handed Justin to him through the opening and followed. Her son was still only making whimpering sounds, his eyes staring vacantly ahead, and the sight of it broke her heart. She stroked his head in concern and asked, "How are you doing, sweetie?"

He lay in Turner's arms like a rag doll, a thumb stuck listlessly in his mouth.

"We've got to keep moving," Turner urged.

"Which way?"

He pointed south. "Away from the road that leads to the highway."

The layers of pine needles provided a soft cushion to absorb their footsteps. The spongy quality made walking a little easier, and Cassandra did her best to keep up with Turner. They had to be as swift as possible without making any noise. The trees would absorb a certain amount of sound, but the deep serenity would emphasize any telltale snapping or rustling noises. And though she doubted Brad's tracking abilities, he might still hear them.

She wondered if they should try returning to the cave. When she made that suggestion, Turner shook his head. The trailhead was in the opposite direction, toward the cabin, he explained, and Brad might be lurking there. Plus the mountainside was too open to risk ascending it from this approach. Brad might see them and follow in pursuit. They had to remain on flat ground and use the thick foliage for cover, while putting as much distance between the cabin and themselves as possible.

They continued bushwhacking for what seemed an indeterminable time to Cassandra. She had no idea how far they had traveled because she couldn't get her bearings. The lookout tower was not visible, and the lake was somewhere behind them. All she could see were trees, and they all looked alike. But Turner seemed confident in charting their route, and that was good enough for her.

She focused on keeping up with him, but the pace began to tell on her. With each succeeding step, her limp became more pronounced and the pain more intense. She missed the crutch Turner had made for her, but desperation kept her moving. She gritted her teeth and pushed on.

Just when she thought she couldn't go another step, Turner stopped and pointed ahead. They had reached the base of the mountain. The forest floor rose almost vertically, climbing the southern slope.

"We'll make camp here," he said.

Cassandra slumped to the ground and leaned against a tree. She took Justin and cuddled him in her arms, stroking his head and looking into his eyes. Her chest tightened when she realized that his eyes were still not looking back at her. A light had gone out. "What's wrong with him?" she asked, her voice filled with dread as she looked at Turner.

He knelt beside her and put a hand on Justin's forehead. "I think he's in shock."

"What does that mean?"

Turner cleared his throat. "It's known as acute stress

reaction. In first aid training we learned about it. It's a psychological condition that happens in response to some traumatic event."

"Like seeing his father attack his mother," Cassandra muttered, her chin trembling. "What can we do?"

"It often resolves itself in time. For now we need to keep him hydrated and as comfortable as possible." He got to his feet. "I'm going to build us a shelter for the night in case it rains again. And it will be good camouflage in case..." He left the thought unfinished.

Cassandra cuddled Justin protectively and watched Turner gather deadfall from the forest floor. He dragged several fallen poles into the clearing and leaned them against a large pine bough overhead. In a short time he had hauled enough to form the framework of a semicircular lean-to. Then he gathered pine boughs and laid them across the poles to complete the walls.

She began to feel thirsty and wondered what they were going to do for water. Turner had mentioned that it was important to keep Justin hydrated, but she had seen no trace of water since they had left the cabin. And they'd certainly had no opportunity to bring water with them.

Glancing up at the sky, she wondered if rain was the answer. Perhaps Turner would dig a hole again to trap rainwater like he'd done at the cave. But the sky was clear and did not promise any precipitation.

Her gaze returned to Turner, and she watched him work. His confidence and efficiency was evident, and she found that calming. She trusted him, and with that trust came reassurance.

"All finished," Turner said at length. "This should work fine."

Cassandra looked at the lean-to in admiration. "Are we going to sleep on pine boughs like they do in the movies?"

"I've never found them as soft and comfortable as survival books claim. A knobby branch always seems to burrow into your back in the middle of the night. No, the forest floor will be more comfortable."

He carried Justin inside the lean-to and set him gently down. Cassandra followed and inspected the interior. "Great job, Turner," she said in admiration. "And it sure smells better than the cave."

Turner chuckled. "Rest here while I look for some water."

She nodded. "Thanks. I was worried about that. You said we need to keep Justin hydrated."

"I'll be right back."

She lay beside Justin and combed his hair with her fingers. As she worked, she sang to him and prayed that she'd see some sign of response. But none came.

Turner returned shortly. "I found some Solomon's Seal near the bottom of the slope, in a shady area."

"What's Solomon's Seal?"

"A flower with large, curved leaves that can hold water. There's some there now from yesterday's rain. Come on."

He picked up Justin and climbed out of the lean-to, leading the way to a stand of tall, graceful flowers. Cassandra accompanied him, relieved to see tiny jewels of water glistening in the hollow space where each leaf met the stem.

Turner broke off a curved leaf and gently poured a few drops into Justin's mouth. The little boy swallowed weakly. Cassandra broke off another leaf and followed suit, and together they sipped the collected water until they quenched their thirst.

They returned to the lean-to and Turner got them settled. Then he left for a short time, returning with a handful of berries. "Here, try these," he said, offering some to her.

"What are they?" she asked.

"Mountain berries. There's a stand not far from here. Chew on them to get what juice you can, but don't swallow the pulp. The berries aren't ripe yet and could give you a stomachache."

She tried one and pulled a face. "They're tart."

"But nourishing."

They ate in silence, spitting out the pulp and savoring the juice until the berries were gone. Once, Cassandra thought she heard a voice calling, long and distant. She glanced at Turner to see if he heard it. He did. The voice soon faded, and they didn't hear it again.

Feelings of regret tormented her as she wondered how many times Justin had seen Brad abuse her, both physically and emotionally. The direct abuse against her was indirect abuse against Justin because he was sensitive and vulnerable. And the direct abuse he had received—being abandoned by his father and locked in the bathroom—had traumatized him severely. Only time would tell how badly he had been scarred.

They laid low for the rest of the day and made a return trip to the stand of flowers before bedtime. Justin still wasn't responsive, and Cassandra was determined to provide for her son's physical needs. She didn't know what to do about his psychological needs.

Back at the lean-to, Turner sat in the open doorway and stared vacantly ahead as the darkness deepened.

Cassandra checked on Justin to make certain he was comfortable and then crawled over beside Turner. "You seem awfully quiet," she said.

"I was just thinking about what happened during the mudslide yesterday."

Cassandra shuddered. "Based on what you told me, it must have been frightening."

"It was. But that's not the part I've been thinking about. When the trail collapsed and that guy and I went careening down the slope, I could see we were headed straight for the cliff. I tried to fight my way out of the mud, but it was impossible."

Cassandra looped her arm through his and pressed tighter against him.

"I thought I was going to die." He paused and cleared his throat. "So I asked God for help because I didn't know what else to do."

"He heard your prayer," Cassandra said, leaning her head on his shoulder. "And mine."

"Just when I was about to give up, a thought came into my mind more forcefully than anything I've ever experienced."

"What was the thought?"

"Don't fight against the current. Swim with it and work your way diagonally toward the edge." He paused and cleared his throat. "I'm a good swimmer thanks to my years at Camp Kopawanee, but the idea of *swimming* with the current would never have occurred to me. But I followed the prompting and worked my way diagonally across the slide and was able to grab onto a bush at the last second. My feet were actually dangling over the edge."

Cassandra shuddered. "I'm so sorry for what you've been through because of Justin and me, Turner. I can't thank you enough for everything you've done."

"I'm not sorry."

She looked at him in surprise.

"Being with you and Justin has been an incredible experience," he continued. "And it's given me a chance to reconsider some things in my life. I'm grateful to...you."

She leaned her head on his shoulder once more. "When you were gone so long, Justin and I prayed for you. We asked that you would be protected and able to return to us. And our prayer was answered." She took his hand. "Miraculously."

He squeezed her hand in return.

"But now we need another miracle, Turner. For Justin. Will you... " She hesitated and then continued. "Will you pray with me for him?"

Turner reached up and brushed a strand of hair from her forehead. "Yes," he replied simply.

They closed their eyes and bowed their heads together. The moon peered over the mountain peaks, washing the trees in silver and filtering through the pine boughs to the front door of the lean-to. And a gentle evening breeze descended the western slope and breathed along the branches, murmuring in approval.

chapter 36

URNER WAS SUDDENLY awake. Someone was shaking him, and it took a moment to clear the sleep from his brain. Cassandra was bent over him, both hands on his shoulders. "It's Justin," she whispered. "He's worse."

Turner blinked away the last of the sleep.

"He keeps moaning, and he's running a fever."

He climbed over to where Justin lay tossing and turning, and put a hand on his forehead. "He's burning up."

A fever, Turner knew, was not necessarily a bad thing. Turning up the heat was one of the body's defense mechanisms in fighting germs that cause infections. It made the host a less comfortable place for them. But Justin's condition was of a more serious nature—he was comatose—and warranted medical attention.

"What are we going to do?" Cassandra asked, her voice thin and urgent.

"We need to get his temperature down."

"How?"

An idea came into Turner's mind. That was happening a lot lately. "We'll carry him to the lake and give him a sponge bath. That will help temporarily. But we've got to get him to a doctor." He looked into Cassandra's eyes. "Brad is going to have to drive him to the hospital."

Cassandra shook her head. "I'm not letting Brad near him."

Turner put an arm gently around her. "It's the only way."

"You're going to be asking mercy from someone who is incapable of giving it."

"I don't see that we have a choice."

She studied his face for a moment and nodded in resignation.

Turner picked up Justin and cradled him in his arms. With Cassandra by his side, they headed for the lake.

It seemed strange that they were actually going in search of Brad, considering what they had already done to escape from him. But as Turner glanced at Justin, the paradox didn't seem so ludicrous after all. The little boy needed medical help fast, and only Brad had the power to see that he got it.

The proposal Turner was going to make was simple and straightforward. He would turn himself and the documents over to Brad in exchange for Justin receiving immediate medical attention and Cassandra being allowed to make a new life. But the proposal was also unrealistic, and Turner knew it. It was naïve to think Brad would attend to his son first before exacting revenge on them, but it was a gamble he and Cassandra had to take. What other choice did they have?

Turner didn't know how much bargaining power he actually had. Would Brad accept his terms or reject them on principle? Did he want the documents badly enough to delay his gratification in exacting revenge? It was a gamble to be sure, and the stakes were high. And personal. But Turner had no intention of dying in the bargain. He would find a way to outwit Brad and escape once more. After all, Brad was in Turner's world now.

When they arrived at the lake, Turner gave Justin to Cassandra while he removed the little boy's shirt and pants, exposing his skin to the cool morning air. Then he scooped up a handful of water and cupped it in an attempt to warm it slightly.

"Shouldn't we just immerse him in the lake?" she asked. "That will cool him down faster."

"True, but the shock could result in convulsions. A gentle application of warm water is best."

"*Warm* water?"

"To keep him as comfortable as possible. Besides, it's not the temperature of the water that will cool him. It's the evaporation of the liquid off his skin. That's why I didn't immerse him, clothes and all. The material would act like a blanket and interfere with the evaporation process."

He gently applied water to Justin's chest, arms, and legs. Despite his efforts to warm the water, he heard the little boy suck in his breath, but otherwise Justin didn't respond. He remained as limp as a stuffed toy monkey.

Cassandra watched Turner, biting her lip in concern.

Justin began to shiver, but Turner could still feel the heat radiating from him. Concurrent fever and chills always seemed like a medical oxymoron.

He applied more water to Justin's chest. The large surface areas were where evaporation would occur the most rapidly.

As he worked, he continually glanced around, expecting Brad to appear at any minute. There was no question that Brad was still in the area. He had not retrieved what he had come for, and Turner knew Brad was desperate. And desperation was a powerful motivator. On several occasions in the dying seconds of a high school football game, Brad had rallied his teammates and pulled off a victory. His compulsion to win bordered on obsessive. And the fact that Turner had given him a taste of defeat by escaping with Cassandra and Justin had to be particularly galling. There was no way Brad would ever admit defeat and skulk away with his tail tucked between his legs.

At length Cassandra said, "Justin's not feeling as hot to the touch."

"Good. We can put his pants and shirt back on him now."

But it was easier said than done. It took their combined efforts to dress Justin because it was like trying to put clothes on a rag doll. When they finished, Turner glanced toward the trail that led to the cabin. "Ready?"

She nodded.

Taking Justin from her, he started up the trail and she followed.

As they approached the clearing, Turner called out, "Brad, it's me! I need to talk to you."

He applied the same rule as when hiking in bear territory: Make lots of noise and let any beast in the area know you're around. He didn't want to catch Brad by surprise and have him start shooting. Brad would naturally be caught off guard by their sudden arrival.

He wished he could sneak into the Explorer and drive away, but he knew Brad wasn't careless enough to leave the keys in the ignition. And since Turner didn't know how to hotwire a car, neither the Explorer or the Mercedes were available for service. He was going to have to convince Brad to cooperate and prove that this was not a trick. No wasps, no lies, nothing up his sleeve.

They entered the clearing.

"Brad!" he called again. "It's Turner. We need to talk."

Brad appeared on the front porch. His face and arms still bore traces of the wasps' attack, and Turner could tell that Brad had spent a sleepless night. Brad folded his arms and glared at them with bloodshot eyes. The gun, which he had somehow retrieved, was tucked in his belt and clearly visible. Turner could almost hear the wheels turning in Brad's brain, deciding how best to deal with them. It was payback time.

"Justin's sick," Turner said. "We need to get him to a doctor."

Brad lowered his gaze to the unconscious figure in Turner's arms.

Cassandra wet her lips and addressed her husband. "I'll tell you where the documents are, Brad. Just get Justin to a doctor. He's our son."

Brad didn't move.

"He's sick," Turner repeated anxiously. "He has a high fever, and we need to get him to the hospital."

Brad eyed them suspiciously. "First, tell me where the documents are."

Turner stepped toward him. "As soon as you drop Cassandra and Justin off at the hospital, I'll do better than that. I'll *take* you to them."

"And I'm supposed to believe that, Pancake?"

"I'm here, aren't I?"

Brad considered Turner's response. "You'll take me to them?"

"Yes."

Mocking Turner's earnestness, Brad said, "Cross your heart and hope to die?"

"Look, they're in a locker at the bus depot," Turner said earnestly.

"And the key?"

Turner shook his head. "Drop Cassandra and Justin off at the hospital first, and I'll take you to get it. Then the documents are yours."

Brad looked at him coldly, and Turner feared they had arrived at the *die* part. Brad drew the gun and fired into the ground beside Cassandra. She gasped and jumped backward.

"The next time it's her foot," Brad said. "Then her leg."

As he prepared to fire, Turner stepped in front of Cassandra. "The key is in the handle of the dustpan in my broom closet."

"Turner, no," Cassandra said, taking Justin from him and cradling him protectively.

"We have no choice," Turner replied, hoping he just hadn't made the biggest miscalculation of his life. Armed with the information he had just provided, Brad could dispose of him, retrieve the key, and try it in every locker door at the bus depot until he found the right one. Perhaps he—Turner—had just outlived his usefulness.

Brad descended the steps of the porch and slowly approached, keeping his eyes trained on Turner. "In the handle of the dustpan in your broom closet, huh?" He looked at Cassandra. "Only you could think up something like that."

Without warning, he lashed out and sucker-punched Turner in the face. Turner fell to the ground and blinked to refocus his eyes, fighting to remain conscious. Through blurred vision he saw Cassandra move anxiously toward him but Brad stopped her.

"Put Justin in the Explorer," Brad said coldly. When she hesitated, he barked, "Do it!"

She strapped Justin in the back seat and then looked at Turner. "We can't just leave Turner lying here."

"Don't worry. We won't."

Turner felt himself being dragged by the ankles into the cabin and dumped unceremoniously on the floor.

"At least put him on the couch," Cassandra protested.

Turner attempted to sit up, but Brad kicked him in the stomach, knocking the wind out of him. Turner struggled to catch his breath as Cassandra cried in alarm and attempted to reach him, but Brad caught her by the arm and motioned toward a dining room chair. "Bring it here into the kitchen and sit down!" he ordered.

"There isn't time," Cassandra replied. "We have to get Justin to a doctor."

"Do it!" Brad shouted.

Cassandra dutifully carried one of the chairs into the kitchen. Brad then grabbed her by the shoulders and forced her to sit down on it.

Turner struggled to recover his breath and watched help-lessly as Brad uncoiled the rope from the backpack that was lying near the closet—the rope Turner had used earlier to haul the backpack up the embankment.

"Brad, you don't need to tie Turner up. He's not going to—"

She stopped midsentence as he looped the rope around her and yanked hard. Gasping in pain, she tried to get off the chair, but he held her down and wrapped several coils around her.

"What are you doing?" she demanded. "We've got to leave right now."

"Not *we*, dear."

She fought against the rope. "Brad, I'm coming with you. You're not taking Justin without me. That was the deal."

"I never made any *deal*." He wrapped more coils around her, pulling so hard that she grunted in pain. She tried vainly to free herself.

Turner attempted to get up to intervene, but he was still too winded.

"You don't have to do this," Cassandra said, grimacing as the rope cut into her arms. "I won't go to the police. I swear."

Brad grinned ominously. "I know you won't."

Although he was still struggling for air, dread crept over Turner at the implication in Brad's voice.

"Untie me," she pleaded. "Please." Her last word was spoken as though it was a petition in a prayer.

Brad wrapped a final coil around her and knotted the rope securely.

"Just drop Justin and me off at the hospital and go get the documents," she said imploringly. "You'll have what you came for."

He looked at her and shook his head as if to say *silly girl*. After checking the rope, he placed a roll of paper towel on the stove and unrolled it the length of the counter.

"What are you doing?" she gasped.

He placed several dishtowels and cereal boxes on top of the paper towel. "Shooting you is too easy. You and your *boyfriend* are going to be the victims of a tragic accident."

"What?"

"You deserve to go together, seeing how you've betrayed me. Only your ashes will be left to tell the sad tale of lust and death."

Cassandra's mouth gaped open in horror. "Brad, you can't mean it."

He turned on the burners, and a blue flame hissed into life.

She struggled to free herself. "Turner! Turner!"

"Call to the loser all you want," Brad taunted. "Like he's going to be any help."

The paper towel on the burners turned brown and began to smoke.

Cassandra spoke rapidly. "I gave a letter to a friend that's to be sent to the police in case anything happens to me. It tells everything, Brad!" She quoted several details from the letter. "You'll go to jail...if your business associates don't get to you first."

He grabbed her roughly by the throat. "Who did you give it to?"

"Untie me and let us go. I'll see that you get the letter back, unopened. I promise."

"You *promise*," he hissed in her face. "Like you promised to keep our wedding vows." He lingered long enough to make sure the paper towel caught fire. "Justin and I will think about you from the Grand Caymans. Maybe South America. Good-bye, sweetheart." He grinned as the flames quickly spread. The cereal boxes and dishtowels ignited, raising a hungry flame that licked the wooden cupboards above. It wasn't long until they too were on fire.

It hurt Turner to breathe and his head pounded like a drumbeat, but he felt his strength returning. He remained still, however, waiting for the opportune moment to strike.

Brad wiggled his fingers at Cassandra in a gesture of farewell. She struggled to get free and called Turner's name repeatedly.

Turner smelled smoke and could feel heat radiate from the cupboards. Steeling himself, he waited for Brad to walk by and then lunged forward and tripped him. Brad fell to the floor but rolled over with catlike quickness, lashing out with a vicious kick, which only grazed Turner's shoulder. The cupboard door took the brunt of the force and collapsed inward.

Brad aimed another vicious kick at him. Turner twisted sideways and staggered to his feet, missing the blow, which shattered another cupboard door.

As Brad reached for his gun, Turner grabbed a flaming dishtowel from the counter and threw it at him. Brad dropped the weapon in an effort to cover his face.

Turner picked up the gun and backed toward Cassandra.

"Think you can shoot me in cold blood, Pancake?" Brad sneered, wiping the sparks and ashes from his clothing and hair.

"In a heartbeat," Turner replied, with as much bravado as he could muster. He had let the nettles, the trees, and the mudslide serve him to this point. But he was certain he could stare Brad in the eyes and blast him into eternity with the mere twitch of a finger if he had to.

Brad took a step toward him menacingly.

"Don't make me to do it," Turner warned.

"You haven't got the guts, Pancake."

"But I've got the reasons. Two of them."

"Oh, that's touching," Brad said sarcastically, advancing another step.

Turner saw Brad's muscles tense. He pulled the trigger at the same instant Brad sprang for him. The sound of the blast mingled with the hiss of the fire, and Brad dropped to the floor and clutched his side.

The fire had reached the window curtains. They exploded in a frenzy of red and yellow, and the flames climbed toward the beadboard ceiling, filling the living room with smoke.

"Turner, help!" Cassandra called.

Turner pocketed the gun and began frantically working on the knots, the number of which demonstrated Brad's anger. He saw a flash of movement from the corner of his eye and turned too late to dodge the attack. Brad crashed into him, and they fell heavily to the floor, tipping Cassandra's chair over in the process. The three of them became a tangle of legs, both human and lathed wood.

A red splotch stained Brad's shirt on his right side. Ignoring the wound, he swung wildly, knocking Turner into what remained of the blackened curtains. Smoke clogged Turner's lungs and impaired his vision, adding to the disorientation. Coughing violently, he staggered sideways in anticipation of another onslaught of fists and feet.

Cassandra screamed as the side cupboards caught fire and flames snaked toward her. Brad stood between them, however, and Turner couldn't reach her without going through him. Nor could he shoot again for fear of hitting her.

He threw himself at Brad in an attempt to bulldog his way past him. But in this desperate game of mano a mano, Brad had the physical advantage. He threw Turner to the ground and attempted to stomp on him. Turner rolled out of the way and scrambled to his feet. Fortunately his momentum had carried him closer to Cassandra, and he hurried toward her.

As Brad moved in to attack, the cupboards above the stove toppled in a flaming crash, forcing him back. This gave Turner a chance to sit Cassandra upright but no time to undo the knots. Instead, he began dragging her, chair and all, toward the front door.

Snatching up a kitchen stool, Brad raised it overhead and rushed forward, leaping through the flames.

"Look out, Turner!" Cassandra shouted in warning.

Turner darted out of the way as the stool shattered against the floor. Grabbing a piece of the broken leg, Turner smashed it across Brad's left shin. Brad yelled in pain and went down on one knee.

"Hurry, Turner!" she cried.

As Turner pulled her closer to the front door, Brad got to his feet and limped toward them, coughing and growling in rage. Turner fumbled to draw the gun, and Brad caught him by the arm and pulled upward, causing the shot to pass harmlessly into the ceiling. The two men struggled for possession, and Turner could feel the gun slipping from his hand. He prayed for strength to hang on, realizing that if he lost control of the gun, he was a dead man.

As the gun inched out of his grasp, Turner suddenly released his grip and dropped to the floor, placing a well-aimed kick at the tender spot on Brad's left shin. Brad howled in pain and fell backward, clutching his injured leg. The gun flew out of his hand and slid across the kitchen floor toward the dining room. Crawling like a wounded crab, Brad scrambled to retrieve it.

The ceiling groaned and chunks of beadboard fell, hissing like flaming meteorites. Ignoring the danger, Brad snatched up the gun and took aim.

More of the ceiling fell.

Turner pulled Cassandra down behind the counter as the bullet sailed overhead. He knew the cupboard's wood paneling would offer little protection from the bullets, and so he kept low and dragged Cassandra into the front entrance.

Brad appeared through a gap in the fire and took aim again. A section of the ceiling fell in a clatter of sparks, igniting the front of his shirt and causing the second shot to miss. The bullet shattered the light fixture in the front entrance as Turner dragged Cassandra outside. A tongue of flame followed them, crossing the porch and greedily licking the Explorer.

"We've got to get Justin!" she cried, as Turner pulled her behind the vehicle and fumbled with the rope.

Seconds later a scream issued from the cabin as the roof collapsed, sending up a tower of sparks and flame, exposing the overhanging branches to the fire. Cassandra flinched as the death cry rose in pitch and then ended abruptly.

Turner worked on the knots, which had become tighter in her struggles to get free. One of the walls collapsed, sending sparks mushrooming into the air. They covered their heads as a swarm of sparks descended, each ember burning with the intensity of a wasp's sting.

"The Explorer's going to catch fire, Turner!" she shouted, above the sounds of engorged flames and groaning wood. "We've got to get Justin."

The last knot finally submitted, and Turner uncoiled the rope from around her. "Stay here!" he replied. "I'll get him."

But Cassandra was already ahead of him, crawling to the side door of the vehicle. He rushed to help her.

Several tall pine trees surrounding the cabin exploded into flames. The sap hissed like bacon frying on the griddle.

Cassandra wrenched the back door open and climbed in beside Justin, who was still not responsive. The front porch collapsed, and the odor of heated tin and melting plastic almost overpowered her as she undid Justin's seatbelt. The Explorer was on fire!

Turner took Justin from her and led the way to the back of

the vehicle as a wave of heat seared the air overhead. "We've got to get down to the lake!" he shouted.

Attempting to reach the main road on foot would be suicide. The fire would overtake them before they made it halfway. Coniferous trees, like pine and spruce, burn five to ten times faster than deciduous trees because of the resin in the bark and needles. And he and Cassandra and Justin *were* in the heart of a coniferous forest!

They scrambled to their feet and headed for the lake.

The cabin was now a funeral pyre. Only one wall remained, a flaming tombstone to its solitary occupant. Ashes to ashes, dust to dust.

They raced down the trail to the lake as quickly as Cassandra's ankle would allow, keeping just ahead of the flames.

"The canoe!" Turner shouted.

When they arrived, he handed Justin to her and picked up the canoe like it was a cardboard cutout. He dropped it in the water and threw the paddles in the bottom. Not bothering with the life jackets, he took Justin from her and climbed into the canoe, steadying it while she followed. He situated Justin carefully at his feet and pushed off from the dock.

A surge of fire shot down the trail and ignited the dock. Flaming fingers clawed the air, reaching...grasping.

Cassandra grabbed the other paddle, and she and Turner worked in rhythm, frantically making their way from shore.

Still not willing to relent, however, the fire moved along the water's edge to a point that jutted out into the lake like a crooked thumb. Steering for the center of the lake, Turner and Cassandra paddled until they were exhausted, not pausing to admire the scenery and appreciate the beauty of their surroundings...which were going up in smoke. Literally.

When they reached the center of the lake, they stopped

paddling and slumped wearily in their seats. The canoe drifted on the red-tinged surface as the fire continued to rage around them.

Turner picked up Justin and held him close, dipping his hand in the water and wetting the little boy's fevered brow. Justin moaned slightly and stirred.

Cassandra turned around in the canoe so she was facing them and looked anxiously at her son.

"The fire's like a giant emergency flare," Turner said. "It will bring help. We'll be able to get Justin to the hospital as soon as emergency services arrive."

She exhaled in relief and looked back at the dock. It was burning now and the front section had collapsed. Then her gaze went to the cabin. She shuddered and her expression clouded over as tears formed in her eyes.

Turner reached for her hand and squeezed reassuringly. "It's all right, Cassandra. You've been holding it in a long while. Too long."

So with Justin cradled safely between them, they sat bobbing on the water as she cried, releasing emotions that had been repressed for years. And in the distance, above the roar and hiss of the flames, came the unmistakable wail of sirens.

chapter 31

ESPITE THE PAIN of his injuries, Turner felt comforted by Loretta's regular visits with him in the hospital. She hovered, fluffed his pillow, filled his water glass, and stood guard so he could rest. One of the nurses jokingly asked when the hospital had been upgraded to a five-star establishment. Turner wondered what the nurse would think when Loretta began supplementing his hospital meals with home cooking.

He was in worse condition than first thought. Cassandra too. They had first- and second-degree burns on their arms and hands that required immediate attention to prevent infection. And Turner had some lacerations on his back and legs he didn't remember receiving. Antiseptic cream and bandages were applied, and painkillers were administered at regular intervals.

They had been airlifted by helicopter to the hospital and put in separate rooms. Justin was taken to the children's ward, which upset Cassandra because she didn't want to be away from him. But the hospital staff convinced her it was for the best.

Loretta shuttled between rooms and gave Turner regular updates on their progress, but the news worried him. Justin was still not responding to stimuli but was in stable condition. He was not able to eat on his own, so he was being fed intravenously.

Visits from members of the Silverthorne police department and the Colorado Department of Forestry and Fire Protection worried Turner too. The forest fire burned for two days before firefighters were able to get it under control, and it warranted investigation. So did the body count. Turner had to make several statements regarding the origins of the fire and the deaths of Slick and Brad. He also told them about Twitch, who was found the following day, wandering in an unburned section of the forest and babbling incoherently. The investigators asked tough questions, and Turner's answers left lingering doubts in their minds: Did the first victim fall off the cliff or was he pushed? Why was the second victim unable to escape the fire in the cabin if he was the one who started it?

Turner couldn't fault the investigators for being confused by the facts. An unfortunate series of fatalities pointed directly to him, and it took some effort to convince the police that he wasn't really a serial killer disguised as a handyman and college student.

They took statements from Cassandra too, Turner learned. She told them about the financial records and documents. The investigators were extremely interested and went to retrieve them. After receiving everything, the interrogation stopped. Turner assumed it meant there was enough corroboration to close the case. Either that or the investigators decided not to ruffle Loretta's feathers further. She clucked around in the background and was as relieved as he was to see the back of their suits.

The following morning, however, several FBI agents arrived, and Turner had to go through it all over again, which perturbed Mother Hen even more. When their questions hinted of accusations, she looked ready to gather her chick under her wings and peck out the agents' eyes.

Harvey came for a visit in the afternoon. He asked how Turner was doing and then promptly launched into an account of his own aches and pains. He ended by saying how much the Mountain View Motel needed Turner back, and he promised no to-do list until Turner was strong enough to resume work. Which, Turner guessed, probably meant the day after his return home.

Loretta scolded Harvey for his lack of bedside manners and handed Turner a glass of water.

Turner took a sip and then set it aside. "I wanted to say I'm sorry about the car, Mama Retta. The Buick was—"

"Don't worry about that old girl," she replied. "It's time we upgraded anyway. What would you think of us getting an SUV?"

"Four-door, V8," Harvey added.

Images flashed through his mind of Loretta behind the wheel of a zippy, high-performance vehicle, running drivers off the road, left and right. "We'll talk," he replied.

"Silver, I think," she mused, obviously in honor of the *old girl*.

Mary arrived just then, allowing for a timely change of subject.

"Please tell me your friend has fire insurance," Turner said, ready to apologize himself hoarse. He had tried to think of ways he could make it up to her friend, short of taking out a loan to rebuild the cabin, but so far had come up with nothing.

Mary pulled up a chair beside the bed. "I spoke with her last night. She does have fire insurance and is meeting with the adjustor tomorrow. She didn't sound worried."

"But the fire destroyed everything. The beautiful scenery that made the cabin so idyllic is now a charred wasteland."

"She's going to put the insurance money into a retirement condo in Palm Springs. She's actually been talking about it for a while. Now, she has an excuse to do it."

Turner shook his head in chagrin. "But the trouble we caused. You let us use the cabin and—"

"We'll have no such foolish talk," Loretta said, planting a fist on each of her generous hips. "Things can be replaced. People can't."

"I agree," Mary added. "The Good Book reminds us not to set our hearts on the riches of this world, where moths and rust can destroy. Or where bad guys can burn down cabins." She winked at Turner. "I threw in that last part. But the point is, things of this world pass away. Treasures in heaven, however, last forever. And you, young man, have a pile waiting for you there. It's a great thing you did, helping Cassandra and that cute little child of hers. I just praise the Lord that you all didn't go and get yourselves killed. I was so worried for you."

Turner looked from her to Loretta. "And I'm so glad you are both all right. I was afraid those guys had used strong-arm tactics to make you reveal our location."

Loretta and Mary exchanged glances, and then Loretta fired a look of disapproval at Harvey. "Do you want to tell him or should we?" she asked.

Harvey looked at Turner sheepishly and cleared his throat. "The PI guy contacted me the other day—"

"He wasn't a PI," Loretta muttered.

"More like a hired thug," Mary added.

Harvey squirmed in his chair. "How was I to know? Anyway, he contacted me the other day and asked if I knew your whereabouts. I'd overheard Loretta talking to Mary, so I knew about the cabin. He told me about the wife running away for her safety and said the police had apprehended the husband and that the wife was needed to testify against him, to keep him locked behind bars. What was I supposed to do?"

Mary politely declined to answer the question.

"Keep your mouth shut," Loretta replied, less politely.

Harvey turned to Turner defensively. "I just wanted you to

be able to come home, so I gave him the general directions to the cabin. Turns out he played me for a sucker."

"And like a sucker, you swallowed the bait, hook, line, and sinker," Loretta muttered.

"He *was* convincing," Turner said, remembering Slick pointing the gun *convincingly* at him.

Harvey turned triumphantly toward Loretta, but she waved her hand dismissively.

They sat in quiet contemplation for a moment. Turner took a drink of water in an attempt to douse the fevered memories of the past few days.

Loretta rolled him gently over so she could fluff his pillow again. Turner didn't protest the treatment. Loretta, as Mother Hen, was a force to be reckoned with, but that was nothing compared to her as Mother Bear, so he kept quiet and let her fluff to her heart's content.

After fussing and fretting for a while longer, she declared it was time for Harvey and her to get back to the motel. Mary said she had an appointment with a young victim of parental abuse—"It just goes on and on," she sighed—and gave Turner a kiss on the cheek.

Turner smiled as he watched Harvey beat them to the door. Hospitals made his boss nervous.

Once he was alone, Turner settled back on his fluffy pillow and tried to close his eyes. But an image of Brad's shirt catching fire pushed its way into his consciousness, followed by the memory of Slick going over the cliff. He lay staring at the ceiling, distracting himself by counting the tiles, but he only got to fifty-three before his eyes began to droop. And then... the images returned.

Cassandra arrived in a wheelchair later that evening. "Hi," she said, approaching the bed. "I just had to come and see you. How are you doing?" She studied his bandages and thought how tired he looked.

Turner propped himself up on one elbow. "Not too bad. It only hurts when I breathe."

Cassandra felt a profound sense of responsibility for Turner's condition. And during the two days she had been confined to her bed, she had thought a great deal about him. Between her concerns for Justin and the guilt she felt for involving Turner in the first place, she had thought of little else.

"How are *you* doing?" Turner asked, interrupting her self-recrimination.

"Pretty good," she replied.

"I agree with the pretty part."

Cassandra blushed and instinctively touched her hair.

"And how's Justin doing?" Turner asked.

She sat up a little straighter. "He's responding to the medication and his fever has finally broken."

"Is he talking yet?"

"No, but apparently that's normal. The doctors tell me it's just going to take time."

Turner held out his bandaged hand, and she rolled forward and gently pressed her fingertips to his. His touch was soft and warm, and she felt a tingling sensation despite the pain of her burns.

"I can't begin to thank you for what you've done for Justin and me," she said, smiling at him. "I don't know what we would have done without you. But I'm just so sorry I got you involved and you got hurt."

"Like I told you before, *I'm* not sorry."

She studied him momentarily and a felt a sense of relief. "I've been doing a lot of thinking over the past two days, Turner. I firmly believe that you were the answer to our prayers. You were the one person who could help Justin and me."

"You're giving me too much credit."

Cassandra shook her head. "I don't think so. I feel we were led to the one person who was prepared to help us. Do you remember the story of Esther in the Bible?"

"Vaguely."

"Esther was a girl who was raised up to be queen of Persia at a time when her people, the Jews, were in danger of being destroyed. But she was afraid to speak in their defense and present herself to the king unannounced for fear of displeasing him and being executed. But Mordecai, her adoptive father and advisor, told her that perhaps she had been raised up for such a time as this in order to rescue her people."

"I still think you're giving me too much credit."

"You worked for four years at that youth camp and learned outdoor and survival skills. You blessed the lives of many young people, but then you were laid off because you were needed elsewhere. And after your mother died, you were led to the motel because Loretta and Harvey needed you, and you needed to register in college and get on with your life. And I believe you were led to us because you were the only one who had the skills to do what you did. You stopped a lot of bad people and illegal activities, Turner, and I believe you were raised up for such a time as this."

Turner stroked his chin pensively. "Actually, I believe you were led here for my sake."

She expressed surprise. "What do you mean?"

"There were some things missing in my life—some things

I needed to learn. Or relearn. And I'm grateful to you, Cassandra, for helping me do that."

"I didn't do anything," she protested.

"You helped me see what was right in front of my face the whole time." He shifted in the bed to get more comfortable. "I told you that when I was in the mudslide, heading for certain death, the thought occurred to me to swim with the current, rather than fight against it. At first I wondered if it came to me because of my survival training. But when I was wrestling with Brad for the gun, in the cabin, and prayed for strength to outmuscle him, a powerful thought occurred to me as though a voice said: *Go for his shin!* So I released my grip and kicked him hard in his tender shin, forcing him to drop the gun. That gave you and me time to reach the door before the roof collapsed. If I had stubbornly tried to outmuscle him, you and I wouldn't be here now. God has been guiding me all along, Cassandra. I can see that now."

She reached out and caressed his fingertips. "It's wonderful to hear you say that, Turner."

"And when I get better, I'm going to make the most of it." He looked into her eyes. "You and I are going to see that Justin gets the best care possible. We'll work together to—"

Cassandra dropped her gaze. "Actually Justin is being transferred to Sunrise Children's Hospital in Las Vegas."

"When?"

"Tomorrow morning. And I'm going with him. The hospital there has a stress therapist for children. Her name is Dr. Courtnall, and she specializes in play therapy, which will allow Justin to deal with the trauma he's experienced. It will give him a chance to work through his feelings naturally and safely, and help him get better." Her voice broke. "But it's going to be hard."

"He's a tough little guy. I know he'll be okay."

"Also, I've got to see a family friend who is a lawyer. He's going to help me with the legal matters relating to the marriage and…Brad's death. There are some other things I need help sorting out, so I have to return home as quickly as possible."

"Then I'm coming with you. Just as soon as I—"

She shook her head. "You need to stay here and get better. You've fallen behind in your studies, and I know there's a pile of jobs waiting for you at the motel."

"They can wait a little longer."

Her eyes filled with tears. "*We're* going to have to wait a little longer, Turner. I've got to go be with Justin and take care of things at home. And you've got responsibilities here."

"But I want to be with you."

"And I want to be with you too. But it will just be until Justin gets better."

He toyed with the edge of the blanket. "I understand why you have to leave. I just wish it wasn't so soon."

She pursed her lips. "I owe a lot of money. The medical bills are piling up, and Brad put us in debt with a series of bad investments. The banks wouldn't carry him, so he borrowed from the wrong kind of people and put us even further in debt." She shook her head wearily "I called the bank this afternoon. The stocks and bonds don't amount to as much money as I was hoping. I'm going to have to sell the house and everything just to get my head above water."

"What about declaring bankruptcy? The debts aren't your doing."

"But I'm still legally tied to them. Besides, the people who loaned Brad money would never leave me alone. The police have the records and charges will probably be laid, but it could take months to get everything straightened out. Meanwhile I'd be hounded for the outstanding amount, and that's not how I want to live. Plus, I'd have a lousy credit rating. No, the only way is to pay back everything and be done with it."

Turner considered her response and then asked, "When everything's taken care of and Justin's better, will you come back?"

She smiled. "Just try and stop me." Looking into his eyes, she held his gaze. "I wish I would have known you back in high school for the person you truly are." She smiled wryly. "And Brad too for that matter. I wish I could have seen both of you more clearly. Things would have been so different." She gently touched his fingertips. "I'm a better person because of you, Turner Caldwell." She leaned forward and kissed him on the cheek and then turned as if to leave.

"Stay a little longer," he whispered.

She maneuvered her wheelchair sideways and placed her head gently on his arm. "I'd like that," she said softly.

chapter 38

*T*URNER RETURNED HOME three days later.

Harvey and Loretta were there to greet him when he arrived. Harvey held a hammer, and his black and blue thumbnail bore evidence that he had been attempting to use it. Turner volunteered to help out, but Loretta wouldn't allow it. Instead she had Harvey carry his suitcase while they walked Turner to his room. On the way she told her husband in no uncertain terms that Turner was not allowed to do any handyman work for three more days. She wagged a finger under Harvey's nose as she made the declaration.

"I can handle things," Harvey said defensively. He shifted Turner's suitcase to the other hand and rolled his shoulder. "But this arthritis—it's acting up again."

"Three more days!"

Harvey exhaled sharply.

So did Turner when Loretta opened his door. A pot of stew was on the stove, and two loaves of fresh-baked bread sat on the counter. His laundry had been done and was neatly folded in a laundry basket. And a Dell laptop computer and a new backpack sat on the table.

"Hey, you guys didn't have to buy me a new laptop," he said in surprise, embracing Loretta.

"You lost yours in the fire," Loretta said. "This is a refurbished one and didn't cost that much money. But now you'll have no excuse. You've fallen behind in your courses and you need to catch up. Right away. We didn't enroll you in college just to have you flunk out."

Turner liked the *we*. "I'll start back first thing tomorrow morning, Mama Retta."

Harvey set Turner's suitcase down in the bedroom and sighed dramatically.

Loretta ignored him and looked around the room, giving it a final inspection. Satisfied, she embraced Turner and held him for a long time. "It's so good to have you back," she said, a catch in her voice. "Now get some rest and good luck at school tomorrow."

"I could use some rest too," Harvey muttered. "This right shoulder of mine—"

"March!" she replied, pointing toward the door. "Turner needs some peace and quiet."

Harvey muttered under his breath as he exited, while Loretta paused to give Turner one more hug.

When he was alone, Turner dished up a bowl of stew and cut a generous slice of bread. Then he booted up the laptop and connected to the motel Wi-Fi. Entering his password, he logged on to his e-mail account. There were four e-mails from Cassandra, beginning the day she arrived in Las Vegas. Sitting at the kitchen table, he ate as he excitedly read them.

Her first e-mail explained that she and Justin had arrived safely in Las Vegas and that Justin was in a private room on the second floor of the Sunshine Children's Hospital. She wrote:

> The pediatricians are excellent, and I am particularly impressed with Dr. Courtnall, the stress therapist. She was thorough in her approach and obtained a complete history of Justin. Then she followed this with an initial clinical assessment and consultation with me. Based on the information, a treatment program has been implemented, and Dr. Courtnall's prognosis is encouraging.

Her approach will allow Justin to deal with the trauma he experienced and give him a chance to work through his feelings naturally and safely. He still isn't responding to physical stimuli, but Dr. Courtnall doesn't seem unduly worried at this point. I'll keep you updated on his progress.

The e-mail also included a brief account of how returning to her house had been more emotionally difficult than she had expected. She continued:

Reminders of Brad were everywhere, and his specter walked the halls. It was too difficult to remain in the house alone, and so I called a friend and asked to stay with her. I packed some clean clothes and other things and also grabbed Justin's teddy bear, at Dr. Courtnall's request. She wants to use Teddy for the next session. I miss you, Turner. Please hurry and get better.

Cassandra's second e-mail was dated the following evening. She recounted how Dr. Courtnall used Justin's teddy bear as a starting point. She created a little story about Teddy, consistently touching the soft fur to Justin's face and arms while relating how lonely Teddy was because he didn't have a friend and would Justin be his friend? The e-mail continued:

During the story, Justin blinked—actually blinked— and Dr. Courtnall took that as a good sign. She told a second story of Justin and Teddy going to the lake and playing together on the beach. They made tunnels and built sandcastles and threw rocks in the water. And they went wading and even had a water fight. Before the story was finished, Justin had his arm wrapped around Teddy, which Dr. Courtnall took as an even better sign. I'm thrilled, Turner, to see even that much progress. I pray every day for Justin...and for you. I know we can get through this.

Her third e-mail gave an account of her visit to see her lawyer friend at Barnes, Randall, and Associates. He was sympathetic to her situation but realistic too. It would take some time to draft up a proposal to her creditors and figure out all her assets and liabilities. But he was confident her debts could be addressed in order of priority, and any remaining unpaid ones could be consolidated into a bank loan, with a manageable monthly payment. But he confirmed what she already knew. If she wanted to get her head above water, the house and two cars would have to be sold. And that was another reason Cassandra felt she couldn't stay in the house alone. It already seemed like it belonged to someone else.

She also explained that she was following Mary's advice and was receiving counseling too. She wrote:

> I'm a victim of spousal abuse of the worst kind—my husband tried to kill me—and I need help in dealing with everything I've suffered. Meredith, my counselor, is helping me work through my issues. She is very insightful and I trust her.

Cassandra's last e-mail had to do with a report that had aired on the news about Brad's death and the fire at the cabin, along with the backstory. Turner was aware of the news report and was not surprised to learn that it had upset Brad's family greatly. They wanted Cassandra to contact the media and set the record straight. Their son was not abusive, they claimed, and he would never have tried to kill her. Her e-mail continued:

Brad's father tried to force me to retract the story reported to the media about his son—it seems bullying runs in the family—but I refused and hung up on him. Later Brad's mother called and tried a different approach. Guilt. My husband—their dear son—was dead and no longer in a position to defend himself. If the story was not retracted, the family name would be sullied. What would people think? I hung up on her before I told her what I thought!

Tears don't e-mail well, but Turner could see them all over Cassandra's last communication. It had to be heartbreaking for her to be the victim of physical and emotional abuse, and yet be perceived as the insensitive and unfaithful spouse in the marriage. Obviously Brad's parents were blind to the fact that their son was an abuser and, worse, a man guilty of attempted murder. But knowing Cassandra as he did, Turner guessed she hadn't told Brad's parents the whole story, allowing the truth to be ceremoniously buried with him. That was the kind of person she was.

Turner felt angry about the injustice of the whole thing and considered writing a letter to the family, exposing Brad for what he truly was. But he decided against it. He would follow Cassandra's example and be the kind of person he needed to be too.

In the den at her friend's house, Cassandra wearily sat down at the computer and logged on to her e-mail account. It was the following day and had been a busy one. Between visits to the hospital to be with Justin and a follow-up visit to the lawyer and to the bank, she was exhausted.

But she perked up when she found two e-mails from Turner

waiting for her. Undoing her ponytail, she finger-brushed her hair and settled back to read them.

The first entry explained that he had visited each professor following his return from the hospital and attempted to explain what had happened. But for the most part, explanations proved unnecessary. The TV news report about his experience lauded him as an everyday hero. He wrote:

> I'm not certain who contacted the media, but I suspect a certain local motel proprietor recognized this as an opportunity to plug the establishment at which I am employed.

Cassandra shook her head. She had only met Harvey briefly when she checked into the Mountain View Motel, but based on what Turner had told her, Harvey was…Harvey. The report may have benefited the motel, but it caused her a lot of grief with Brad's family.

Turner's e-mail continued:

> A news team came to the hospital and interviewed me. Lights, camera, action. The whole nine yards. They also interviewed Harvey, who plugged the Mountain View Motel shamelessly, and Loretta, who mentioned that my hospital bills were enormous and that a "local hero" shouldn't be strapped with a financial burden for trying to do the right thing. And would you believe it? Since the news feature aired, money has come rolling in. People from everywhere have been sending donations, and at the rate things are going, our hospital bills—that's right, yours and mine and Justin's—should be paid for. What a blessing!

Cassandra stared at the computer screen in disbelief. The news report had a silver lining! To have her hospital bills cleared was more than a blessing. It was a miracle. She had worried endlessly about the mounting medical costs, not that she begrudged the treatment Justin was receiving. But knowing it would take the rest of her life to pay for it was a daunting reality. And now this. Tears of relief and gratitude flowed, and it was a few minutes before she could see well enough to read the rest of Turner's e-mail.

> And there's another blessing too. As a result of the news feature, my professors have been practically falling over themselves in an effort to be accommodating. One even volunteered to be in a news feature that focused on me as a college student. Perhaps he saw this as an opportunity to plug the college at which I'm enrolled. But because of the distractions involved in my "fifteen minutes of fame," I didn't do especially well on my latest assignments, although I did receive passing grades. And my outdoor education professor was particularly complimentary on how I outwitted the men, using the natural environment to my advantage. I didn't tell him that God should get most of the credit.

Cassandra paused to reflect back on the young man she had met the night she and Justin first appeared in his apartment. Turner had been kind and helpful, but she had sensed an undercurrent of bitterness in him. She learned that the loss of his four-year job as a counselor at the Christian youth camp and the death of his mother had shaken him to the core. But through another set of potentially faith-rattling experiences, he had rediscovered his lost faith. Once more she considered how God was always at work behind the scenes.

Turner's second e-mail was more personal. He explained

that Loretta, after inspecting his healing injuries, had finally granted permission for him to resume his handyman duties. The list Harvey handed him rivaled the Constitution and its amendments for length and detail.

Cassandra chuckled and kept reading.

> My first job was to fix a dripping faucet in Room 21. It was the unit you and Justin occupied. I remembered how beautiful and yet troubled you looked when you answered the door. I remembered the safety chain and the drinking glass and how Justin, his thumb stuck securely in his mouth, clutched the stuffed monkey. The current guest probably wondered why my eyes suddenly misted over and I fumbled with the wrench. I miss you, Cassandra, and pray for you and Justin. If he's not better soon, I'm coming to Vegas. I have to see you guys.

Her smile faded as she read the last two sentences again. *If he's not better soon, I'm coming to Vegas. I have to see you guys.* She had been anticipating this and now paused to consider her response. Then clicking the new message button, she exhaled slowly and began to type.

chapter 39

*T*URNER ARRIVED HOME later that evening from his last class and opened the door to his apartment. The room was empty and quiet, just as it had been before Cassandra and Justin arrived. He glanced around and noticed that everything was in its usual place, which had not been the case when Justin was there. How Turner wished he could see something out of place—proof that little hands were healthy and active.

After popping a frozen pizza into the microwave, he took his laptop out of his backpack and sat at the kitchen table. This was his favorite time of day—the time to check his e-mails. Cassandra had written him daily, and he was anxious for each new installment. She sounded positive and things were improving steadily, although not as fast as anyone wanted. But there was progress, and he expected more of the same in her latest communication.

The e-mail began as a fulfillment to his wish.

> What wonderful news about the financial donations. It makes me realize that there are a lot of good people in this world. Especially a certain college student I know, who happens to work part time as a handyman.
>
> Justin's making excellent progress with play therapy and is already making sounds. He's not speaking yet, but the sounds show improvement. He is beginning to gesture for things too, like when he wants a glass of water. But Dr. Courtnall says we're not to give it to

him until he articulates his request. Already he's saying, "Wa" for water. He's becoming increasingly responsive to physical stimuli and is able to return my embrace when I hug him. He isn't smiling yet, but the corners of his mouth twitch when I tickle him. It might just be wishful thinking, but I'm sure his eyes brighten when I come into the room. I pray he'll continue to return from the deep, dark place he's retreated to and become the wonderful child he used to be.

Pumping his fist, Turner said, "Yes! Way to go, little man." The timer on the microwave beeped and he went to check on the pizza. It was ready. He put it on a small plate and carried it back to the table. Pausing to say grace—something he had started doing since returning from the hospital—he took a bite and continued reading.

I've been meeting regularly with my counselor—Meredith—and feel that I'm making progress too. She's helped me see that I did not deserve the treatment I received from Brad. Apparently many victims accept the abuse, feeling they warrant it for faults and failings on their part. They think they aren't loveable or worthy of something better, while others accept the abuse because they don't know what else to do. They have no alternate source of income or security and so they stay for the sake of their children. That was me. But not anymore. I know I can work through this and heal so I can be there for Justin. And that's what I need to talk to you about, Turner.

The last sentence ended ominously, and Turner felt his chest constrict. He drew in a deep breath and continued reading.

Meredith is helping me analyze the incredible experience you and I went through together. She says we
were forced to rely on each other, and that bonded us
in a special way. It's what survivors feel toward one
another when the crisis ends. They have a special and
unique bond that outsiders simply can't share. In our
case everything happened so fast. We jumped from the
frying pan into the fire...literally. And we didn't have
time to do anything but react and keep reacting. Every
moment we spent together was in crisis. And now that
it's over, we feel a certain obligation toward each other.

"It's more than an *obligation*," Turner muttered aloud. "It
goes way beyond that." He took another bite of his pizza and
chewed slowly.

I was a married woman on the run—one who wasn't
looking to start a new relationship. Meredith has helped
me realize that you and I didn't meet under normal circumstances. We didn't even have time to get properly
acquainted—or reacquainted, really. Our lives were in
constant danger. And now that it's over, she's advising
me—us really—to take time to work things out and not
rush into anything. You can't build a future together
when the past is the only thing you have in common. I
know—Brad and I tried.

"But I'm not Brad," Turner protested to the kitchen walls. He
didn't want a future based on the past either. But how could
you build a future if the present remained at arm's length?
Scowling in frustration, he read the last section.

My head is telling me that circumstance brought us
together, but necessity forced us to rely on each other.
And though we were bonded by our circumstances, it

was a matter of survival, not love. On the other hand, my heart is telling me that I have grown to love you. I love the person you are and what you did for Justin and me. I'll never forget you, and I'll make certain he doesn't either. Please be patient while I work things out between my head and my heart.

Meredith says that love on the rebound is always risky because it's built on an unstable foundation. But I know what I felt when I was with you. As you can see, I'm in a quandary. My physical injuries are healing nicely, but Meredith says I'm still wounded emotionally and that I'm very vulnerable right now. She says I need to take more time to figure things out and not rush into a relationship until I heal more on the inside. So for now I'm not coming back to Lakewood, Turner, and I ask you not to visit me here. I pray you'll understand and respect my wishes. Give my love to Loretta and Harvey and Mary.

Turner sat back in his chair and stared vacantly at the emptiness around him. He chewed on his lip and considered his response to her e-mail. His chin trembled, and he struggled with his emotions. Finally he pursed his lips and typed Cassandra a one-word reply. Pausing briefly, he hit the send button and then went to bed.

Cassandra stared at the single word displayed on the computer monitor.

Okay.

Although it was only one word, it spoke volumes. It suggested acceptance and support, but also hurt and rejection.

The single word answered her request, true, but its curtness said much more.

She had hurt Turner. But the irony was she was doing it so she *didn't* hurt him. A little pain now would prevent a larger hurt later. She and Turner had been thrust into a life-and-death situation, so it was only natural they would develop feelings for each other. But based on what? Meredith had cautioned her about love on the rebound. She had even quoted the old maxim: *Two wrongs don't make a right* and had warned Cassandra about not making the same mistake twice.

But with Turner, it hadn't felt wrong. In fact, *everything* about him felt right. The strength of his character, his kindness and gentleness, the warmth of his touch, and the way it made her feel when he smiled at her. At first she had been oblivious to these things because she was a married woman and wasn't looking for a new relationship But in time his traits had become impossible to ignore. He was everything Brad was not. And with her marriage now over, what was she waiting for? What was she afraid of? Was she afraid of returning to Turner, only to discover that they didn't have anything in common other than the memory of their experience together? Was everything she had felt based solely on the urgency she experienced at the time?

These were tough questions to be sure. And until she knew the answers and healed on the inside, she was going to follow her counselor's advice and—wait.

chapter 40

*D*URING THE NEXT few weeks Turner patched holes, repainted walls, unclogged toilets, repaired air conditioners, oiled squeaky hinges, and installed safety chains. As each item on the list disappeared one by one, Harvey's blood pressure responded accordingly.

Turner also threw himself into his studies. He did some bonus assignments and was able to improve his marks. He was even selected to be a student counselor for an upcoming three-day camp for his outdoor education class. That alone guaranteed a good mark.

He still received regular e-mails from Cassandra. In her latest communication she said:

> Justin's now saying words and has to verbalize what he wants before he's allowed to do it. For example, if he wants to play with the toys in the playroom, he has to say exactly that. He's smiling and laughing now and is becoming impatient with being cooped up. That's the best sign of all, according to Dr. Courtnall.

The e-mail was good news, of course. But Turner's heart sank as he noticed there was no mention of when she would return to Lakewood and no invitation for him to visit Las Vegas. And of course he couldn't raise the subject in his e-mails to her.

He began taking evening walks in the park. Fall was in the air, and the leaves were beginning to turn color, and he enjoyed witnessing the change. His room was too quiet and the walls seemed to close in claustrophobically. And the evening news held little appeal. It had become two-dimensional, showing only the length and breadth of the world, whereas he had plumbed its depths and was no longer placated by mere facts and figures. So he satisfied his craving for a deeper interaction with life by walking in the park and experiencing the world unfold around him in 3-D.

On one occasion he saw a young couple stroll hand in hand through the park, and he thought of the touch of Cassandra's hand in his. He could still feel her head on his shoulder and smell the fragrance of her hair. The memory of her lips on his cheek was seared in his brain. He sat down on a park bench nearby and stared off in the distance…remembering.

On another occasion he watched a young boy chase a small flock of ducks and laugh with glee as they waddled into the pond. Turner thought of Justin and the joy his little buddy had found in simple things: the stuffed monkey, the pillow fight, the canoe ride, the flowers and insects around the cabin.

Reminders were everywhere, in everything Turner saw and dreamed.

Cassandra and Justin were dream determinants of the first order. It seemed that she, in particular, was destined to be a lifelong subject of his dreams, featured in HD. His high school memories were painful, and he had gone to great lengths to suppress them. But thoughts of her were equally painful, though not in the same way. They affected a different region of his heart—a place that felt as empty as an unfurnished motel room, languishing from lack of occupancy.

The experiences at the cabin with Brad and the hired thugs were dream determinants too. Turner frequently awoke in the night as dark and frightening images swirled inside his head. Sometimes Twitch was trapped in the fire, and Slick was the one having a bad experience in the nettles. Other times it was

Brad who was flailing his arms to keep from going over the embankment. The jumble of distorted images and fragmented memories was disturbing.

As a result, he got very little sleep.

Loretta noticed and finally took matters into her own hands. She invited Mary to come for dinner the following Sunday afternoon. After a delicious meal of fried chicken, scalloped potatoes, steamed vegetables, and banana cream pie for dessert, the two women sat him down in the living room and gave Turner a chance to vent. Harvey was sent to watch television in the bedroom, where he promptly fell asleep.

Turner talked for a long time, sometimes asking a question and then answering it before Loretta or Mary could reply. Other times he left the question hanging in the air because it was unanswerable. He talked about his fears and worries, his hopes and dreams, and Loretta put an arm around him while he plumbed the depths of his soul. There were tears shed, mostly his, and she wiped them away with a handkerchief. When he was finally spent, he looked at Loretta and Mary miserably and said, "She's not coming back, is she?"

Loretta pursed her lips thoughtfully. "I believe Cassandra came into your life for a purpose, and I know you do too. But just how this will end, I can't say. I can only hope. And I do hope, Turner. I hope for your happiness and for hers. But this much I can say: Any young woman out there would be lucky to have you. And they had better measure up too or they'll have me to deal with."

"Amen," Mary replied, eliciting a chuckle.

"In the meantime you're going to have to let go of some things and hang on to others."

He looked at her quizzically. "What things, Mama Retta?"

"You'll know when the time comes."

"As human beings we have an amazing capacity that way,"

Mary added. "Trust in the instincts the good Lord gave you. And right now I hope your instincts are telling you that you're the victim of abuse too, young man. Just like Cassandra and that precious little child of hers. I told her and I'm telling you that it's important to work through the steps that lead to healing. You can't ignore or minimize the pain and trauma. Feelings and memories buried alive never die. They just fester and consume you one bite at a time, from the inside out."

They talked for another hour, sharing experiences and shedding tears. They also laughed. Loretta shared humorous anecdotes, mostly about Harvey, that helped lighten the atmosphere.

When it was over, Turner hugged both women good night and promised to talk to Mary again and continue his own journey of healing. Then he went to his apartment and took the Gideon's Bible from his dresser drawer and sat on the bed. Thumbing to the Book of Esther, he read the account and pondered what Cassandra had told him about it. Cassandra maintained that he had come into her life for a special purpose and that events had placed him in a position to help her and Justin. She also maintained that it was all part of the plan, that things didn't happen by chance or coincidence. He had once argued with her about the idea of a plan, but now he felt differently. He believed that she had been placed in a position to help him too. And just who had helped whom the most, he couldn't say.

He closed the Bible and leaned back against the headboard, wondering if they had been brought into each other's lives for that one occasion only. He didn't know the answer...yet. He could only be patient and let the plan unfold.

chapter 41

IVE WEEKS AFTER returning to Las Vegas, Cassandra emerged from the law office of Barnes, Randall, and Associates. She held a file folder that contained receipts for the sale of her home and the two automobiles, as well as a detailed outline of bills paid on her behalf. The money from the sale of her assets had not been sufficient to pay every creditor, including her lawyer. But it turned out Brad had a life insurance policy and that, along with the money Loretta had sent from the donations collected following the TV news broadcast, was enough to clear the outstanding debts. There was even money left over, and for the first time in years, she felt truly free.

She stopped in the middle of the sidewalk, causing people to bump into her and hurry on unapologetically. But she didn't care. She felt deliciously happy and resisted the urge to throw her arms in the air and shout for joy. And despite the sounds of traffic and the hustle and bustle around her, she felt at peace.

Justin was home from the hospital and hardly showed any signs of the trauma he had experienced. He was running around, as active as ever. And talking up a storm. Her friend was babysitting him right now and had been adamant about letting them stay with her as long as necessary. Still, Cassandra thought, it would be nice for Justin and her to get an apartment of their own soon. In time she'd find a job and put money away for his college fund, but that was down the road. Today she was going to celebrate.

She caught a taxi to her favorite restaurant, Alexis Gardens, and had to wait twenty minutes for a table. While she waited, she studied the menu and remembered being stuck in the cave with Justin, cold and hungry. She had dreamed of sitting down to a sumptuous meal and eating whatever she wanted, and now she no longer had to dream. She was going to feast.

After being seated at a table near the window, she placed her order and then watched the people on the sidewalk rush by. Each person had somewhere to go and something to do. Each one had hopes and dreams.

She ran a hand across the file folder and thought about how it represented the fulfillment of *her* hopes and dreams. Her debts were paid and her name was cleared. And a celebratory meal was being prepared at this very moment.

She decided to e-mail Turner tonight and share the good news. And what an e-mail it would be. Chock-full of nothing but happiness. Justin was doing great, her legal affairs were complete, and she was going to end the appointments with her counselor. Could things be any better?

Her meal arrived, and she sat patiently while the waiter poured her a glass of wine. She unfolded her napkin and placed it across her lap. Then she took a sip of the wine and held it in her mouth, savoring the bouquet. She dabbed the corner of her mouth with her napkin and reached for the salad fork. She ate in silent contemplation and reflected on the circumstances that had brought her to this point.

She finished her salad and began the main course. As she ate, she frequently glanced at the file folder and considered what it represented. Progress. Freedom. Independence.

A gale of laughter distracted her and she turned to see a wedding party enter the restaurant. The bride wore a floor-length, strapless, white satin gown, and the groom was dressed in a black tuxedo, complete with a red cummerbund.

They held onto each other passionately, unwilling to let go for even a second. The rest of the wedding party followed behind, laughing and talking excitedly as they were ushered to an adjacent banquet room.

Cassandra tried to concentrate on her meal, but her eyes continually wandered to the bride and groom at the head table, who kissed each other at every opportunity. They looked happy and complete, absorbed in the moment as if nothing else mattered or existed.

She watched them a while longer and then glanced at the file folder. If it represented the successful culmination of everything in her life to this point, why did she suddenly feel so empty? She pushed away from the table and signaled the waiter for the check.

Moments later, clutching the file folder, she hailed a taxi and climbed in the backseat, anxious to get home and be with Justin. An occasion like this shouldn't be celebrated alone anyway. Right now she needed to be with him.

Justin was already in bed when she walked in the door. So after greeting her friend, she tiptoed in to kiss him good night.

His eyes popped open at her approach. "Mommy, I didn't have a bedtime story."

She smiled and stroked his head. "Okay. What story would you like to hear?"

"One about Turner and me."

She stopped abruptly and looked at her son. Turner's name had come up various times during Dr. Courtnall's play therapy sessions, but to hear Justin speak his name so casually caught her by surprise. "What story is that?" she said.

"One about Turner and me hunting for bears. We find one and it chases us and tries to eat us."

"Really? And then what happens?"

"A nice squirrel shows us its tree and we climb up it."

"And that's the end of the story?"

"Nope. The bear climbs up and tries to get us. So Turner wrestles the bear, and it runs away."

"So Turner saves you?"

"Yeah." Justin yawned and began to close his eyes. "I miss him, Mommy."

"So do I," she said, admitting what she had been hesitant to acknowledge for weeks. In counseling, Meredith had warned her about love on the rebound and that she shouldn't rush into a new relationship. But what was love anyway but an exciting and frightening calculated risk, all rolled into one? There were no written guarantees, no failsafe switches, no ironclad clauses to ensure success. Love was a gamble—but a gamble worth taking.

She kissed Justin good night and went into the den. Her head pounded with questions as she sat down at the computer. Had she waited too long? Turner could have any girl he wanted and was talented enough to be anything he wanted to be. Was their recent experience together the only thing they were meant to share because other people were being prepared to come into their lives? Maybe she and Turner would eventually find fulfillment...but just not with each other. Was love something that happened to you or was it something you made happen...with God's help?

She logged onto her account and entered Turner's e-mail address. Fingers hovering above the keyboard, she hesitated and stared at the blinking cursor in the blank message box. What to type? There were news events to relate and memories to reminisce about.

But she didn't start there. Instead she typed:

> Justin asked me to tell him a bedtime story tonight. It
> was about you and him hunting bears. He had the story

all figured out. It ended with you wrestling the bear into submission and it went running away. That was his version. In my version the bear isn't the only one who's been running away. But my version is incomplete, and I don't know how the story ends. I need help finishing it…

Cassandra sat back in her chair and read over the message. Then with a determined expression, she hit the send button.

epiLogue

*T*HE SUN WAS setting and a thin layer of red-tinged clouds skirted the horizon as Turner drove east on I-70 in Harvey and Loretta's new silver Buick Enclave CXL. True to her word Loretta had purchased the latest model, with all the bells and whistles. She had even signed up for driving lessons, much to everyone's relief.

Turner sang along to the radio and tapped the steering wheel to the beat as the tires hummed in harmony. A few minutes later the GPS unit interrupted him, prompting him to take the Airport Boulevard exit. He eased into the right lane and slowed to let a car nudge ahead of him. Then he continued up Airport Boulevard as it headed north and finally turned east once more, ushering traffic to and from the Denver International Airport.

Fifteen minutes later the GPS unit announced, "Arriving at destination." He drove to short-term parking and pulled into a stall away from other vehicles. A scratch in the paint or a door ding would be catastrophic. Making certain the Buick Enclave was locked and secure, he hurried into the terminal building and checked the arrivals board to make sure flights were on time. They were.

He worked his way toward the large water fountain in the center of the terminal that graced the waiting area. A crowd of people had already gathered, huddled in groups and looking toward the escalators that delivered arriving passengers to the reception area. Turner moved to the outside edge of the crowd and fidgeted in his pockets as he watched arriving passengers make their way toward the escalators.

A tall man, an elderly woman, a teenage girl with pierced lips, and a middle-aged man came up the escalator first. They were greeted by waiting family and friends, embracing and sharing smiles.

Other people followed. A teenage boy with green hair, a woman with a crying baby, a large man who was finishing off a sandwich. They too were greeted by family and friends, or they simply walked by on their way to the baggage claim area.

A gap in the line occurred and then a little boy appeared at the top of the escalator. When he saw Turner, he broke out in a grin and ran toward him so fast he almost lost his balance. "Turner! Turner!" he cried, extending his arms.

Turner scooped him up and swung him around, causing Justin to squeal in delight as several passengers glanced at them in bemusement. The circle of Turner's swing momentarily brought a woman into view. She had reached the top of the escalator and took a step toward him. The next rotation brought her into view again, and he saw a smile spread across her face. The tears began to flow.

Holding Justin against him, Turner extended his hand and rushed toward her, smiling in response.

Cassandra Todd had returned.

Also Available From Darrel Nelson

The Anniversary Waltz

PROLOGUE

October 2006

WOULD YOU DO me the honor, Miss?"

Adam Carlson stood beside his wife, Elizabeth, who was still seated at the dining room table. He presented her with a single white rose, which he brought out from behind his back. She held the flower close in order to savor its sweet fragrance. Adam extended a wrinkled hand and looked at her expectantly, the question lingering in his smile.

Elizabeth laughed lightly and put the rose on the table beside her plate, pausing to smooth down her white hair and adjust the two-strand pearl necklace around her slender neck. She placed her hand in his, and together they walked slowly into the living room, followed by family members who gathered around the perimeter of the area rug.

The living room was decorated especially for the occasion. A banner that read *HAPPY ANNIVERSARY* stretched above the doorway, and crepe streamers hung from the center of the ceiling, radiating to the corners of the room like the spokes of a wheel. Balloons were taped to the walls in clusters, and below each cluster was a hand-drawn picture that showed two stick figures holding hands, with the words *GREAT-GRANDMA LOVES GREAT-GRANDPA* printed across the bottom in irregular block letters. A brass floor lamp stood in the far corner, casting a warm glow throughout the room. A floral arrangement in a ceramic vase sat on the fireplace mantel, and a small pennant attached to a thin wooden stick protruded from the leaves and bore the message *HAPPY 60TH*, written in glitter paint. An old picture frame holding a photograph of Adam and Elizabeth on their wedding day sat on the coffee table, and an album containing photographs of past anniversaries lay open beside it.

When everyone had assembled in the living room, Adam held Elizabeth in formal waltz position. He cleared his throat and said, "It's only fair to warn you that I have two left feet. I hope I don't step on you with either one of them."

She reached up and gently stroked his cheek with her thin hand. "I'll risk it, sir."

They moved slowly in a small circle in the center of the area rug as he softly hummed "Believe Me, If All Those Endearing Young Charms," a song that had become *their* song years ago. It was a simple waltz to even simpler accompaniment, but tears formed in Elizabeth's eyes. Adam produced a handkerchief from his pocket and gently dabbed her tears.

Several family members brought out handkerchiefs too and wiped their eyes, as they did every year at this moment.

Adam and Elizabeth's youngest great-grandchild, a little girl with a ribbon in her hair and wearing her Sunday dress, glanced up at her mother in concern. "Mommy, is Great-Grandma sad?"

"No, dear," came the subdued reply. "She's happy."

The little girl looked puzzled. "Why is she crying?"

"You'll see."

Turning her attention back to her great-grandparents, the little girl watched them intently.

Adam held Elizabeth close, and their steps became smaller and smaller until their feet stopped moving altogether. They merely swayed back and forth on the spot. Dropping the formal dance position, she rested her head against Adam, and he wrapped his arms around her frail shoulders. Humming in a mere whisper now and pausing more frequently to catch his breath, he held her against him until the song ended. Then he tilted her face up to his, and they exchanged a tender kiss.

The family members applauded, the little girl the most enthusiastically of all.

Several cameras appeared, and Adam and Elizabeth held on to each other so the moment could be captured and added to the photo album.

Conducting his wife over to the couch, Adam helped her get seated. "Thank you for the dance, Elizabeth," he said.

"Thank *you* for the dance, Adam," she replied. "All sixty years."

He sat beside her, and they held hands. The family members gathered around, as they did every year on this occasion, to hear Adam and Elizabeth relate the story of the anniversary waltz.

about the author

ARREL NELSON IS a retired schoolteacher and lives with his wife, Marsha, in Raymond, Alberta, Canada. They are the parents of four children and are proud grandparents. Darrel is the author of *The Anniversary Waltz* and *The Return of Cassandra Todd*. He is currently working on his next novel, *Following Rain*.

Correspondence for the author should be addressed to:
Darrel Nelson
P.O. Box 1094
Raymond, Alberta, Canada
T0K 2S0

Or you can visit his website (www.darrelnelson.com) and post comments there.

FREE NEWSLETTERS
TO HELP EMPOWER YOUR LIFE

Why subscribe today?

❏ **DELIVERED DIRECTLY TO YOU.** All you have to do is open your inbox and read.

❏ **EXCLUSIVE CONTENT.** We cover the news overlooked by the mainstream press.

❏ **STAY CURRENT.** Find the latest court rulings, revivals, and cultural trends.

❏ **UPDATE OTHERS.** Easy to forward to friends and family with the click of your mouse.

CHOOSE THE E-NEWSLETTER THAT INTERESTS YOU MOST:

- Christian news
- Daily devotionals
- Spiritual empowerment
- And much, much more

SIGN UP AT: **http://freenewsletters.charismamag.com**

8178